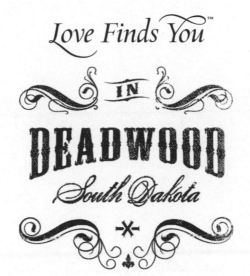

Love Finds You

IN

DEADWOOD

South Dakota

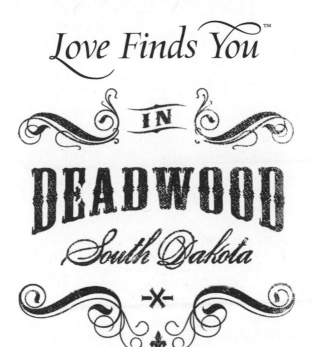

Love Finds You™

IN

DEADWOOD

South Dakota

BY TRACEY CROSS

summerside
PRESS™

Summerside Press™
Minneapolis 55438

Love Finds You in Deadwood, South Dakota
© 2010 by Tracey V. Bateman

ISBN 978-1-61129-105-6

Scripture references are from The Holy Bible, King James Version (KJV).

The town depicted in this book is a real place, but all characters are
fictional. Any resemblances to actual people or events are purely
coincidental.

Cover Design by Lookout Design | www.lookoutdesign.com.

Interior Design by Müllerhaus Publishing Group | www.mullerhaus.net.

*Summerside Press™ is an inspirational publisher offering fresh, irresistible
books to uplift the heart and engage the mind.*

Printed in USA.

Dedication

....

For Jesus, who makes all things new.

Acknowledgments

. . . .

It bears repeating that no book is accomplished by the efforts of one person. It takes a village, or in my case, a small continent to take it from basic idea to finished product.

Thanks to:

Stephanie Grace Whitson—for a wealth of information and places to look. I fell in love with your books when I read *Walks the Fire* many years ago and have been a fan ever since. Thank you!

Frances D.—my mom for helping flesh out the tough spots during a crazy deadline.

Chris and Angie—for reading the book and at least *telling* me you loved it.

Carlton, Jason, Rachel, and Ramona, my Summerside team—you guys are the best!

Kids—Cat, Mickey, Stevan, and Will, for doing extra chores without complaining too much, for cooking suppers (especially you, Cat), and working out many of your own issues. You continually amaze me with your love and dedication to God and to me. I love you so much.

Rusty—my soldier husband. Come home soon; we miss you.

Deadwood, South Dakota

DEADWOOD. THE NAME CONJURES UP COLORFUL VISIONS OF THE Wild West. Hollywood has produced exciting musicals and TV series based on this town—but do they portray Deadwood as it really was? The year was 1876 when a miner name John B. Pearson struck gold. He might have run up and down that canyon, waving his hat and yelling in excitement. Or maybe he glanced around furtively, in fear of thieves. The one thing we know for sure is that the canyon walls were lined with dead trees, which gave the site the name Deadwood Gulch.

Prospectors soon converged on the area with dreams of striking it rich. But after a few initial mining successes, the gold was mostly gone. All that was left was a town filled with the rough and the lawless—folks like gambler and gunfighter Wild Bill Hickok, who was shot dead in 1876 during a poker game in Deadwood's Nuttal & Mann's Saloon. Decent folk shied away from the town, and the few who tried to brave it often regretted their decision. This era of Deadwood came to an end in 1879 when a raging fire swept through the business district. The election of a new sheriff and the rebuilding of the city brought law and order to Deadwood. In 1890 the railroad came, and the community changed forever.

Today the town of Deadwood, population just over 1,300, is the seat of Lawrence County. Overlooked by the famous Mount Moriah cemetery, the resting place of both Wild Bill and Calamity Jane, it boasts museums, tours, more than sixty casinos, and tales of the past.

Tracey Cross

PART ONE:
THE HOMESTEAD

Chapter One

. . . .

Early April, 1879

It had simply never occurred to Jane Albright that Tom might be dead. Gracious, if she feared for his life each time he failed to arrive home in a reasonable amount of time, she'd spend every waking minute in an absolute state. After all, the trip to Deadwood took a month, and that was only one way. With weather upsets, the swollen North Platte, and breakdowns, she never expected to see him within three months of each departure.

So, although he was two weeks overdue, she'd hardly given his absence a thought until late last night when Hank Barnes came rolling in on the freight wagon with Tom in the back, covered from head to toe with his bedroll.

Standing next to her husband's grave, Jane barely found the grace to speak a psalm over him. Even as she said a closing prayer, she found the words automatic and insincere. Were it not for her son, Danny, standing next to her, fidgeting like only a five-year-old could, she might have foregone the funeral altogether and just told Hank to bury him without paying final respects. But she couldn't have her son remembering that she hadn't given his pa a proper burial.

Hank, Tom's partner, stood respectfully by the grave he'd tended to himself, his battered hat clutched in calloused hands that had worked much too hard for it to all end this way.

Jane's amen brought his head up, and, as one, they turned away from the gravesite of the man who had caused such upheaval for them both, leaving them to salvage what they could of the ruins.

"How long before the lender calls in the note?" Jane stared at the grizzled bullwhacker, trying to wrap her head around the fact that her husband had left them with nothing. Less than nothing, in fact. He'd left them in debt, which was the worst thing he could have done.

Hank cleared his throat and stopped walking when they reached the doorway to the sod house. "Mr. Lloyd has been patient for too long already, ma'am. He—um—it was due in full three months ago. Tom never made even one payment."

A wave of nausea seized Jane's stomach. Her mind refused to believe that there was nothing to be done. Mama Rose had always said, "Where there's a will, there's a way." That might have been the only thing the nasty woman had ever taught Jane, but the lesson had been well learned.

Jane squared her shoulders and tilted her head a little to look Hank in the eye. "We'll just have to convince him that you and I are not of the same inclinations toward sloth and drink as Tom was. Any reasonable man will be willing to give us a bit more time to gather the payment. How long do you think it might take to catch up?"

Realizing she was doing all the talking and Hank wasn't holding her gaze, Jane frowned, scrutinizing him. It couldn't be a good sign that his boots shifted. The forty-year-old man was squirming worse than little Danny when he was about to get into trouble. "What aren't you telling me, Hank? Whatever it is, just come right out with it."

"I hate to have to tell you this, ma'am. 'Specially when you got that boy to care for and the…" He glanced at her midsection, then darted his gaze to his worn-out boots.

Heat rose to Jane's face, and irritation crept through her. Tom must have been bragging about the baby. She hated to think ill of the dead, but what kind of man announced his wife's pregnancy? That was just—common.

But that wasn't Hank's fault. Stuffing back her frustration, she patted his arm. "Come inside and have some dinner. Together, we'll figure out what to do."

He shook his head. "I reckon I best be getting on before dark."

"Are you going to try to make a start for Deadwood this late?" Jane's eyebrows lifted. With impending darkness, all sorts of cutthroats and thieves would be lurking about. Not to mention Indians. "Surely you can wait until morning. You're welcome to sleep in the barn."

"Miss Jane, I hate to do this to you, but I got a wife of my own to take care of." The misery on his face, a combination of sympathy and panic, touched Jane's heart.

"I know, Hank. How is Tildy?"

"She's packing." Finally, he made solid eye contact. Jane wasn't sure she liked the message written there.

"Packing? But what do you mean? Where is she going?"

"Not just her. We're moseying on west. To Oregon."

A gasp made its way to Jane's throat. "But what about the freighting? The oxen and wagons? How are we going to pay the loan back if you're not here to help?"

"I'm sorry, Miss Jane. Tom took the loan in his name."

Narrowing her gaze, she searched his red face. "What exactly are you trying to say?"

"I'm free and clear to take my family and go."

Words failed Jane at the utter coldness of his statement, and the equally cold implication. He would not be held responsible for the loan, even if he had benefited from the debt. After all, he had taken his share of the freight money.

"You're leaving it all to me? Is that what you're saying?"

He kept his gaze averted as he nodded. Then he glanced up, embarrassment clouding his face. Good! He deserved every twist of guilt the Lord sent to convict him of this unbelievable sin and lack of character.

"You and the boy are welcome to come along with us."

"Leave our land?"

The very thought seemed ludicrous. Leave her homestead? The place where she'd fought blizzards and drought and loneliness while Tom was gone? Where she'd nearly starved to death that first year? No. This was her land, and she wasn't giving it up. One day she would leave this place to her children. If she left now, what would she have to give them? With no husband and no prospects? She'd end up in another marriage of convenience—maybe to a man worse than Tom had been. No, Hank couldn't possibly be serious. Even if he truly believed she might consider such a ridiculous offer, Jane knew the invitation was nothing more than an attempt to assuage his guilty conscience.

There was nothing to do but let him go. She gathered a deep breath. Why demand what he wasn't going to give? "Hank, you've been a good friend to me these last few years. If you hadn't taken Tom under your wing, I don't know how we'd have survived. I won't pretend to understand your abandonment. But I'll make out all right."

After a brief wince over her use of the word *abandonment*, Hank's features gave way to relief, and he found his voice. "I'm dreadful sorry to be leaving you like this."

"It's no matter. I bear you no ill will."

"That's mighty kind of you, Miss Jane." He seemed indecisive, as if he was about to stay after all.

Jane held her breath and watched his inward struggle play out in his expressions. When he looked her head-on, she knew she'd lost.

She offered a half smile. "Please give Tildy my best and write when you reach Oregon."

"You sure you won't change your mind? They say single women are scarce out West. You'd find yourself a right good man quick as you could snap a finger."

Shaking her head, Jane took a step back as though he might snatch her up and force her to go. "I'm determined to make a go of it right here. This land belongs to my children, and I'm not about to walk off and let it go."

"At least you won't have those beasts to tend to all alone." He nodded toward the pen, where a pair of oxen made short work of what little grass remained.

"I'm not sure I know what you mean."

"I reckon I haven't mentioned it yet." He cleared his throat. "I'll be taking those oxen off your hands for the trip."

Jane's jaw dropped at the audacious statement, said so matter-of-factly, as though she had no say in the decision. "You're going to do *what*?"

"I'm planning on taking those animals. You won't be needing them, and I reckon I'll hitch them up to take us on to Oregon."

"Wait just a minute, Hank."

"Yes, ma'am?"

She gathered all the courage she could muster, shaking her head vehemently. "You can't have them. Those oxen are part of the freighting business. I'm keeping them."

His anger flashed. "What good are they to you?"

"Well, I have to find some way to get the freight running again."

An indulgent smile played at the corners of his lips. "How do you plan to do that? All the hands quit because Tom owes three months of wages. You can't do it alone, and you've no way to hire anyone on." Without waiting for her answer, Hank resumed his walk toward the animals.

"I–I'm not sure, but I'll figure it out somehow, and I'm going to need the oxen when I do."

Watching him disregard her completely and continue to walk toward the oxen—*her* oxen—was too much for Jane. She snatched up the shotgun by the door and leveled the barrel at him just as Hank gathered the leather straps of the oxen. "Hank! You're not taking my property."

He turned, and his eyes widened. "I never would have thought it of you, Miss Jane."

"You're leaving me no choice, Hank. Now you have a choice. Stay here and help me raise the money the company owes to Mr. Lloyd, or walk away and leave me with the burden. But I can't let you steal from me."

"Steal?" His face twisted with outrage. "These animals are mine as much as yours."

"No, sir, that isn't true." She shook her head so hard, some of her hairpins loosened. "The oxen are part of the freighting company."

He gave a short laugh. "Truth be told, they ain't the company's either. Lloyd is going to come take them away. Technically they belong to him."

"We'll see about that." Jane set her jaw and stared him

down, determined not to waver. "And even so, Mr. Lloyd's claim on them is another reason you aren't taking them and leaving me to explain why he isn't getting his money or the oxen. Have you no scruples whatsoever?"

He scowled. "How about if I buy them from you?"

Jane blinked and stared. If he had cash to purchase oxen, why hadn't he paid the lender instead?

As if reading her mind, Hank answered the unasked question. "We sold our land. That's how I got some cash money to outfit our journey west."

"Who would be foolish enough to purchase a homestead when there's so much free land for the taking?"

He shrugged. "Could be because there's a soddy on the land and a wood barn already built. So what do you say about me buying those two?"

"Unless you're offering me enough to pay off the loan so my home is safe, then I'll have to say no."

"Miss Jane, you got to be reasonable." He took a step in her direction but stopped when she cocked the gun. He scowled. "I can't get to Oregon with my horses. I need those animals."

"Too bad. Go buy some oxen in Sidney. I'm not going to tell you again. And don't think you'll come steal them from me after I go to sleep, because I intend to stand guard all night."

"You're being stubborn." Hank's lips twisted in a sneer. "The way I see it, I'm doing you a favor taking them off your hands."

"The way I see it, those oxen are the key to my children's future. If you test me, I won't hesitate to shoot. And I don't believe the law would blame me."

Jane's legs shook violently under her heavy skirt. She had never pointed a gun at a human being before, and she didn't like the feeling. She wasn't entirely certain she could squeeze the trigger, so she prayed Hank wouldn't call her bluff.

Thankfully, he didn't. "You win. Keep the beasts. They've seen better days anyhow."

As she watched him mount his horse and ride away, Jane had never felt so alone.

Only a tug at her skirt forced her to shove away the tears of self-pity and focus on her boy. She looked down and smiled. Danny had removed his shoes and shirt, and his trousers were rolled up to his knees. He wore the headband and feather she had made him weeks ago.

"Can I play Indian?" Danny asked. His chubby hands held up a pot of rouge for her to take. Why Tom had ever thought she'd wear face paint was beyond her, but he had brought it home as a gift after a trip to Deadwood. But the paint had served to offer hours of play for Danny, so all in all, she'd felt it was money well spent.

"*May* I play Indian," she gently corrected, setting the rifle back in its corner just outside the door.

Danny grinned. "May I?"

"Of course you may. But it's too cold still for you to go barefoot. You'll have to put your boots back on before going out."

"Indians don't wear boots."

She smiled and tweaked his nose. "Well, Indians have cold feet, then. You must wear boots."

"Aw, Ma."

As she painted his face, Jane couldn't help but find it sad that the boy didn't even mourn the loss of his pa. But Tom Albright had been a harsh man, a drunkard, with never a kind word for his son. His death at the hands of a two-bit gambler seemed fitting somehow.

In life he had abused and neglected them and in death left them destitute. But Jane was determined to turn all that around. She had no idea how but held a steady confidence the Lord would show her the way.

* * * * *

Early May

Dusk was settling over the Nebraska plains when Franklin Lloyd finally spotted the Albright homestead. It had been a long ride from Deadwood, and he already felt the relief to his bones that his journey was coming to an end.

A beautiful orange sky had begun to fade at the edge of the prairie line, but the view still took away Franklin's breath, filling him with hope that perhaps here, in this part of the country, he might find some peace at last. Perhaps living where there was no filth and human greed or any other human vices, he might be able to reconcile Martha's death and learn to fellowship with God once more. The two years had dulled the pain of losing his pretty bride, but God had never explained the necessity of taking her, and Franklin needed to understand why.

He kept his horse to a walk as he approached the soddy. Glancing around, he couldn't help but frown. This was not what he had been expecting to find. It appeared the place had been well-kept. A pen toward the barn detained a pair of oxen. A clothesline was hung between two posts, and a woman's dress whipped about in the mild evening breeze. *A woman's dress?*

Frank mentally kicked himself. He must have come to the wrong homestead. Or perhaps squatters had taken up residence. He was about to dismount and make an inquiry when the door opened. A young boy stood there, looking up. Between chubby hands he held up a stick like a bow, pulled back a pretend arrow, and shot him.

Sliding from his horse, Franklin grinned at the lad's outlandish Indian getup.

"Ma falls down when I kill her," the lad scolded.

"I'm terribly sorry." He reached out his hand. "My name is Mr. Lloyd. What's yours?"

"Mr. Albright." The lad slipped a dirty, chubby hand inside Franklin's.

"Albright?" Franklin's eyebrows went up in spite of himself. "Is your pa here?"

The lad nodded and pointed. "Over there."

"Danny, who are you talking to?" The voice started before the woman appeared. Large blue eyes widened when she saw him, and she stopped short and gasped, eyeing the rifle next to the door. Her blond hair was pulled into a loose bun and strands had come loose, whipping around her mouth and neck. Bare toes peeked out beneath her skirts, and a streak of flour smudged her cheek. He found the entire image disturbingly attractive.

Franklin held up his palms. "Don't worry. I'm not a threat."

She tucked the boy behind her skirts, but he peeked around, watching Franklin.

"I'm sorry to be so bold," he said, "but I'm looking for Mr. Tom Albright. The boy said he was over there, but I'm not sure what he meant."

"He was referring to my husband's grave." The woman's face hardened. "We buried him a month ago."

She looked overwhelmed and weary. Franklin knew it wouldn't take much for her wall to crack. But he had no desire to be the hammer.

"Please accept my deepest sympathy."

She kept her gaze steady on his. "May I ask your business with Mr. Albright?"

The last thing Franklin wanted to do was tell this woman she and her child would be expected to leave the homestead as soon as possible. "It's a delicate matter, I'm afraid."

She turned to the child. "Danny, please go play. But don't go too far. It's almost dark."

"Yes, Ma! Come on, Cheyenne!" The child dashed around Franklin's legs, screeching as he pretended to be an Indian. A big gray sheepdog mix loped after him, barking in a deep, excited tone.

"Now, Mr. Lloyd, perhaps you would be so kind as to state your business."

Franklin turned back to Mrs. Albright.

Her voice shook a little, but she leveled her gaze at him. "You'll forgive me if I don't invite you in."

The shadows beneath her eyes told of sleepless nights and worry. She looked exhausted and perhaps a little ill. He hated to keep her standing.

"Of course. Let me explain why I've intruded."

"You needn't bother." She expelled a heavy breath and swayed. "I assume you must be Mr. Lloyd?"

Surprised, Franklin nodded. Perhaps this wouldn't be as awkward as he'd feared. She breathed out. Franklin peered closer, frowning at her flushed cheeks and glassy eyes. "Please excuse me for being so forward, but are you all right, ma'am?"

She lifted her chin. "I am quite fine, sir. Let's get on with this."

A breeze sent a chill down his spine that wasn't entirely inconsistent with her icy stare. Clearly, this woman had formed an opinion of him long before the moment of their meeting. "I'm not sure what your husband told you before he passed away."

"Tom told me nothing. His partner Hank explained that you are owed a debt, and my husband put up the freight wagon and oxen as collateral."

"That's correct." He dreaded the next few words because she evidently didn't know the extent of the debt owed by her husband. "But that isn't all."

"I'm sure I don't know what you mean, Mr. Lloyd. What else is there?"

"Ma'am, I'm sorry to tell you this, but along with the freighting business and the store in Deadwood, your husband put your land on the loan as well."

"I—I didn't know there was a store."

"Not much of one. A tent really, behind a rough storefront."

"But the house and land."

Miserably, he nodded.

The woman's face blanched. "Are you saying Tom used our home as collateral?"

Feeling like a complete cad, he nodded. "The home and the business."

A moan bubbled from her lips, and she swayed. Franklin reached out and caught her just before she hit the ground in a dead faint. Lifting the unconscious woman, he called out for Danny. Heat smoldered through the fabric of her dress.

The boy came running. When he saw his mother in Franklin's arms, he did what any decent youngster would do. He began kicking and hitting for all he was worth. "Put her down, you varmint! Get him, Cheyenne!" The dog barked, playing the game.

"It's okay. She fainted." Franklin's shins smarted from the kicks, but he couldn't blame the lad. "Can you take me inside and show me where she sleeps so I can lay her down?"

His face scrunched, and he shook his head. "Ma wouldn't like that."

Franklin was positive she wouldn't like it, but there was nothing to be done about that now. "We'll apologize when she wakes up. I think she'd rather wake up in her bed than with me holding her like a baby, don't you?"

Danny hesitated, as though considering the scenario, then nodded. "Yes, sir. I reckon she'd rather just go on to bed."

The soddy was small, cramped, and barely tall enough for Franklin's full height. As he followed Danny inside the one-room dwelling, he noted the rag rugs on the dirt floor, the clothing neatly hung on pegs, and books placed in an orderly fashion on a shelf in one corner of the room.

"Danny, pull back the quilt, please."

With clumsy movements, the lad did as instructed, and Franklin lowered Mrs. Albright to a feather mattress. He was a little surprised she hadn't come to yet, but if she was half as exhausted as she appeared to be, she probably needed to sleep.

Glancing around, he wasn't sure what to do. He knew the woman would likely be mortified that he had carried her inside and even more so if he stayed, but he noticed a pot of stew simmering and the dough already made up for biscuits.

He could certainly finish cooking supper. After all, he'd spent a year mining and a year living alone in Deadwood, so he knew how to cook a meal. Only in the past year had he hired a cook and a housekeeper.

He caught Danny's gaze and grinned. "Guess I'm going to finish cooking for your ma. What's on the stove?"

A wide grin spread across the boy's mouth. "Rabbit. Ma shot it, and she even let me help pull out the innards."

Franklin laughed out loud, then remembered to keep his voice down. He glanced at the bed, and his heart nearly stopped as her eyes opened.

"Mr. Lloyd!" she said, her voice still weak. "Just because you are taking my home doesn't mean you have the right to move in before I move out." She sat up slowly. "I'm afraid our talk will have to wait until morning as I am not feeling well."

Her expression revealed her shaky condition. If she tried to stand, Franklin knew she was going down again. Her condition had to stem from more than simple upset over his revelation of the extent of her husband's indebtedness to him. "Mrs. Albright, I don't mean to behave ungentlemanly, so please forgive me. But you have no business getting out of bed. You're burning up."

"I—was baking earlier and became too hot."

Rushing to her, Franklin pressed the back of his hand to her forehead.

She pulled away, weakly. "How dare you touch me!"

"I'm sorry, ma'am. But you have a fever. A high one."

He knelt on the floor, so he didn't tower over her, hoping the action would help her feel at ease with him. He met her eye to eye. "I know this is awkward, but you are sick and exhausted and must sleep. You don't know me, but I'm not going to harm you or the boy. I'm giving you my word, and you are going to have to accept it. If you don't stay in bed, you'll get sicker, and then what's Danny going to do?"

Tears filled her beautiful blue eyes, and her lip trembled as she nodded. "Okay, Mr. Lloyd. And thank you. Please don't sleep in the house. There's a nice loft in the barn. Take two quilts from the trunk over there. It still gets very cold at night."

She lay back and covered herself. Franklin couldn't resist reaching out and tucking the quilt in around her shoulders.

"You have my word. I'll make sure Danny is fed and put to bed, then I'll go."

"God must have sent you to us." A wisp of a smile touched her lips as she closed her eyes and drifted back to sleep.

Franklin stood, feeling more than a little baffled at the turn of events. He'd had no idea Tom Albright was a married man. Judging from the man's conduct at Bedlow's Saloon, he'd apparently forgotten that little fact himself. A man like that didn't deserve any woman, let alone one as capable as the one he'd found.

Tom Albright had been worse than a fool. But that wasn't his wife's fault. Franklin hated to call in the note and evict the woman and her son. Especially now that he knew they existed and rather liked them both.

Perhaps Mrs. Albright would allow him to put her and the boy on a train headed east. Either way, this land and the land adjoining were where he intended to raise his cattle and get away from Deadwood once and for all. There was no room in his plans for a woman and a little boy.

They would have to go before the first of the herds arrived from Texas in the next few months. But he wouldn't allow himself to think of the hardness of what he must do. For now, he had biscuits to finish and a hungry boy to feed.

Chapter Two

....

Jane came slowly awake to the aroma of bacon and coffee. The combination seized her stomach and rolled it over, forcing her to lie very still or risk retching right then and there. She took two deep breaths. As the nausea subsided, clarity slowly shifted across her mind, and she sat up.

The stillness of the room might have caused her to think she'd merely dreamed up the handsome Mr. Lloyd and his presence in her home, but on the table a single plate of food, covered with a kitchen towel, defied the hope.

Oh gracious, he had tucked her into bed. What would Mama Rose say if she knew? Right now the old dowager must be rolling in her grave.

Jane pressed her palms to her flaming cheeks and closed her eyes, taking stock of the events she could remember. Mr. Lloyd had shown up to tell her he was taking not only the oxen and wagon but the homestead also.

At the rush of memory, tears threatened, clogging her throat and stinging her nose, but there wasn't time to give in to despair. The door opened, and Danny bounded in. He turned his beautiful brown eyes in her direction, and his face lit up. He tossed a few sticks of kindling in the wood box. "Ma! You're up. Are you all better?"

"Much better, darling."

He threw himself into her arms, knocking the wind out of her and nearly sending her back on the bed. But she didn't mind, despite her weakness. Laughing, she squeezed him, then held him out at arm's length. His hair was unkempt, and dirt smudged his cheek, but all in all he was a wondrous sight.

Mr. Lloyd followed Danny inside, carrying an armload of wood.

Jane, keenly aware of Mr. Lloyd's attention, couldn't resist meeting his gaze. She resented his command of the room. He looked completely at ease, as though his hands had worked at pick and shovel to cut out the home. As though he had soaked his own blistered palms in stinging salt water as a result. As though he had fought storms and shaken with fear when Pawnee came right up to the house and stole livestock and pots.

Yet, despite her resentment, something twisted her stomach as he smiled, a gentle smile that nonetheless reached his eyes. The type of look she'd always dreamed a man might bestow.

Then she remembered: if Mr. Lloyd had his way, she and Danny would soon be out in the cold. She forced herself to look away.

"Mr. Lloyd let me swing the ax." Danny's words acted like a bucket of cold spring water.

"He let you swing an *ax*?"

"Yep, and I didn't cut off a toe or a finger or a leg or an arm."

"Lucky for you." She said the words to the boy but directed them to Mr. Lloyd.

He grinned in a most unapologetic manner. "It didn't have the head on it." He chuckled. "I was just showing him how it's done." He nodded toward the table. "You haven't eaten your breakfast. Do you feel up to sitting at the table, or shall I bring it to you?"

"I'm not very hungry."

"You need to eat." A frown pushed his eyebrows together. "Do you realize how long you've been sleeping?"

"Thirteen or fourteen hours?" What must he think of her lying abed, leaving her chores and her child for him to tend?

"Two days."

Jane's jaw dropped. Surely he must be joking. "That's not possible."

"I'm afraid it is. Your fever shot up pretty high that first night and all the following day. Yesterday you slept. But"—he peered closely—"you don't remember asking for water yesterday?"

Jane shook her head, still trying to gather her thoughts to include this impossible information. "I can scarcely believe I've been asleep for so long. And you took care of my home and my son...."

He opened the stove and fed the flame without looking at her. "I was honored. Think nothing of it."

The impropriety of the unlikely situation hit her full in the stomach, sending another wave of nausea through her midsection.

As if sensing her discomfort, Mr. Lloyd did the gentlemanly thing and walked toward the door. Jane noted he barely stood at his full height in the low-ceilinged sod home without scraping his head when he walked. "I'll finish up the chores outside and give you a chance to compose yourself." He paused. "You can be assured that I didn't—that is, nothing—" He swallowed hard. "If there had been anyone else to place the cool cloths on your head and help you other-wise, I never would have put either of us in such a difficult position in regards to modesty. But I only cared for you as was necessary to your condition and did not take advantage in any other way."

His ears flamed red, as did his neck. Without awaiting an answer or casting a glance in her direction he ducked through the doorway and fled the soddy.

"Can I go too, Ma?"

"Yes," she whispered.

As Danny bounded out the door after Mr. Lloyd, who had apparently become her son's new hero, Jane closed her eyes and shook her head, determined to force the horrible "Mr. Lloyd" situation from her mind. When she opened her eyes, she glanced toward the table to the plate of food, suddenly finding herself ravenous. She needed to eat soon for the baby anyway, if it had been two full days since she or her little one had received nourishment.

She stood carefully, pressing her palm against the sod wall for support as the blood rushed to her head. Once she gained her footing, she went to the table and sat, removing the cover from her plate. The ham was a little cold, but that didn't stop her from wolfing down every bite and then tackling the two biscuits.

Her legs felt as though she were walking through waist-high water in heavy skirts as she took her plate to the counter. She was about to bend and lift the bucket to pour water into the washbasin when Danny rushed back inside. "Ma, Mr. Lloyd said to tell you not to worry about tidying up your dishes. He will be inside directly to tend to that."

"Oh he did, did he?"

"Yes, ma'am."

"Well, little mister, what does Mr. Lloyd suggest I do?"

"He said to tell you you should probably go back to bed and rest up so you can get strong again."

Yes, he wanted her strong again. So he could snatch up her land, her belongings. He could just forget it. "I expect I'll make my own decisions regarding *my* own home. I refuse to leave dishes undone." She reached down and lifted the bucket. Weakness overcame her arms, sliding downward, robbing strength from her fingertips. The full bucket slipped from her grasp. Water splashed to the ground, mixed with the dirt floor, and quickly turned to mud.

To Jane's horror, Mr. Lloyd made an appearance in the doorway at that precise moment. He released a sigh as Jane bent to pick up the now empty bucket, bracing herself for a scolding.

But the censure never came. Instead he spoke in a soft tone. "Let's get you back to bed." He slipped his arm around her waist and gently guided her across the small room, deftly steering her away from the mud.

Too weary to resist, Jane allowed the ministrations as far as the side of the bed. She held up her palm. "Will you please turn around while I get back into bed?"

"I understand why you're embarrassed, Mrs. Albright. But my intentions are completely honorable."

"Yes, please, don't talk about it anymore and—don't look at me."

"As you wish." Obligingly, he turned his back.

Now that her stomach had food in it, sleepiness nearly overcame her. But she turned her gaze toward the man who was soon to throw her out of her home. "Mr. Lloyd, you needn't stay. We'll be fine. Danny is a very capable little boy." But even as she said it, her concern for her son won over her need for modesty. "No, I'm sorry. Don't leave until I can see to him—only please do not sleep in the house." She hoped she wouldn't sleep all day.

"I wouldn't dream of it, Mrs. Albright."

Vaguely aware she was drifting to sleep, she murmured a "thank you" that she wasn't sure she had the energy to put voice to.

When she awoke later, the soddy was dark, except for a soft glow at the table where Mr. Lloyd sat bent over papers.

Frowning, she sat up, still weak, but knowing she was getting better. In the other corner, Danny lay on his pallet, staring up at the ceiling, hands behind his head, elbows to the sides, as if he'd just been sent to bed.

"Mr. Lloyd?" She stood on weak but steady legs, her gown wrinkled from three days' wear. She pushed at the wrinkles as she padded across the room. Mr. Lloyd had spread hay on the wet spot to soak up the water.

"You look better," he observed. "On the mend, I'd say."

"I think so."

"Hi, Ma," Danny whispered from his bed. "You slept the day away again."

Mr. Lloyd chuckled.

Jane walked to her son and knelt beside him. Her arms ached for the feel of his body in her arms. "I know the rule is that you don't get up once you're put to bed, but how about bending a little? I could sure use one of your hugs."

"Sure! That okay with you, sir?" He glanced around Jane to the man at the table.

"Fine with me." Mr. Lloyd grinned. "I suppose you ought to do whatever your ma says from here on out."

Danny slid effortlessly into her arms. Jane drew him close, then wrinkled her nose. "What day is today?"

"Friday."

"Good. Tomorrow is bath day! You need one."

He lay back down, screwing his face into a scowl. "I hate baths."

Jane giggled and reached down to tickle his tummy. "I know you do, but you smell much nicer after you've had one." She tucked the cover up around his shoulders and bent to kiss him. Her head spun as she sat up.

"You okay?"

She'd almost forgotten Mr. Lloyd was still in the room. Had he been watching her?

"I'm fine. Just moved a bit too fast."

Before she could try to stand, he was at her side, offering his hand.

She had no choice but to take it and did so, wishing his hand weren't so warm and comforting. He released her as soon as she was steady on her feet. "I have some stew set back on the stove for you. It should be mostly warm."

"Thank you. That was thoughtful." Considering why he was here.

"If you sit down, I'll get it for you."

"No thank you, Mr. Lloyd. I can get my own."

He scrutinized her for a second, then shrugged. "Suit yourself."

Fighting a wave of dizziness, she forced herself not to sway or close her eyes. Instead, she walked forward blindly past the dark spots in her vision. After a few gulps and deep breaths, the dizziness passed, and she dipped the stew into a bowl.

She sat at the opposite end of the table and bowed her head. Silently she thanked the Lord for her food, then ate just as silently, allowing Mr. Lloyd the privacy of working on his papers.

Finally, he looked up and glanced to the corner where Danny now slept soundly. With a serious expression, he said, "I suppose we should discuss the original reason I arrived unannounced on your doorstep."

Dread gripped Jane, robbing her of appetite. She pushed away the half-eaten bowl of stew. How would she ever convince Mr. Lloyd to give her time to raise the money he was owed? If he wanted the homestead so badly he'd travel almost 280 miles from Deadwood, she doubted very much there would be any reasoning with him. But for Danny's sake, and the sake of the little one inside her, she had to try.

"Your husband approached me approximately one year ago and requested a sizable loan to expand his freighting business into a general store."

"A general store?" Jane felt foolish. Her husband had never confided the addition to his freighting business. "I had no idea."

Mr. Lloyd nodded. "He wanted to buy his own freight and sell mainly dry goods. Men do it all the time. Some succeed. Some don't. I'm sorry to say, your husband's venture was an abysmal failure."

Jane closed her eyes for a second. Of course Tom had failed. "I see."

"He hired a man who couldn't stay out of the saloons, who squandered every dime the market brought in. By the time your husband came back to Deadwood with his last load of freight, the man had been killed for cheating at cards. That's when I reintroduced myself to Mr. Albright. He believed his clerk had been paying my fees each month. However, when we compared accounting books, his was vastly different from mine."

Jane hoped with all of her heart that Tom had truly believed the payments were being made. Otherwise he was an adulterer, a liar, and a thief to boot. She didn't want her son's name associated with such dishonor. "How much have you been repaid, Mr. Lloyd?"

Before he answered, she remembered Hank had already told her.

His face reddened. "Nothing."

Jane stood and walked to the counter. She poured a cup of coffee and offered some to Mr. Lloyd. He slid his cup over and nodded his thanks.

"I know this is a terrible shock coming to you at such a time. Your husband is dead, and now to learn you've lost your business and your home…"

Jane set the pot heavily on the stove and whipped around. She walked around the table, forcing Mr. Lloyd to move back a little to look her in the eyes. "I don't understand how a homestead can be part of your business deal with my late husband. It's a homestead."

"I'm sorry, Mrs. Albright. Your husband signed it over to me three months ago. It's mine now."

"But it still belongs to the government. We haven't worked it long enough to have a clear deed."

"Yes, ma'am, I am aware of that. I will take over the soddy, the outbuildings, and the fields and homestead for the rest of the time remaining on your claim."

Danny stirred and cooed as he slept.

"My husband had no right to put up this land, this home. He didn't work this land. I did. We hired the well dug. He never lifted a finger. You don't own the rest of the time on this place. You won't own a soddy and a barn and garden. You'll own my blood and sweat. Sir, if you take this place, you'll be stealing my son's legacy right out from under him."

Breathless, she slid into her chair, refusing to meet his gaze. Her hands shook as she brought the mug to her lips and took in a fair gulp of the lukewarm coffee.

"Forgive me, Mrs. Albright." He cleared his throat and closed his ledger book. "I'm a businessman."

"And I, sir, am a mother. What would you have me do— a woman alone in this land?"

"I'm glad you asked. I—"

Jane's stomach twisted as he faltered in his conversation. "I won't enter another marriage of convenience," she said quickly. "I know you're fond of Danny. But I'm determined to keep that resolve." With renewed courage she stared him head on.

His lips twisted into a smirk. "And if I had intended to propose, I would be as determined to persuade you to change your mind—seeing as I am so fond of the little man. However, my proposal was of a different nature."

Jane's face burned. She pressed a cool palm to her neck as embarrassment speared through her like shards of burning rocks. "I apologize for my presumption. What did you intend to propose?"

He reached forward and covered her other hand with his—warm and altogether uncomfortable. Jane jerked away, knocking the table and sloshing both cups of coffee. Mr. Lloyd snatched up his ledger, removing it from the path of a line of threatening liquid.

Jane jumped to her feet, retrieved a cloth from the counter, and sopped up the mess. "I'm so clumsy. Please forgive me."

He took hold of her wrist. Gently. Slowly she looked down into a kind face. "Sit down for a minute. There's no harm done here."

Slowly she inched back down until her body folded into the wooden chair. "Mr. Lloyd, you have done a great deal for my son and myself during the last couple of days. And I am grateful Danny was not left to his own devices during my illness. But I cannot possibly give up this homestead. Not while there's breath in my body and my child depends upon me for his well-being."

Mr. Lloyd's eyebrow slid upward, giving him a rakish appearance. Jane's heart raced as he folded his arms across his chest and thrust his long legs out in front of him. He tipped the chair back until it balanced on two legs. "Indeed? And how would you stop me from claiming what is legally mine?"

"But it's not yours. It's mine. My husband barely even knew how to find his way home he was gone so much."

His gaze darted to her hand and back to her face. "I am

sorry to distress you. But I'm afraid I have plans for the land that are already set into place. There's nothing I can do."

A short laugh jutted from her throat. "Nothing except throw us out with nowhere to go? I suppose I can try to go to the Fort and take in laundry."

But in that instance she knew the so-called laundresses following the army usually performed other unsavory and unacceptable services as well. She would never stoop so low.

The front legs thudded on the dirt floor. "Don't be ridiculous."

"What is it to you where we end up?" she challenged. "Since you have no intention of doing the honorable thing."

"And what would that be? Give you my rightful property?"

"*My* property."

His shoulders rose and fell as he took a steadying breath. "As I've been trying to say, I am not tossing you into the mud, Mrs. Albright. In fact, I'm offering you fare to anywhere you'd like to go. East, west, Texas. Anywhere you and Danny might call home."

"We call this place home."

A scowl marred his face, and he stood. He lifted the coffeepot, offering her some. She shook her head. He poured himself a cup and sat back down.

Clasping her hands together to keep them from trembling, she rested her forearms in front of her on the table. She swallowed hard. "Mr. Lloyd, I appreciate your kind offer. However, I would like to make a counter-proposal."

In the month following her husband's death she had spent time caring for the oxen and studying the freight wagon. She had been forming a plan, should this day ever come. Inwardly, she prayed for mercy. *Please, let this work.*

"Oh?" He sipped his coffee, scrutinizing her over the chipped rim. The calculated look intimidated Jane, but she straightened her shoulders with determination. Danny's future was worth putting forth the effort of negotiating.

"Perhaps you would allow me to deliver freight to and from Deadwood as your employee until the homestead portion of the debt is paid."

Silence permeated the room as he stared at her, as though waiting to hear the part of her proposal that made sense. Finally, he shook his head. "Mrs. Albright, I'm not sure I understand. The note combines the homestead and the business. They're not two separate loans."

"Yes, I understand. But I don't believe I'd want to keep the freighting business. As a matter of fact, the law requires that I live on the homestead and keep it up. I couldn't do that if I were gone all the time. So this is just until my homestead is clear of debt. You may have the wagon and the oxen."

"But the homestead has already passed into my hands. It's already mine. Even if I were of a mind to hire a female to deliver freight, which I am not, mind you, there is no point in the exercise. The debt is paid by the transfer of property."

Every time he said the homestead belonged to him, Jane wanted to scream. To shove her calloused hands toward his face. To show him the bruises on her body from the hard labor of caring for this place. What right had he?

"Besides, how on earth would you handle freighting? A woman isn't cut out for that kind of work." His eyes examined her, as though trying to picture the scenario.

A glimmer of hope ignited deep inside, but she forced herself to remain stoic. Perhaps he was beginning to soften to the idea. "Tom told me once of a woman freighter. If you hadn't noticed, Mr. Lloyd, I am anything but small and soft. I'm strong, sturdy, and tall for a woman."

"Yes, but freighting is hard work. Heavy work, and not only loading freight. The oxen are large and stubborn; you have to know how to crack a bullwhip."

"Mr. Lloyd, I have been feeding the oxen every day. I think they like me."

He chuckled from his chest. "You think they like you? Mrs. Albright. It simply isn't possible."

Standing, he tucked the ledger book under his arm and reached for his cup. He set it on the counter and turned, slid his chair back under the table, and leveled his gaze at her. "Tomorrow I'll be leaving for Deadwood to get some things in order. My offer of train fare for you and Danny still stands. Kindly begin packing your things, and be ready to move in three months' time. That's when I'll arrive back here—with the marshal, if I must."

Bitter disappointment muted Jane. All she could do was nod.

As she lay in bed that night, she tried to picture a place where she and Danny could start over. In a city, she'd be working many hours in a factory or as a domestic. She knew how many torturous hours she would be forced to work to provide the most meager of livings for the children. She would never see them. After living with Mama Rose in the county orphanage most of her life and being denied maternal affection, Jane was fiercely determined that her children would never be left to fend for themselves. So a city was not even a consideration.

The other choice was to try to homestead herself. She could file another claim, but she didn't have the strength to build her own house of sod. At the very least, Tom had done much of the heavier chores early on. She couldn't afford to hire a man to help.

Despair sat heavily on her chest, like a fallen tree, as she considered her last option. One she'd sworn never to consider again. Marry again. Tears slipped down her cheeks as she imagined beginning another chapter in her life with another strange man sharing her bed.

It was too much to bear.

Chapter Three

························

Franklin awakened with a start. What was wrong? His heart raced, and he sat up, reaching for his pistol. Light streamed in through the cracks in the barn walls the same as it had for the last two mornings. Still, something seemed—different.

From his pallet in the loft, he glanced over the edge into the barn's ground floor. The horses didn't seem upset, but his gut tightened with foreboding. And his gut was hardly ever wrong.

He noted the oxen hitched to the wagon. What was she up to?

The smell of frying bacon tempted his hollow stomach. Perhaps he only felt strange because he had been the one doing the cooking the past couple of days. Jane—he couldn't quite think of her as Mrs. Albright when alone with his thoughts—was well and clearly attending her child and home. Still, something felt off.

He slipped on his boots, kept his senses alert and pistol in hand as he climbed from the loft. As he stepped out into a brilliant spring morning, everything seemed still, as though he were the only human being in the world. He'd felt this way only one other time. Those childhood memories flooded back to him as though no time had passed between the day his mother had died and now.

Deep down he knew he wasn't in the same moment. He knew where he was, but the lines between past and present blurred. His bootsteps picked up pace. He ran to the soddy and flung the door open.

Jane spun around from the stove, flinging bacon to the floor. "Mr. Lloyd! You gave me a start!"

"I'm so sorry." Franklin scanned the tidy room. Nothing seemed amiss, other than the bacon on the floor. He stepped forward quickly, before Jane could retrieve the meat. "I'll get that. I'm so sorry. I thought—" He shook his head, walked with greasy bacon in hand to the door, and tossed it out to the dog.

"Is everything all right, Mr. Lloyd? You seem upset. I hope you aren't coming down with my illness." She frowned, searching his face. "Sit down. I'll pour you some coffee. Breakfast is almost ready."

Franklin wasn't accustomed to being told what to do, but he obeyed without question, stopping at the washbasin to clean his hands before sitting down to breakfast.

Jane's smile of approval sent rays of sunshine to his heart.

"I'm sorry for bursting in on you that way."

She set a cup in front of him and poured from the pot. "It's no matter." A slight smile tipped one corner of her mouth. "Cheyenne is pleased, I'm sure."

He chuckled and sipped his coffee, admitting that her brew was vastly superior to his own. "Why is the wagon hitched up?"

"I was practicing with the oxen. You were right. They are stubborn animals."

Staring at the formidable woman, he forced back a comment about her own stubbornness. "Why are you practicing?"

She shrugged. "I hoped a good night's sleep and a hearty breakfast might change your mind."

He swallowed another sip of the bitter brew. "May I have a bit more sugar, please?"

"Certainly."

He glanced around. "Where's Danny?"

"I sent him to gather eggs. He should be back soon."

"Would you join me for coffee?" He pushed out the chair catty-cornered from him.

Her face darkened to a pretty pink, but she shook her head. "I have to watch the breakfast, or the dog will be getting a lot more than he bargained for, and we'll go hungry."

This woman surprised him with her kindness. After their last conversation, he'd fully intended to be given a cold shoulder this morning. "You seem to be feeling much better."

She smiled. A touch of gray still ringed her eyes, but her steps seemed quick and sure as she went about preparing the meal.

He, on the other hand, was feeling strange. His eyes wanted to close, and his vision was beginning to blur.

"Are you all right, Mr. Lloyd?" Jane stood over him, her eyebrows furrowed in concern.

"I must have taken a touch of your illness, I'm afraid."

"Oh, dear, perhaps another cup of coffee might help. Unless you intend to return to bed, as I did."

That was out of the question. He pushed his cup toward her, amazed at the colorful blur that followed the action. "Please."

"Of course." She filled his coffee once more.

The cup shook, sloshing coffee onto the table as he tried to lift it to his lips. "I beg your pardon," he said, barely able to hear his own voice. Or was it too loud?

"Think nothing of it." Jane's voice soothed him. "Let me help." She covered his hand with hers and steadied the cup as it reached his mouth. The hot liquid slid down his throat. "That's it. Just a little more."

Her sweet voice was the last thing Franklin heard before his head hit the table.

* * * * *

Jane tugged at the stubborn oxen, walking beside them and praying they would cooperate. She had only been on the trail for three hours, but already her muscles ached as though she'd put in a week of work without a break for sleep or food. Tears quickly approached the surface of her resolve, but she knew her boy was watching, so weakness was not an option.

"Danny, sing a song for your ma."

Danny had wandered just a little ways from the wagon, with Cheyenne following happily. Jane would have felt much better if Danny had stayed in the back of the wagon, where she could keep a better eye on him, but he was a strong, energetic boy, and Jane knew she couldn't keep him confined. It wouldn't be fair. After all, he hadn't asked for his father to be a poor manager of their home and his business.

Danny started singing a silly, made-up song about the oxen and how silly Ma looked, trying to get them to move. Jane smiled but found her mind wandering. And then the guilt poured in. Only desperation had driven her to put laudanum in Mr. Lloyd's coffee this morning. Thank goodness he hadn't insisted she have a cup with him after she'd refused the first suggestion.

Mama Rose had given her the bottle of medicine when she'd agreed to become Tom's bride. He had arrived at Mama's home for orphans, looking for a young woman of marriageable age who might want to go west with him. Mama had shown him the door, but Jane had run after him.

Heat burned her face at the memory of his critical perusal of her large frame and too-big blue eyes. "I reckon you'll do," he'd said.

Within a day they were married, and Jane knew the regret only a woman who married a stranger in haste could know, and the bruises attested to her disappointment.

"Take this," Mama Rose had said, slipping a bottle of laudanum into her hand. "Use it to keep him off you. If it gets to be too much, use the whole bottle, and he'll never bother you again."

She had never been able to bring herself to use the medicine on Tom, although she'd been sorely tempted more than once.

The freighting business had been a mercy and, Jane believed with all of her heart, an answered prayer. She would have been forced to leave him for her son's protection if he hadn't been gone so much.

Fort Sidney was just ahead, thank goodness. If one could call it a fort. It was more of a town, with soldiers guarding the citizens and the railroad. It was crudely known as "wide open," with bawdy houses and saloons and shows twenty-four hours a day.

"Look at the soldiers, Ma!"

A tall soldier with muscles straining his blue shirt turned at Danny's cry. His face held the hardness of someone who has seen his share of struggle. Still, his expression softened when he saw Jane and the animals. He motioned for another soldier.

The young man came immediately. "Yes, Sergeant?"

"Help the lady and get these oxen to the corral."

"Yes, sir." The young soldier climbed up, grabbed the bull-whip, which Jane had been too timid to even attempt to use, and effectively moved the animals forward.

Jane held tightly to Danny's hand and followed the wagon on foot. She nodded to the sergeant. "Thank you."

His hand touched his cap. "My pleasure, ma'am. If you don't mind my asking, what brings you alone to Fort Sidney?"

Before she could speak up, Danny piped up. "She ain't alone. I'm with her. Can I see your sword?" Cheyenne pressed in closer to Danny as the fearless little boy stepped closer to the soldier.

"Daniel Thomas Albright!" Mortified, Jane's face burned with embarrassment at the lad's lack of manners.

"It's okay, ma'am. The lad's right. You're not alone." The soldier chuckled and pulled his saber from the sheath. "Lookee here, son." He held it balanced on his palm and crouched down eye level with Danny.

Danny walked forward slowly, keeping his eyes on the saber as though hypnotized by the thing.

"Don't touch it, Danny."

"Aw, Ma."

"Better listen to your ma. One touch could slice off one of those little fingers."

Danny slipped his hands quickly behind his back. "You ever stuck that in an Indian?"

"That's enough, Danny. We need to let the sergeant get back to his post."

The soldier winked boldly at her and chuckled again. "A pleasure to meet you, ma'am. And Danny." His eyes sought hers. "We don't get too many ladies at the fort. If you need anything, ask for Sergeant Roland. And be careful with that dog. If he gets into mischief, he'll be shot."

"Thank you for your kindness." She smiled at the barrel-chested soldier and followed after the freight wagon. The fort teemed with life. Soldiers, straight-backed and respectful, tipped their hats as she passed by, though she could see curiosity in their eyes. As the sergeant had said, they weren't used to seeing women who weren't for sale. Her face warmed, and she did her best to keep her gaze averted from anyone who might seek to cause trouble.

The wagon stopped before a livery stable next to a corral. Her heart sank as she read the rough-hewn sign hanging on the stable door.

ANIMAL BOARDING:

2.00 PER DAY

WAGONS 1.00

Jane patted the waistband of her skirt. She had exactly fifty dollars to her name—her savings from doing seamstress work before her marriage to Tom. She would have given him the money. Had planned to present it to him on their wedding night as a wedding gift. But after the brutality of that night, she had decided to keep it hidden in case she needed to escape.

A sweaty, potbellied man stepped out of the livery stable and spoke to the soldier, then motioned to the corral.

"Excuse me, Private," she called out as the soldier began to unhitch the oxen from the wagon. "Please keep the oxen hitched to the wagon."

The liveryman turned and scowled. "You can't leave 'em hitched up all night." He looked her up and down, then had the grace to remove his hat, revealing a thinning, greasy cap of gray. "Name's Wilder. I own the livery. I don't allow animals to stay hitched all night. It ain't right. No disrespect intended."

At least he tried his hand at manners. Jane smiled. "None taken, Mr. Wilder. It's just that I am unable to meet your price for boarding."

The soldier started. "Ma'am, by the time you load up, it'll be getting on to dusk."

He was right, of course. But what else could she do? She had no intention of wasting three precious dollars. The liveryman averted his gaze and spat a stream of tobacco juice on the ground. Jane's stomach threatened to rebel. "I understand. I suppose I'll have to take my chances and camp outside the fort."

The soldier reached up and swiped at the sweat on his brow. "Yes, ma'am. But that's just it. They won't let anyone out after dusk. Renegade Indians. A woman like you with a youngster…"

The meaning of his omitted words was all too clear.

She glanced back at the liveryman, eyeing his ragged clothing and his approximate measurements. He looked about Tom's size. "I can't help but notice your shirt is ripped and stained, and your trousers are worn through in—places." Only these dire circumstances could have induced her to set aside propriety and admit such a rude observation, so she hurried on. "My husband passed away a short while ago. I brought his clothes with me to sell in Deadwood. I'd like to propose a trade."

"Why would I want a dead man's clothes?"

"Because I made them." She smiled. "Before my marriage I was a seamstress by trade. I had more orders than I could fill. After my marriage I used those skills to keep my husband in sturdy clothes. You look to be about his size. I will trade you two shirts and one pair of trousers to board my oxen and wagon for the night."

The liveryman scratched at the stubble along his jaw. "I never thought much about my clothes, but I reckon these are wearin' out."

"We have a deal, then?"

He turned his head and spat again, then wiped his mouth on the back of his sleeve. He gave a curt nod. "Sounds like a fair trade."

It took all of her willpower not to show her relief. "Thank you." She looked from the liveryman to the soldier. "Now, may I ask either of you gentleman where I may find a fair-minded freighter who will hire me to drive my wagon to Deadwood?"

Mr. Wilder pointed. "McMillan's Freighting is looking for a new hauler. He lost two wagons to the Barry gang last week." The liveryman narrowed his gaze. "You intending to haul freight on your own?"

Jane's back straightened as though it had a mind of its own. She would not be dissuaded just because she had no idea what she was doing and had never handled a bullwhip in her life. Those were things she could learn. She'd never failed to do something well once she set her mind to learning it. "Yes, Mr. Wilder, I do intend to haul freight to Deadwood. And no, I'm not alone. I have my boy here."

"I'm strong, ain't I, Ma?"

"You certainly are, Danny. About as strong as any man."

His chest puffed, and Jane felt a twinge of guilt at the lie, but she had to save face and appear strong, or someone would try to take advantage of her.

Mr. Wilder must have gotten the hint, because he merely nodded. "I wish you all the luck in the world."

Jane knew luck would have nothing to do with it. If there was even a small chance that this was going to work, it would be nothing less than divine intervention.

Chapter Four

It was his own fault. He had let down his guard, trusted a female, and gotten himself drugged. At least that's what he assumed had happened. Franklin kicked at the ground with the toe of his boot. He had no one to blame but himself.

The wagon tracks led in the direction of Fort Sidney. Foolish woman. What was she up to? His heart raced at the very memory of her suggesting she might move to the Fort and take in laundry. But she had to know better! She had to know what those women truly were. At least at most forts and that one in particular.

Despite the fact she had drugged him and left him sleeping while she stole his oxen and wagon, he knew she was desperate, and his heart beat with concern for her. He wasn't used to this confusing mix of emotions. Anger and worry rolled together into one massive knot in his stomach, and he wasn't altogether sure what he would do when he saw her. He was leaning toward throttling her.

To make matters worse, a clap of thunder opened the sky, and rain began to pour over the earth. It ran down his neck, soaked his clothing, and dripped from his chin and nose. Wiping it away did no good; neither did searching the horizon for shelter. Tryst, the four-year-old brown gelding, protested and picked up the pace.

Franklin understood the animal's desire to hurry. After all, the faster they went, the sooner they'd reach their destination. But the ground was beginning to turn to mud, and it would take only an instant for Tryst to slip and go down. Franklin couldn't take the chance of losing his horse, so he reined in the spirited animal.

By the time he reached the outskirts of Fort Sidney, he was soaked through and in a foul mood. A group of soldiers camped a few yards outside town. A burly sergeant nodded to him. "What's your business in Fort Sidney?"

"I've come after a woman."

The soldier's eyes grew hard. "That so? Any woman in particular?"

The suspicion in his voice and eyes annoyed Franklin. Did he look like the sort of man bent on hurting a woman?

He gathered a calming breath. After all, it would do no good for him to be at odds with the first person of authority he came across. If provoked, this man could keep him out of town and in the pouring rain. "I am following a certain woman. You might have seen her. I tracked the wagon here to the fort. She had a little boy with her. About five years old. Smarter than most youngsters."

Recognition lit the sergeant's eyes, but it was clear he wasn't ready to divulge information. Franklin didn't blame him. There was something about Jane that drew a man.

Maybe her eyes, or her gentle face, with a hint of a dimple in each cheek, or her long, smooth neck…

"What do you want with her?" The sergeant's gruff voice broke through Franklin's thoughts. Thankfully.

"She took something of mine. I'm here to get it back."

An unpleasant puff of air left the sergeant's lips. "Don't reckon I believe that. She's about the nicest gal I seen in two years. What's your real reason for following her and that little boy?"

"How about you mind your own business? If she's inside the fort, I'll find her myself and take care of things."

In a flash the sergeant had his pistol drawn, the nose pointed at Franklin's heart.

Franklin realized he had no choice but to prove he had the right to pursue Jane Albright. He reached inside his shirt.

"Easy, now," the sergeant warned, keeping the gun at a steady aim.

"Just getting a document out of my pocket. It'll prove Mrs. Albright owes me the property she has in her possession. Her husband took out a sizeable loan with me and failed to pay."

"Her man passed. That's what she claimed."

"Yes, but he had already signed everything over to me." He handed the document over to the sergeant.

"What kind of gentleman takes from a woman with a boy to raise?" The sergeant's condemnation was nearly palpable. It flew like an arrow and hit the mark.

"I never claimed to be much of a gentleman," Franklin

shot back. "What I am is a businessman." He opened his hand, and the sergeant slapped the paper into his palm.

"Well, I can't rightly keep you out of town. But I don't think it's right."

"And if I had any other option, I'd take it."

"You could marry her. She's a comely woman. The lad's a friendly sort. A man could do worse. She'll likely have ten proposals before the day's up."

Franklin's face warmed at the suggestion. It wasn't as though he hadn't considered the possibility. After all, women like Jane were a rarity out here. But he couldn't ask a woman to marry him before he was set up to give her a decent life. That was part of the reason he was so insistent on getting the homestead. The desire for a wife and children had been creeping up on him for some time. But lately, he dreamed about a family day and night.

"Mrs. Albright has made it clear she's not interested in entering into that sort of contract."

"So you asked her."

"No. But I didn't have to."

"Well, what women say and what they mean ain't always the same thing. She probably figured you didn't want to marry her and beat you to it."

Franklin shook his head. Sitting atop his horse in the rain, which thankfully had lessened to a drizzle, and discussing what women were thinking was just about the last thing he could imagine that he wanted to do. "I'll keep that in mind," he said to the sergeant. "Now, if I have your permission to go, I'd like to get my horse into a warm stall somewhere."

"All right. Go ahead." He peered closer, his eyes stern. "But I don't want no trouble. You don't hurt that woman or her boy, or you'll be answering to me and every soldier in Sidney. That clear?"

What did he think Franklin was going to do? Of course, Franklin didn't know what he was going to do himself, but in any case, he certainly wouldn't harm Jane and Danny. The most he might do was turn her over his knee for drugging him. Then he would put her on a train back East and be done with his responsibility.

* * * * *

The rain had made a mess of the street, and Jane's skirts dragged in the muddy sludge, weighing her down and making her miserable in general. She had visited McMillan's Freight, Andy's Freight, Barker Boys' Freight, and Jones and Sons. It seemed as though just about everyone in town made a living either in the saloons, on the stage, or in freighting. The problem was, not one man was willing to give her a chance. She could haul freight as well as any man, but she needed someone who was willing to see past the skirts and the little boy and give her a chance to prove it.

She walked into Solomon's Freight and Goods, her emotions past tears and at the point of anger and determination. Her boots clicked on the wood floor, and her wet skirts swooshed so much she knew she made a pathetic figure rather than the confident woman she'd hoped to portray. She click-swooshed up to the counter. "I'd like to see the manager or the owner or whomever is in charge."

The young man glanced up and his eyebrows raised.

"Well?" she said. "Don't just sit there. I said, bring out the manager."

"Is there a problem, ma'am?"

"Yes, as a matter of fact there is. A huge problem." She glared at the scrawny, bespectacled clerk and took out all of her frustrations on the first man she figured she could take in a fair fight. "I am in need of a run to Deadwood. I have a perfectly sturdy wagon, two reliable and equally sturdy oxen, and not one man in this incredibly filthy town will even speak to me, let alone allow me to haul."

A chuckle came from across the room, and Jane turned. A tall, lean man, wearing a jacket that would probably pay all of Jane's debts and purchase enough feed for the animals and seed for the entire next planting season, was smiling at her.

She scowled. "What do you find so funny, sir?"

"Your assertion that not one man in town will speak to you."

"Well, it's true." She drew herself up with all the dignity a bedraggled, forlorn woman could have and glared. "And I defy you to prove me wrong."

"Please do not be offended. I only meant that a woman as beautiful as you was likely inundated with offers for dinner and very likely a few proposals of marriage, unless I grossly underestimate the wisdom of Sidney's male population."

Danny tugged on her skirt. "Is he talking about those men that wanted to marry you, Ma?"

Jane's cheeks grew hot as the man's grin widened. "Yes, Danny. That's precisely what he is talking about. But he should know that I am not referring to foolish men trying to marry the first decent woman they've seen in only the dear Lord knows how long. I am referring only to the men in the freighting companies who will not allow me to haul their freight into Deadwood."

The man straightened and quickly closed the distance between them. He stretched out his hand. "Please allow me to beg your pardon. My manners have been deplorable. My name is Trent Bedlow."

Jane accepted the smooth, proffered hand. If this man had ever done a day's work, it hadn't been recently. The feel of the soft, smooth hand turned her stomach a little. But that wasn't all. The way he looked her down, then up, made her feel uncomfortable and unclean. "Nice to meet you, Mr. Bedlow."

He turned his attention to Danny and held out his hand. Danny scowled but politely shook, then let go as quickly as possible.

Jane turned back to the clerk. "Are you going to go get me the manager? Or shall I go exploring until I find him myself?"

The clerk's ears turned red. "But ma'am, he's—"

"What Lawrence is trying to tell you is that I am, in fact, the proprietor of this freighting company. And it would be my pleasure to discuss an arrangement over dinner, if you would allow me to escort you and the lad."

"No thank you," Jane said decisively, though her stomach rumbled at the mere mention of food. They hadn't eaten since lunch many hours earlier, and she was certain Danny was just as hungry as she. To his credit, though, he'd never said one word of complaint.

"Are you certain? I am headed out to eat now. If you'd rather wait, we can speak in the morning."

"In the morning?"

"Yes, we are getting ready to close." He smiled, but it never quite reached his eyes.

She recognized his intent. She could either go to dinner with him to discuss the freighting, or she could wait until morning. Feeling helpless, Jane released a breath. "I suppose…"

The door flung open. Jane whipped around and came face to face with Mr. Lloyd.

"What do you think you're doing?" he demanded.

"Mr. Lloyd!" Danny's joyous shout filled the room. "You woke up. Ma said she thought you were so tired you'd probably sleep all the way until tomorrow."

Mr. Lloyd stared at Mr. Bedlow. "It's a good thing for your ma that I'm a light sleeper."

"To what do we owe this pleasure, Frank?" Mr. Bedlow's words were like ice.

"It's none of your business why I'm here."

"Indeed? And likewise it is none of your affair if I escort a lovely young woman and her son out to a nice meal."

"It is when the lady in question is Mrs. Albright. I'll thank you to remove your hand from her arm."

Jane stared from one man to the other, trying to make sense of the exchange. "You two know each other?" She waited for Mr. Lloyd to demand the return of the oxen and wagon. She could kick herself for being so frugal with the laudanum. She hadn't wanted to risk giving him too much. Clearly she hadn't given him enough.

Mr. Bedlow increased the pressure on her arm. Almost painfully so. "Frank and I go way back. When he first made an appearance in Sidney preaching hellfire and brimstone. Of course it was quite a different man who rode into Deadwood a year later."

"Preaching?" Jane turned her question to Mr. Lloyd.

"That was a long time ago. And it isn't the reason I can't allow you to have dinner with him."

Jane's ire rose. Who did he think he was? "You won't allow me? Excuse me, sir. I may owe you a debt, but that certainly does not give you leave to choose my dinner companions for me." She turned her head sharply. "Thank you for your kind invitation, Mr. Bedlow. I would be delighted to accept on behalf of Danny and myself."

Mr. Bedlow turned a triumphant grin to Mr. Lloyd. "Spunky, isn't she?"

"Wait a minute," Mr. Lloyd said. "Have you forgotten why I'm here?"

The depth of his determination filled the room, as did the silence that followed. Jane's face burned. "I haven't forgotten, Mr. Lloyd. But Danny still has to be fed."

"Then I will take the two of you to dinner myself."

Mr. Bedlow drew her closer. "I have to object." His voice remained calm, but the challenge in his eyes was undeniable.

Mr. Lloyd stared back, equally challenging. Wide-eyed, Danny stared between the two men. He slipped a chubby, clammy hand inside hers. Jane knew she needed to settle the issue in such a way that Danny wouldn't be upset.

She was just about to open her mouth to speak when Mr. Lloyd spoke first. "I have a legal matter to discuss with Mrs. Albright." He turned his attention to Jane. "I won't be put off, Jane. I'm in no mood to track you down again."

Jane pulled herself from Mr. Bedlow's grasp and gave a sigh. "You win, Mr. Lloyd." Turning to the other man, she gave a nod. "I appreciate your thoughtfulness, but I suppose I will have to come by in the morning and talk business then."

Mr. Bedlow's eyebrows rose in amusement. "Certainly. I shall be here at seven." Reaching forward, he traced her jaw with his finger. "I would love to see you then."

Jane stepped back sharply, away from his too-familiar

touch, and backed into Mr. Lloyd. His hands moved to her shoulders. "She won't be here."

"No, I don't suppose she will be." Mr. Bedlow winked at Jane and left the building.

The clerk cleared his throat. "I'll be closing up now."

Mr. Lloyd took her arm and led her to the door. Jane held tightly to Danny's hand as they stepped out onto the street that still bustled with activity, even more than earlier, despite the late hour. On the homestead, she would dish up supper, they would clean up the dishes, wash before putting on pajamas, read a chapter from the Bible, say prayers, and be in bed by eight o'clock.

Jane tried to yank her arm from Mr. Lloyd's grasp, but he held tightly. "Do you want to tell me what you think you're doing?" she demanded.

"First of all, I'm not giving you a chance to run away from me again." He glanced at her, his eyes dark beneath a furrowed brow. "With or without drugging me."

Jane frowned and motioned her head toward Danny. "Listen, Mr. Lloyd, about the coffee," she whispered.

"The coffee? I should have known when you weren't drinking any."

"Please accept my apology. It was unforgivable."

"No."

His short reply startled Jane. She sidestepped a wad of used tobacco. "No?"

"No. I do not accept your apology. It was only asked for

based on your new predicament. If you had gotten away, you never would have given me another thought."

He was wrong about that, but she would never admit to him that he had filled her thoughts since the moment she awakened and found him taking such tender care of Danny. "Are you taking me to the authorities?"

"No. Not that you don't deserve it."

"Where then?"

"I'm taking you to get something to eat," he said as though speaking to a child.

Danny's steps faltered, and Jane stopped short, causing Mr. Lloyd to scowl as her arms slipped from his grasp. She bent down and gathered the little boy in her arms.

"Here, give him to me."

Danny went readily into Mr. Lloyd's arms and giggled as he was swung up onto strong shoulders. Cheyenne gave a yelp.

"Look, Ma," Danny yelled. "I'm bigger than you."

"You certainly are!" She smiled, then lowered her voice, addressing Mr. Lloyd. "Be careful with him."

Without a reply, he turned into the next building. Jane looked up and her eyes opened wide as she took in a two-story home, much like the orphanage where she grew up. It was whitewashed and tidy from the outside. A rocking chair sat, gently swaying in the breeze. She longed to sink into the chair, which had a floral print pillow on the seat.

As if reading her thoughts, Mr. Lloyd motioned to the

chair. "Go ahead and sit down with Danny. I'll go talk to the owner of the boardinghouse and see what we can do about getting you a place to sleep tonight."

"Mr. Lloyd, I can't." Humiliation burned in her cheeks. The last thing she wanted to do was remind this man that she already owed him more than she could likely pay in five years. Why would he even bring up such a matter? Was he being deliberately cruel in his effort to repay her for this morning's actions?

"The owner is a friend. Family, in a way."

She drew herself up to her highest point of dignity without standing on tiptoes. "I can't allow you to pay for mine and Danny's keep, sir."

"And I have no intention of suggesting such a thing. As I mentioned, the owner is family. I'm sure we can work out an arrangement." He scrutinized her. "Are you up to doing domestic work to pay for room and board?"

Relief flooded her. She'd rather scrub a hundred floors than be further beholden to anyone. "I am able to work for our keep."

He gently lowered a droopy-eyed Danny to the porch. Jane gathered the boy into her arms and sat in the rocking chair.

Mr. Lloyd wiped his boots on the mat outside the front door as he rang the bell. A little girl of no more than eight or nine years answered the door. Her face split into a wide grin. "Uncle Franklin! Miss Bess! Come quick!" She stamped her foot and grinned broadly. "What are you doing here?"

Mr. Lloyd laughed and swung the child into his arms. "Would you believe me if I said I came to see you?"

"No, sir, I would say you're telling a falsehood. And you know what Miss Bess says about those." She tapped his shoulder. "Besides, I'm too big for you to pick me up like this."

Chastised, he set her down. "You are getting to be quite the young lady, aren't you? Well, are you too grown up to hold my hand and take me to Miss Bess?"

The door closed on the reunion, and Jane drew Danny close to her and rocked. Her heart lifted in prayer. *Lord, what will we do now that Mr. Lloyd has found us so quickly? However will I care for my boy?*

A breeze floated across the porch. Danny sighed, and she looked down at him. A thought came to her worry-ravaged mind. God loved Danny even more than she did. He wouldn't leave them helpless.

Chapter Five

. . . .

"For heaven's sake, Franklin, why don't you just marry the girl? It's time you settle down anyway. Martha wouldn't have wanted you to stay alone the rest of your life."

The words twisted like a saber, deep and slashing. "I know." Staring at Jane sound asleep with her son nestled in her arms, Franklin couldn't deny—to himself anyway—that he was tempted to suggest the arrangement to Jane.

But the image of her slaving away on that dirty homestead flashed through his mind, and Franklin shook his head at his sister-in-law, Bess Crawford. "I'm in no position to marry again until I can build a proper home."

She gave a huff. "I've never seen a man so in need of a wife. You're getting so set in your ways, you'll wake up one day and find yourself just like Uncle Nathan."

"And I'll get around to finding one as soon as I'm settled on my homestead and can be a proper husband and father and not before. So let's not talk about it anymore."

He hadn't intended for his voice to rise. But it had, and Jane's eyes popped open. She glanced between Franklin and Bess. "I must have fallen asleep."

With characteristic nurturing, Bess reached down. "Let me take the boy. We'll lay him down in your room."

"Gracious," Jane said, standing. She smoothed her skirt. "You must be ready for my help in the kitchen."

Bess frowned. "Don't be silly, honey. Supper's been ready for ten minutes."

"Oh, well. I suppose I'll help with dishes and anything else you need from me. I appreciate you putting Danny and me up for the night."

"Your presence here is payment enough." Bess waited while Franklin opened the door. "It's very rare indeed that I have the opportunity to speak to a lady."

"How is it you came to be here?" Jane asked, her arm brushing against Franklin's as she followed Bess inside ahead of him. She looked at him as though to apologize, then turned back to Bess. "I mean, if there aren't many women who aren't…" Her face turned a becoming shade of pink. "Perhaps it's none of my business."

"Not at all. I came out with my twin sister when she got married." Her eyes cut to Franklin, but she didn't tell the secret that wasn't hers to share. "When she died a year later, I stayed on and took over her house and turned it into a boardinghouse."

"You and your husband?" Jane asked.

Bess chuckled. "Heavens, no. I'm still waiting for my man to find me." She led the way up the narrow steps and down the hall into a neat bedroom.

"You're forgetting Coop," Franklin said, amused.

"You're forgetting Coop is about the biggest heathen I know. When he decides to settle down and let God do a work in him, then I might consider one of his marriage proposals."

Noting Jane's look of confusion, Franklin took initiative. "If you're wondering about the children peeking out from different rooms, those are children Bess has taken in from here and there. She's like a beloved old aunt." He grinned fondly at her.

Bess chuckled as she laid Danny on the bed. "I may be an old maid of twenty-four, but God has given me children anyway."

"Where do the children come from, Bess?" Jane asked, sitting next to Danny's feet, removing his dusty boots.

Bess darted a gaze to the doorway where four or five children peeked in. Jane followed her gaze and nodded. Explanations would have to wait.

"Children, go get ready for bed. I'll be up to hear your prayers after we adults have our supper." She shooed them away. "The children eat in the kitchen earlier than the boarders," she explained for Jane's benefit. "Some of our boarders don't enjoy the laughter of children."

Franklin smiled at the children as he left the room. Bess and Jane followed to the dining room. The boarders were already seated and the table set. Nathan Crawford boarded with Bess and paid a fair price for his room and meals. Several other boarders were family men looking for a decent place away from the bawdy houses or the hotel above the saloons. Two of the boarders were performers. The women sat properly, but their gowns were too low-cut, and the paint plastered across their faces seemed indecent. Franklin hated that Bess rented rooms to them. But she was adamant. "If I don't, they'll end up in the saloons. Performing is bad enough, but at least they aren't doing worse."

Franklin held out a chair for Jane. She gave him a shy smile. "Thank you." Taking her napkin, she set it gently in her lap. Bess folded her hands and bowed her head. "Lord, once again we thank You for the bounty You have set before us."

Franklin shifted. Long ago he'd stopped praying, and now he felt like a hypocrite. He kept his eyes focused on the china plate in front of him. The china Martha's mother had passed down to her the day of her wedding. Franklin had laughed when Martha had insisted upon bringing it. "We're going to the basest of towns. If there's a rougher town out West, it's Deadwood."

She had smiled with her green eyes and kissed him on the nose. "Then, my darling, you bring the Scripture, and I shall bring the culture. We'll each have our part to play in God's marvelous plan for Fort Sidney."

Three years had come and gone since that moment, and though the pain had eased greatly, he still couldn't quite forgive the one who had taken his Martha. He had moved to Deadwood and struck it rich in mining. But he tired of that life quickly. He had made his fortune, hired men to mine his gold, and kept a steady income for himself and several family men, whom he paid good wages. Deadwood itself was rife with moneymaking opportunities. Men hoping to strike it rich paid the exorbitant prices charged by the freighters who risked life and limb to bring food and supplies to the dusty mining town.

Freighting companies were springing up in Sidney as fast as a man could blink, and Franklin saw no reason he shouldn't begin his own. So with the help of his uncle, Nathan, and his brother, Coop, he had started the business in Sidney. They ran Lloyd Brothers Freighting from Sidney, and he oversaw the goods from the store in Deadwood.

"Franklin?" Bess's voice brought him back from his memories. He glanced up and took the bowl of potatoes she held out. "We said amen."

"I beg your pardon." He took his potato and passed the bowl to Jane.

Franklin sat silently as the talk around the table buzzed. He rarely allowed his mind to recreate the past, but when it did, only time could remove the fullness of it and allow other thoughts to push it back. But Bess's next words jolted him back to the present. "Jane, what are your plans?"

Without missing a beat, she said, "I intend to meet with Mr. Bedlow in the morning. He said he would be at the freighting office at seven. I hope to persuade him to hire my wagon and me with it to haul supplies into Deadwood."

Bess frowned. "Meet with Bedlow? He's a despicable man. Besides, why on earth would you want to haul freight?"

Jane's cheeks reddened. "I thought him pleasant enough." She quickly sipped her water.

Uncle Nathan scowled. "Bedlow's a crook and a liar. If he wants to talk to a pretty thing like you, it ain't freighting on his mind." The silverware clinked together as his fist came down on the table to emphasize his point.

Jane's shoulders squared, and Franklin recognized her stubborn streak setting in like a determined sun peeking through clouds. "I do not know what sort of man Mr. Bedlow is, but he is the only man in any freighting company willing to give me a moment of his time." Her lips trembled. "I must find someone who will allow me to haul freight to Deadwood. I have a little boy to take care of."

Uncle Nathan shook his head and pointed his fork at Jane. "Stay in Sidney two days, and you'll get yourself a dozen proposals. Shoot, I'd marry you myself if I wasn't so old and ornery." He grinned, showing a mouth with only half the teeth God had given him.

"Thank you for your advice, sir." Jane's voice had taken on the icy tone she used when she had her mind set. Franklin hadn't known her long, but he knew her well enough to know that she didn't care for Uncle Nathan's suggestion. "But I have no intention of getting married until I pay off certain debts my recently deceased husband left me with."

Bess cleared her throat. "Yes, but we know Mr. Bedlow's character, Jane. He is not a good man where women are concerned. He owns other businesses in Sidney as well as Deadwood. Most of them cater to the—er—baser side of human nature."

The air around the room thickened with a tense silence as Jane clearly took in Bess's meaning. Her face fell. "Then I suppose I shall have to find someone else to hire my wagon."

Franklin wanted to remind her that the wagon didn't technically belong to her, but what was the use?

Uncle Nathan stared at her as though this was the first time he had really considered her presence. "You know how to crack a whip, ma'am?"

"No, sir. I have been attempting to learn from the memory of my husband's handling of it, but so far I have not been successful."

He scowled and gave a frustrated huff. "Then how do you expect to move the oxen? You have to know how to handle a whip if you're gonna haul freight."

Franklin frowned. What was Uncle Nathan doing?

"I—I don't know. I had hoped I could learn as I go along. I've been watching the freighters all day. It seems to be a precise movement of the wrist and shoulder."

"You can't learn by watching." Uncle Nathan speared a bite of meat from his plate and shoved it into his mouth. "Meet me in back of the house before breakfast, and I'll give you a lesson."

Jane's eyes grew wide. "You will?" Her hope-filled voice shot a dart of shame to Franklin. He had done nothing but discourage her since their meeting. But if she had any idea what she was attempting to get herself into, she would surely take him up on his offer of train fare back East for her and Danny.

Uncle Nathan nodded. "You say you got a wagon?"

"Yes, sir. My husband left it heavily in debt. I don't have much money to purchase supplies to haul, but I could get enough for a start."

"What I have in mind won't cost you a plug nickel."

"Just what do you have in mind, Uncle Nathan?" Franklin didn't want to believe the worst about his uncle, but what was this sudden interest he'd taken in Mrs. Albright?

"I reckon that's between me and the widow here." Uncle Nathan scowled pointedly. "Don't you think it's right admiresome that a woman like this little thing wants to work like a man to pay off her dead husband's debts?"

"Thank you, sir," Jane said before Franklin could answer. Franklin turned to her. Jane's eyes were full of unshed tears. "I shall meet you and gratefully accept your kind offer of a lesson in handling the whip."

"Ma! Ma!"

At the panicked scream from upstairs, Jane shot to her feet, then grabbed onto the table as she swayed. "Excuse me, please." She steadied herself for a second, then hurried from the room.

After she left, Franklin turned quick attention on his uncle. "What do you think you're doing?"

"Helping out a little lady I took a liking to." Uncle Nathan sipped his coffee. "What do you care?"

"I just want to know what your intentions are. Why teach her to crack a whip? She'll never find a freight company willing to allow a woman to haul supplies. It's too difficult."

"No, it ain't. I know a woman with four wagons to her name and a couple of men working for her."

"I know Sal. She's rough and strong. Jane isn't."

"Jane?" Bess's voice broke in, filled with amusement at his slipup.

"Mrs. Albright," he corrected.

Now that Bess had entered the conversation, she stayed in. "What are you thinking of doing, Uncle Nathan?"

"I'm going to let her run with me. We can pay her a fair wage. It wouldn't hurt to add another wagon. Coop was planning on bringing it up anyway. We were actually thinking another ten."

Franklin nodded. He'd been thinking the same thing. Deadwood was quickly evolving from a mining camp to a town, and with that came building, and building required wood. But that didn't mean he wanted Jane to be one of those freighters. Besides the fact that he didn't believe she could ever be suited to such difficult labor, he didn't want her to pay the debt. He'd already collected the homestead, and the cattle he'd purchased would be arriving sometime in the fall if all went well. If he allowed her to pay the debt, he wouldn't be able to connect her land to the adjoining homestead. Consequently, he wouldn't have enough land for the cattle.

"Her husband was in debt to us. Her so-called wagon is ours anyway."

Bess's mouth dropped. "You mean to tell me you're the one she's in debt to?"

His ears burned as all eyes at the table accused him. "Not really. I've already taken possession of the freight business as well as the homestead, and I have no intention of taking the payments and returning the land. That's what she wants. The homestead."

The two actresses glared at him, their eyes giving him a full accounting of their collective opinion of him—as if he cared what two painted floozies thought of him. Still, it stung being on the receiving end of everyone's disapproval.

"Mr. Lloyd has kindly offered my son and me train fare back East."

Franklin rose quickly, knocking over his chair, at the sound of Jane's voice. "That's right. Wherever they want to go, as a matter of fact, and enough to sustain them until she is able to find employment and suitable accommodations."

One of the actresses snorted. "Take the offer, honey," she said. "Get that boy out of this place."

"I have no intention of taking Mr. Franklin's offer. I don't want his money. I want my land. And I intend to pay back every cent my husband squandered and get my son's inheritance back."

"For Pete's sake, son," Uncle Nathan piped in, "give the lady back her land. You don't need it."

Franklin smarted under the harsh judgment of his own family.

Jane took her seat with a sleepy Danny in her lap. She began to fill her plate again, presumably for Danny. "I appreciate everyone's concern," she said with a sweeping glance that included everyone who had championed her. "But I do not want Mr. Franklin to give me anything. The homestead wouldn't be fully Danny's if I don't pay what we owe."

Admiration filled all eyes that settled on Jane. Franklin found himself admiring her all over again too. He glanced down at Danny. The lad didn't return the smile. Rather, he glared. Apparently, the boy had heard enough to surmise what they were saying. For the first time in his life, Franklin was the villain.

Inwardly he squirmed under the child's silent admonishment. He turned his gaze on Uncle Nathan. He supposed he could take a payment out of her salary until the homestead was paid off. "All right, Mrs. Albright. You have six months to cover your husband's debt. At the end of that time, if you haven't paid in full, you agree to accept fare back East, and I retain the land."

Jane's solemn blue eyes settled on him. "That sounds fair. Shall we put it in writing?"

Uncle Nathan laughed. "You have a table full of witnesses. He won't cheat you."

"All right then." She held out her hand. "I suppose we should at least shake on it. And, Mr. Lloyd, I will not lose my land."

In that moment, he believed her. She had won. Formidable woman. There was nothing he could do but sit back and wait for her to earn enough to settle back onto the land or quit once it became clear to her that freighting was dirty work, filled with danger and hardship.

He lay in bed that night trying to figure out how she had managed to use his wagon, his freighting company, and the salary he would be paying her to buy back a homestead that legally belonged to him and that he had no desire to lose. Bess was right. He should have just married her. A smart, pretty, godly woman. What more could a man want in a wife?

* * * * *

Jane met with Nathan Crawford before breakfast as he'd instructed. After two hours, she felt she could at the very least lay the whip on the backside of the oxen, should they fail to cooperate with her instructions.

"Now you get cleaned up and have your breakfast," Mr. Crawford instructed, as though she were one of his nieces and nephews. "Then we'll go down to the office and set you up. Where's your wagon?"

"Boarded at Wilder's Livery, with the oxen."

"Fine. I'll have them picked up and brought to our offices."

"No." Jane's heart lifted into her throat. "I'd like to settle up with Mr. Wilder and thank him personally for his kindness."

Mr. Crawford appeared confused. "Suit yourself."

As she made her way inside, through the kitchen, she

snatched two biscuits from the basket on the counter. She was about to walk out when someone gasped. "She stole them!"

Whipping around, she met the gazes of three girls and a boy. "I didn't exactly steal…"

One of the girls, a freckled, tiny thing of no more than six or seven, stepped forward. "Miss Bess says there's no need to steal, because God always provides more than enough to feed us all."

The kitchen door swung open, and Bess entered. She quietly took in the scene, then asked, "What happened?"

"She took biscuits."

Bess glanced up and captured Jane's gaze. There was no reason to explain. From the quiet understanding in the woman's eyes, it was clear she knew why Jane had done it. "Children, Mrs. Albright and Danny are guests in this house. She is going on a journey today and likely took the biscuits so they won't get hungry later."

"Yes, of course, that's right." Jane smiled at the children. "I am so sorry I didn't ask permission. It was wrong of me."

"Well, I think we should make a full basket for Mrs. Albright and Danny to take on their journey," Bess said, her eyes bright and smiling toward the children. She reached inside a cabinet and pulled out a basket. She folded a cloth from another cabinet and set it inside the basket. "What do you think? What shall we send with them?"

The children caught the joy of giving, and everyone made suggestions. By the time they were finished, Bess had shoved a basket filled with goodies into Jane's hand: sandwiches made with thick slices of ham, a jar of apple cider, peach preserves, several more biscuits, and leftover cobbler from the night before.

"All right, children," Bess said. "Please go to the table."

When they left, she smiled and handed Jane the basket. "There now," she said quietly. "This is a much better fare." She gave Jane a quick hug. "The trip to Deadwood is over two hundred and fifty miles, so the food won't last long."

"We'll be fine. I can hunt and fish."

Bess shook her head. "We have room here. You could stay on. From the looks of your and Danny's clothes, I'm guessing you're more than efficient as a seamstress. The saloon girls always want new costumes. And they pay well."

Jane's face warmed at the suggestion. She shook her head.

"Are you sure?" Bess asked. "There is more than one way to pay a debt. It doesn't have to be freighting."

"It's the fastest way to pay him back. You heard what he said. Six months." Her baby would be here before then, but she was determined. If she had to haul freight with a son at her side and a baby in her arms, that was exactly what she would do. Jane knew the urgency. Mr. Lloyd had been clear that he would be using the land himself. If she didn't pay him sooner than later, he would be settled into her house and tending her fire before she could shake a stick.

"Frank is reasonable—and a gentleman. You could do worse."

"I could do worse, what?"

Bess smiled. "You're being deliberately naïve. Frank was devoted to my sister until her death. I've never seen such a good, caring husband. I can see he has taken a liking to you. With a little bit of encouragement from you—"

A gasp escaped Jane's throat. "I could never marry him to pay a debt. Why, why, that would be—it would make me no better than those fancy women in the bawdy houses. I won't do it."

"All right, simmer down." Bess wrapped her arm around Jane's shoulder. "I understand your point of view. I don't agree with you, but I do understand." She walked her through the kitchen door and the back way around the dining room, to the stairs. "I assume you don't intend to take Uncle Nathan up on his offer of joining Lloyd Brothers Freighting."

The knot in Jane's stomach tightened. "No. I can't allow Mr. Lloyd to pay me wages that I owe him in the first place. I need to take care of this on my own."

Bess smiled affectionately. "As silly as that sounds, I understand your stubborn reasoning."

"You won't say anything, will you? I want to meet with Mr. Bedlow and make an agreement with him before Mr. Lloyd can object again."

Worry dimmed the light in Bess's eyes. "Are you sure you know what you're doing?"

Jane wasn't at all sure. But she knew Mr. Bedlow was the only freighter in town who had given her the time of day. "I suppose we'll find out," she said.

Bess reached out and wrapped her into a quick hug. "Be careful. I'll try to stall Frank as long as I can. He'll be angry when he discovers you're gone again." She chuckled. "Personally, I think it's good for a man to chase a woman. He who finds a wife finds a good thing."

"Well, I'm not looking for a husband, and even if Mr. Lloyd is looking for a wife, he's certainly not looking in my direction. He's made that abundantly clear."

"He has?"

"Just—something he said when he offered to pay our fair back East."

"Frank doesn't know what he wants. But I have a feeling he's going to find out as soon as you're out of his sight." She winked. "Make him chase you, but go slow so he can catch you."

"You're hopeless, Bess." If they'd met at a different time, they definitely would have been friends. "I'm so glad we met. Thank you for your hospitality."

"I have a feeling we're going to meet again."

They said good-bye, and Jane hurried upstairs to collect her already packed bag and Danny. With the basket of food on her other arm, she made her way to Solomon's Freight office. She had no idea why Bedlow called his business Solomon's but wasn't curious enough to ask.

"How come we left without having breakfast?" Danny asked.

"Because I have to see Mr. Bedlow, remember? We met him last night."

Danny's silence spoke pretty loudly. Jane felt chastised by her own child. She was sure his opinion of Mr. Bedlow had been shaped by Mr. Lloyd's rather obvious dislike. She had her own misgivings but wouldn't allow herself to be misled. After all, she was a grown woman.

The door was unlocked when Jane arrived at the freighting office ten minutes before seven. She ordered Cheyenne to stay outside the door and stepped inside. Lawrence, the clerk, was nowhere to be found. Jane was glad for Danny's presence at least.

"Ah, not only punctual, but early." Mr. Bedlow smiled. "A praiseworthy trait in a woman."

"In anyone, I'd venture to say."

His smile broadened, and he waved her to a chair. When he offered Danny a candy stick from a dish on the desk, Danny reached, but Jane stopped him with a firm hand on his little arm. "He hasn't eaten his breakfast yet."

Mr. Bedlow winked at Danny. "Later then." His focus returned to Jane. "Shall I send out for breakfast?"

"No, thank you. I brought food enough for a couple of days. What I need from you is for you to allow me the opportunity to haul freight between Sidney and Deadwood."

"And why, pray tell, would a woman like you wish to do such hard work?"

"We are all designed to work hard," she insisted. "I've done so for as far back as I have memory. This is simply another sort of hard work."

Pressing his fingertips together, he pierced her with his gaze. "What if I could offer you a position where you can make double the money freighting would bring you?"

Jane's shoulders straightened, and she sat a little higher in her chair. "Then I would say you are about to insult me. In which case, I will walk out of your office and never think a kind thought about you as long as I live."

A chuckle rumbled his chest, and he opened a silver box on his desk. Lifting out a cigar, he observed her as he removed the end and lit the nasty thing. "I certainly couldn't live with myself if you didn't think kindly of me."

The front door slammed, and telltale bootsteps sent a shot of dread through Jane's stomach. The door to Mr. Bedlow's office flew open, and Mr. Lloyd's frame filled the doorway.

"What do you think you're doing?" he bellowed.

Jane rose on trembling legs. "I should think it's fairly obvious. Mr. Bedlow and I were just about to come to terms of my employment."

She turned to Mr. Bedlow, whose eyes shone with conspiratorial amusement.

"What sort of game are you playing, Jane?" Mr. Lloyd stepped across the floor. "You came to an agreement with me last night."

"Indeed?" Mr. Bedlow puffed on his cigar but remained seated.

"The arrangement I made with you was merely to pay the debts my husband left." Jane turned to Mr. Bedlow. "Our agreement will allow me to honor the agreement I made with you."

"You agreed to come work for me and Coop."

"I don't even know Coop."

"Don't twist this, Jane." He reached out and grabbed her arm.

Mr. Bedlow was on his feet in a flash. "Let the lady go, Frank."

Mr. Lloyd sneered. "You wouldn't know a lady if your own mother walked into the room."

"It so happens my own mother wasn't a lady." Mr. Bedlow's voice was cold as ice. "But Mrs. Albright is, and I won't have her manhandled in my office."

Mr. Lloyd's gaze swept Jane's face. She was trying hard not to cry out from the pain of his fingers. Immediately he turned her loose. "I'm sorry, Jane. I didn't mean to be so rough. But you can't work for Bedlow. He's bad news."

"You are incorrect, Mr. Lloyd. I may work for whomever I choose."

"There you have it." Bedlow's gaze never left Mr. Lloyd's. "I'll thank you to leave my office. And for pity's sake, don't insult me in my own establishment. It's bad form."

Jane turned her back in an effort to avoid Mr. Lloyd's intense brown eyes.

"All right, Mrs. Albright. If this is the way you want it, I'll see you in Deadwood."

His boots stomped across the room and through the front

waiting area. When he left the building, he slammed the door so hard the building shook.

Suddenly Jane felt the urge to run after him and tell him she'd changed her mind. That she would work for him, if he wanted her to. She turned toward the door and almost reached for Danny to do just that, but Mr. Bedlow's voice stopped her. "Well, now. Shall we talk terms? I'd have preferred another position for you, but I see you are set in your ways and won't be satisfied with anything other than a freighting position. There is an expedition beginning this morning. Get your wagon and bring it back here so we can get it loaded." He glanced at Danny. "Where's the boy going to stay while you're on the road?"

Jane drew in a breath at the question. "He'll come with me, of course."

Mr. Bedlow studied her face briefly, then nodded. "It's your choice, but you alone will be responsible for his well-being. His meals come out of yours."

"I alone have taken care of my son since the day he was born, and I have no intention of passing along his care to anyone else." Jane held out her hand. "I thank you for the opportunity to haul supplies for you. You've done me a great service."

He took her hand, turned it over. "These are hands that have seen hard work."

"As I told you."

He traced her calluses with his fingertip. "If you decide freighting is not for you, I can give you a more suitable position in Deadwood."

Jane didn't even want to surmise what position he might find suitable. She jerked her hand from his. "No thank you."

"You misunderstand. I'm making you a fair and almost honorable proposition."

"Sir, I don't know what you have in mind but—"

He gave a short laugh. "Nothing, Mrs. Albright. I am jesting at your expense. Forgive me."

Jane studied his face, wondering why he backed away from what he'd been planning to say. Whatever it was, she was grateful he had changed his mind.

She nodded. "I shall return soon with my wagon and oxen. Come along, Danny." With her head high, she left his office.

Six months—that was how long she had to save her home for her children. She couldn't fail. She would not. She clasped Danny's hand tightly and placed her other hand on the soft spot where her baby grew. These children would not grow up without a home, a place where they knew they belonged. If she had to work blisters into her hands and knots into her muscles—whatever it took, she would not let Mr. Lloyd take her home away.

PART TWO:
DEADWOOD

Chapter Six

....

Early June

Tomorrow the wagons would reach Deadwood. Jane nearly wept with relief at the very idea. For the past two days, even the oxen seemed to sense they would soon have a few days to rest, for they moved without as much hesitation.

Camp tonight was a cheery affair with music and dancing.

When Mr. Bedlow spoke of a line of wagons, she had been concerned about spending a month alone with freighters whose morals were questionable. But as he had promised, he had "taken care" of the situation, and the men left her alone in favor of the three saloon girls Mr. Bedlow was sending to Deadwood. He had gone on ahead by stage to open Bedlow's Saloon and had taken two of his favorite young women with him to start things off.

Oh, how she hated the high-pitched laughter and drunken slurring of speech. How she abhorred the very idea that Danny had to be exposed to such debauchery. She had to remind herself daily that he was very young and would likely not remember any of the trip. And when she returned to Sidney for the next load of supplies, she had every intention of leaving Danny with Bess Crawford. The good thing for Danny was that the men and the women doted on him, so to him, this new adventure was like Christmas.

The music ebbed quickly tonight, and Andy Armor began to play softly. Jane moved toward the fire to gather the dishes. The three-fingered harmonica player nodded when she approached. Noting his tin cup was empty, she lifted the coffee pot from the fire and refreshed his coffee.

His eyes twinkled his thanks, and without stopping, he slowly began to play "Amazing Grace." Jane took a deep breath, fighting tears, and sank onto the log the men had laid out to sit on. She closed her eyes and allowed the music to wash over her. How long had it been since she'd spent time in real prayer? They rose before dawn and often didn't get to sleep before midnight. Most nights, she fell asleep as soon as she took her place on the pallet next to Danny. *O Lord*, she silently prayed. *I haven't been behaving much like a woman covered by Your grace. Forgive me for neglecting You.*

As she poured out her heart to God, the new life inside her made its little presence felt. "Oh!" She hadn't meant to speak out loud. Her hand went to her stomach, and her eyes flew open.

Mr. Armor stopped playing and stared. "Something wrong, ma'am?"

A tiny smile touched her lips at the goodness of God. "No, Mr. Armor. Everything is wonderful. Thank you for playing that song. It was a beautiful reminder to me that God is with me. I'm not lost at all from His sight. He found me and knows exactly where I am."

He cleared his throat and looked away. "Glad you liked it. Wish I'd known. I'd have played it every night."

"No you ain't!" Bob Thacker growled from his bedroll. "I ain't listenin' to no church music."

"What's a-matter, Bobby?" Sarah, a buxom woman with hair too red to be real, teased. "Afraid you'll get religion?"

"That ain't never gonna happen!" He glared at the woman and sneered toward Jane. "Besides, give this one a week in Deadwood, and she won't be askin' for no church music, neither."

Refusing to engage in an argument with the half-intoxicated freighter, Jane picked up the stack of dishes and stood. "Good night, all of you. Pleasant dreams."

She peeked in on Danny and then dipped the dishes in the cool, sudsy wash water. She would finish the dishes, then crawl in beside her little boy. Her aching muscles strained for the moment.

It was unfortunate that Bob held such a disdain for the hymn. He led the wagons and had been put in charge, so it was unlikely Andy would defy him and play "Amazing Grace" again. But that wouldn't stop her from humming it if she chose.

And she did. When she was halfway through the pile of dishes, she heard a branch crack and lifted her head sharply. One couldn't be too careful out here. There was always the threat of Indians and outlaws. But neither of those proved to be the case. Molly, a young prostitute of no more than sixteen years old, walked toward her, smiling. "The men are asleep. I thought you might like some help with the dishes. It's not fair that Bob makes you do them."

Molly was rosy-cheeked and cheerful naturally, not from opium or alcohol—as far as Jane knew, anyway. "There's a towel right there. You could dry if you want."

She nodded and began to dry. "I liked the way Andy played 'Amazing Grace.' It took me back to the days when I lived on my grandma's farm in Kansas."

"How did you happen to find your way to Sidney?"

Jane had never asked before. Had barely spoken to the women on private terms like this. But the question seemed natural, so she didn't hold back.

Molly sighed. "It was just my grandma and me. Ma left when I was little—nearly broke Grandma's heart. I tried so hard to be good to make up for my ma's wicked ways. After Grandma died, the bank said there was nothing for me, and the land had a mortgage, so I had to leave."

With her arms up to her elbows in suds, Jane could only nod. "I am facing similar circumstances. Only I'm widowed. So I'm forced to haul this freight until I pay off my debt and clear my land."

Molly gave a short, humorless laugh. "I answered an advertisement for a housekeeper."

"Let me guess—someone wanted more than housekeeping."

"Yes. Mr. Bedlow. He said I owed him for the fare out here and the new clothes he had sent me, and I had to do what he wanted or he'd set the law on me."

"How long have you been with Mr. Bedlow?"

"Three years."

Jane gasped into the night air. Anger shot through her. "Are you telling me you were only thirteen when you came to Sidney?"

"Yes ma'am." She ducked her head as though ashamed. "But Mr. Bedlow didn't make me entertain until last year. I only cleaned and served drinks before that."

This young, innocent girl had been raped over and over every day for a year. "Oh, Molly. Have you paid your debt?"

"Yes. I am free to go, so he says. But others have tried to leave, and Mr. Bedlow doesn't take kindly to it."

"So what if he takes kindly to it or not? I know, come back with me when I go to Sidney. You can find a position as a seamstress or domestic somehow. I'm sure Bess Crawford will help you."

Molly wiped the last dish and set it on the stack. "It's too late for me to do anything else."

"Don't be silly. It's never too late. A bright girl like you could find a position. Or maybe you can find a decent man and settle down."

When Molly fixed her lovely eyes on Jane, suddenly Jane felt as though she were the child.

"Thank you for speaking with me, Miss Jane. It was nice. I've wanted to a lot, but Mr. Bedlow told us to stay away from you." Her eyes grew worried. "I hope you won't say anything to him about this."

Outrage shot through Jane. How dare that vile man taint these women and then cause them to feel as though they were somehow untouchable. On impulse, she reached out and drew the girl to her. Molly's arms remained at her side. Embarrassed, Jane pulled back.

"Good night, Mrs. Albright. And good-bye. Once we get to Deadwood, it won't be proper for you to speak to me."

She watched Molly, knowing that only because of God's grace had she escaped the same fate. Orphaned at a young age, Jane had been taken in by a greedy, lazy, fat old cow who made her and the other children in the orphanage call her "Mama Rose." Mama Rose had forced Jane to apprentice in the shop of a seamstress, where she'd learned quickly and become in such high demand that Mama Rose eventually allowed her to leave the shop and commission dress orders herself. She shuddered to think where she would be if Mama Rose had been inclined toward ungodly practices.

Jane lay down next to Danny and pressed her hand to her fluttering stomach. It had been a month now. If Mr. Bedlow kept his word, she would have half the money by this time tomorrow. When she got back to Sidney, she could give it to Mr. Lloyd and load up for one more trip like this one. Then she'd never ever have to leave her home again.

She drifted to sleep, dreaming of the little soddy waiting for her to come home and build the rest of her life.

* * * * *

The relentless sky opened, dumping another hard rain on the saturated town. The streets were already inches deep with mud. Horses and oxen struggled to lift one leg after the other. The freight coming in today was going to be a mess. Still, he had every intention of meeting Bedlow's wagons and taking Danny and Jane away from the riffraff as soon as they climbed down.

Impatiently, Franklin turned and walked back toward the counter. He hoped the wagons would arrive soon. Behind him, the bell over the door clanged, and the aroma of cinnamon filled the air. He turned to see Mam Truman, an old Negro woman, shuffling into the store, a cloth-covered basket over her arm. The red bandana covering her nearly white hair was soaked, and she wiped a wrinkled hand across her dark face.

"I swan! I think I saw a few dawgs and cats comin' down out of the sky."

"Hello, Mam." Franklin chuckled. "Is that what you've got in your basket? Because we don't need any more dogs and cats roaming the streets of Deadwood."

She laughed and waved a hand at him. "Nawsir. Sumpin' better than cats in here. Got my twisty cinnamon bread."

"Umm. That's what I'm smelling."

Casey, his apprentice, usually handled this type of business transaction, but Franklin had sent the boy on an errand an hour ago, and he still hadn't returned. He tossed her a dry rag from beneath the counter. "Here, set your basket down and dry yourself off."

While she patted her face, neck, and head with the towel, Franklin raised the cloth off the basket and counted the loaves out on the counter. Mam's bread was famous in Deadwood, and he understood why. His Chinese cook, Cheng, insisted on making his own bread and pastries for the house and was insulted when Franklin had brought several of Mam's delicacies home. So, rather than force the issue, Franklin enjoyed some of the bread now and then at the store.

He opened the cash register and counted out the right amount of coins into her hand.

"Thank you kindly, Mistah Franklin. I gotta get goin'. I'll be back later in the week."

"Don't go out in this downpour, Mam. Wait until it lets up."

"Naw. I gwine be late if I don't scurry. I still have two more general stores and a café to deliver to."

He stood at the door and watched as she climbed into her wagon and flicked the reins at the sodden mules.

At another rumble of thunder, Franklin checked his watch again. The wagons should be rolling into Deadwood by now. His scout had come back yesterday with the news that they were within eight miles of town. His stomach dipped and dove at the thought of seeing Jane again. For the life of him, he couldn't figure why. But he was anxious to make sure she was well and no harm had come to her.

The scout had assured him she seemed well, but he wouldn't be satisfied until he saw for himself. Most likely the rain had delayed their progress.

His own wagons were a full day behind Bedlow's. He had more supplies and had chosen to take a slower pace to preserve the animals.

He put all the bread in a bread basket for customers to choose from. At the first shouts from the townsfolk and rattles from the oxen and wagons, Franklin stepped out of his office and headed over to Bedlow's General Store. Most of the supplies would be unloaded there.

He searched from wagon to wagon but didn't see Jane or Danny. He heard a woman's voice, strong, commanding, confident. With a shock, he realized he'd overlooked her driving the first wagon. Beneath a large hat that covered her mass of blond hair, Jane's face remained tense with concentration as she called to the oxen and cracked the whip with precision, demanding that they move through the sludge. He couldn't hold back a grin. Pretty Miss Jane had proven him wrong. She was as capable as any man, just as she had predicted.

The manager of the general store, an unlikely businessman with chaps and a six-shooter, was outside to greet the wagons. Craig Shewmate was just about the meanest man in town, which was saying a lot for a town like Deadwood, and a crook to boot. The only man he hadn't tried to swindle was Bedlow, and that only because Bedlow was powerful and wouldn't blink before putting a bullet through Craig's head.

Jane pulled to a stop and Franklin moved forward to help her from the wagon. Before he could make his presence known to her, she stood holding the whip. He stopped short, observing her transformation from the young woman he'd met a month earlier. First, she had set aside proper female attire in favor of trousers, a red plaid top, and a fringed jacket made by the Indians. She must have purchased it from one of the Indians at Fort Sidney who came to trade for dry goods. The second surprise in her appearance was that she seemed to have gained several pounds—an unusual occurrence on the trail. Bedlow must be feeding his crew pretty well.

Craig glanced inside the wagon. "Are any of your personal things in there?" he asked.

Jane held up a burlap bag from the wagon seat. "This is it."

Franklin hung back and waited while Craig looked around inside the wagon. After a few minutes, the store manager jumped down. He gave a grunt and spat a stream of tobacco juice.

"All right then. You're free to go if you choose. The wagons move back out in three days, but Mr. Bedlow will expect to see you in the morning."

A frown puckered Jane's forehead. Clearly she had no idea what she should do during the interim.

Franklin stepped forward, and Jane finally spotted him. She didn't speak, but Danny, who had been peeking from behind the canvas, now jumped out. "Ma, look—it's Mr. Lloyd!" He fell into Franklin's arms.

"Danny, be careful!" Jane admonished.

"We made it, Mr. Lloyd. Look at us."

Cheyenne emerged from under the wagon, his tail wagging as he nosed forward, trying to get attention. Franklin obliged and scratched the dirty dog's head.

"Ma says I grew an inch while we were on the trail. Do you think I did?"

"Only an inch? I'd say an inch and a half." Franklin set the boy down and reached for Jane. She settled into his arms, and he slowly lifted her down. He had dreamed of her for weeks. Now, even dirty, wet, and dressed like a man, she stirred his heart. "How was the trip?"

She pushed gently out of his arms. "As well as can be expected, I suppose."

"Come to my house. I have a room made up for you and Danny, and my housekeeper is drawing you a bath."

He could see the hunger that came into her eyes at the mention of a bath. But she shook her head. "Aren't you angry with me?"

"Not so much angry anymore. But concerned for your safety and unnecessary work."

"I don't think it's unnecessary."

Franklin lifted her hand and squeezed. "Please, let's don't fight. Bess made me promise to take care of you while you're in Deadwood, so I came over to invite you to stay in my home while you're in town. I'm not going to try to talk you out of working for Bedlow."

Her eyes squinted as suspicion walled the openness of her expression. "What do you mean, stay in your home?" A crack of thunder made her jump and she squealed, proving that even in man's clothes she was still very female.

He grinned. "I assure you I have nothing improper in mind. Deadwood isn't the most virtuous of towns, and I want you closer, where I can keep you safe."

"I'm sure you're very noble, but I can't stay in a man's home. It isn't proper."

"Your only other option is a hotel. We don't have boarding-houses here like Bess's. There are no matronly women who will invite you to stay with them out of pity for you and fondness for your attractive little boy."

She scowled at him and lifted her eyebrows in that stubborn way she had. He had never known a woman so easy to read.

"Well, I suppose I shall have to stay in the hotel then."

Franklin pointed across the street to the saloon with a hotel above it. "That's your choice."

"There are no other hotels? Nothing that isn't above a saloon?"

"That's it." He took a deep breath. "That isn't entirely true. There is the Grand Central Hotel. But it's expensive and not well-built."

"Well, I can't afford expensive."

"Then there's your option."

As if by design, two men came swaying out of the saloon singing at the top of their lungs. They were so drunk they leaned heavily on each other—even at barely three in the afternoon.

"Imagine what it will be like in there when you're trying to sleep." Franklin looked back at Jane.

"Well"—she hesitated—"I can't take Danny into such a place and, like you said, your place is no more improper than staying in a hotel above a drinking establishment."

"If it makes you feel better, I have two other men working for me. One is a cook, and the other the housekeeper."

"Why would it make me feel better to know that I am not only staying with one man in the house, but three? I was better off on the trail. At least there were other women along."

"Other women?" Outrage shot through him like an arrow. "Do you mean to say there were—"

She nodded, pressing her finger to her lips and staring pointedly at Danny.

Franklin could throttle Bedlow for sending prostitutes on the trail with Jane and Danny. The man probably thought it a hilarious joke to have those women accompany a lady. "Are you ready to come along, then? I instructed my housekeeper to prepare a bath for you."

She nodded. "That sounds lovely. As long as I can be back here early in the morning."

"To see Bedlow?"

"Yes. We need to settle up, and I can give you half what I owe for the homestead."

"Half? That much?"

"Yes. After you gave me six months, Mr. Bedlow figured how much it would take to pay you off in the allotted time, and he is paying me accordingly."

Franklin had no idea what Bedlow had up his sleeve, but

he knew even a generous man, which Bedlow wasn't, would never pay that much for freighting. She was being deceived.

"Jane—"

"Don't say it. I mean it. I know how you feel about Mr. Bedlow. But he's my employer, and I have to maintain my respect for him." She grimaced. "For now anyway. If I begin to despise him, I won't be able to retain a proper attitude when we speak. And that could get me dismissed."

"Good—then forget all of this. Sell the oxen and wagon. That will get you some profit."

"They're yours. Or have you forgotten?" She grinned. "Any profit from them is already yours."

"Well, then, I give you permission to sell them to pay me."

Shaking her head, Jane gave a weary sigh. "It can't work that way. I want my children to be proud of their home and to know that no one gave it to me. I earned it for them." She glanced around. "Anyway, I thought Mr. Bedlow would greet the wagons. But apparently he's decided not to do so."

"He's down the street in his saloon."

"His saloon?"

"He owns two saloons."

"Oh. Of course. I knew that." Her face grew pink. "And he's in one of them?"

"Yep."

"You don't think I'll have to go talk to him in the saloon tomorrow, do you? Surely he'll come to the general store."

He didn't have the heart to tell her that Bedlow's office

was indeed in the saloon. He rarely visited the general store. Instead Franklin grabbed up Danny and swung him up to his shoulders. "Let's go, then." Cheyenne loped along after them.

They slogged through the mud until they reached Lloyds' Mercantile. "Let's go in here. I have a few things to take care of before I can leave for the rest of the day. And we have some fresh cinnamon bread that our baking lady just brought in less than an hour ago. That should ease the sting of having to wait on me."

Jane shrugged. "It's all right. Take your time. It's just nice to be out of the rain and to know I'll soon be clean."

Franklin finished up a few accounts he had open and was just about to close everything up when gunshots blasted outside. Jane gasped and Danny ran to the window. "Danny!" Franklin hollered, rushing across the room and snatching up the little boy. He retreated to a safe place on the other side of the room, then held the boy up so they were eye to eye. "You have to stay away from the window when there's a shootout because too many times a wild bullet breaks the glass. We don't want anything to happen to you, do we? What would your ma do without her little man?"

The little boy was wide-eyed, and his body shook with fear.

Franklin held him closer. "Hey, it's all right. I don't hear any more shooting. It must be over now."

"Give him to me." Jane frowned. "He wasn't scared of the shooting. He was scared of you."

"Of me?"

"You yelled at him and grabbed him. How was he supposed to know you weren't going to hit him?"

Franklin stared at her. Did she honestly think he'd harm Danny? "Why would he think such a thing?"

"His pa wasn't kind. He often got rough with Danny. It's why the freighting wagon was such a glorious opportunity to have him out of the house most of the time."

Franklin wasted no time. He stepped closer to Jane. "Danny, I'm sorry I scared you. I promise I'll never harm you. Do you believe me?"

Danny gave him a wary nod.

Anger burned in him at the thought that Tom Albright had been such a harsh man, his child was still afraid of him months after his death. Had he ever hit Jane? Franklin couldn't even bear to think about it.

He locked up the office and walked outside to the wagon he'd hitched and left waiting over the last hour. He helped Jane into her seat and lifted Danny in so that he sat between them. As they drove to his house, he couldn't help but wonder what sort of man would have this precious gift and not value what he had.

Chapter Seven

....

Jane fingered the books on the shelves, testing the spine of each edition. Shakespeare, Dickens, Thoreau, Edgar Allan Poe. She sighed at the richness and diversity of the books.

"Choose one if you want."

Jane turned at the sound of Mr. Lloyd's voice. "Thank you. I'd enjoy that."

"Danny sleeping?" Mr. Lloyd asked.

Jane nodded. "His eyes shut as soon as he lay down, and he fell right to sleep."

She could feel Mr. Lloyd's eyes on her back as she perused the shelves. Jane was glad she'd brought her Sunday best dress, even though she hadn't been to a church meeting in years and even if her best wasn't very good. After weeks in men's trousers, the soft cotton petticoats felt lovely, the corset, suffocating. But she enjoyed the appreciation in his eyes when she'd walked into the dining room, hair drawn up with little tendrils hanging about her neck and cheeks.

The long soak in the tub had helped to ease some of the stiffness in her muscles. That, combined with a full stomach, now left her feeling cozy and drowsy and delicious.

"I know I wasn't very gracious earlier, but I do thank you for inviting Danny and me to stay."

After observing Deadwood, the saloons, the fighting, shootings, and overall filth, she was more grateful than she could possibly convey to get Danny away from that atmosphere and tucked safely into bed for the night.

"You're more than welcome."

A pregnant pause seemed just the right time for her to turn around and face him. Her face warmed under his scrutiny. "Your home is lovely, Mr. Lloyd."

"It's more than I need." His wistful tone caught her full attention. "I bought the house a year ago from a man who built it for his bride." He grinned. "She took one look at Deadwood, hopped back on the stage, and refused to spend one night here."

"I can't say I blame her. I don't know what I'd have done without your hospitality."

His eyebrow went up. "That's the chance you take when you decide to be stubborn."

A spark of irritation ignited within her. Why did he have to ruin her grateful moment with such a superior attitude? "I don't think wanting to pay my own way and build a decent, stable home is stubbornness. Personally, I think it's admirable."

"What do you think you're going to do with the land once you pay off the debt? You're not going to be able to plant and harvest alone with a little boy. You can't afford to hire a man to do it, and even if you could, who would you get? All the men are either mining or homesteading for themselves, with no time to hire on somewhere else."

Jane walked to the end of the large bookcase to distance herself from him as much as possible without being too obvious. She knew he had a valid point. It was something she should be concerned about. The farm couldn't subsist without a means of support. Sowing and reaping: that's how God made the earth to sustain itself. Without sowing, how would she reap?

She shrugged. "I will consider that once I actually pay off the debt and have my home back."

He looked annoyed. "You know I was perfectly within my right to call in that note. Your husband was three months past due for when the entire amount was to be repaid. I was patient, considering I never received even a single penny. Bedlow would have had him killed and then tossed you off your land without thinking twice."

"Then I suppose that makes you a better man than Bedlow."

A scowl marred his otherwise handsome features. "That's not what makes me a better man than Bedlow. You should never have gotten involved with that man. He is cruel—a thief and a murderer."

"I find that difficult to believe, Mr. Lloyd. Mr. Bedlow may be sinful and even cruel to the young women he employs, but surely the sheriff would have arrested him by now if he were truly such an outlaw." Jane had no idea why the two men seemed to be at odds, but Mr. Lloyd's animosity wasn't a very attractive quality. "Honestly, you seem almost jealous."

Mr. Lloyd stood. "You think jealousy is motivating my concern for you?"

Horror filled Jane. He thought she meant he—

"I assure you, that isn't what I meant. I only meant you're wealthy. Perhaps not as wealthy as Mr. Bedlow, but…" She realized how daft she sounded. "I'm sorry. I shouldn't have implied any such thing."

Taking her by the shoulders, Mr. Lloyd forced her to meet his gaze. "Jane, listen to me. Mr. Bedlow is not just a wealthy man with too much time and money at his disposal. He is motivated by greed. Every decision he makes is about what he can attain. I can't guess why he took you on unless it was to spite me. But even that doesn't seem likely. He doesn't do things that don't benefit him. I just want you to be careful. And as for the sheriff, don't ever think you can run to him if you're in trouble with Bedlow. Bedlow owns the sheriff and most of the town."

The intensity in his eyes took away her breath. Jane's mind shifted back to those few days in the soddy when he took care of her and Danny. How could she have such conflicting thoughts and emotions about a man?

"Why does it matter to you?" she whispered, unable to look away from his beautiful brown eyes that, for all indications, were sincere. "Danny and I are strangers—strangers indebted to you at that."

He didn't speak for a moment but searched her face. Then he dropped his hands from her arms and walked back to his seat. "I don't know why I care. Maybe it's guilt."

"Guilt for taking my land?"

He gave a wry grin and shook his head. "Guilt for hoping you can't raise the money to pay the debt."

"That's terrible." Her lip trembled, and she turned away so he couldn't see.

"Maybe so. But I have cattle coming in the fall with nowhere to graze. Your dream is to leave a legacy to Danny. And mine is to build a legacy to pass on to any children I have in the future. So you see we have the same thing in mind. The difference is, I own the land."

She slid a poetry book from the shelf and turned to face him. "Not for long." But his desire to ranch explained why he had fought so hard to convince her that going east was the best option for her. "You have Hank's land. Raise your cattle there."

"I intend to have a lot of them. Many more than the adjoining land can sustain."

"You could always rent the land from me." She'd said it as a flip alternative.

He brought his head up. "You would consider that?"

Jane caught her breath as the possibility became real. "Well, I hadn't before this, but it might serve us both well. And maybe my son can learn ranching from you. But you would have to agree to move your cattle off the land by the time Danny is ready to start his own herd."

"I could agree to that."

"In writing."

"Don't trust me?" He laughed.

"I'm learning that everything should be put into writing."

He nodded. "You're right." His eyes twinkled. "I'll go with you to tell Bedlow."

Jane frowned. "Tell him what?"

"That your first trip with freight was your last."

Jane fingered the book, hugging it close. "Why would I tell him that?"

He started to speak but closed his mouth. Then his eyes lit with revelation. "You want it in writing first. Fine. I'll have my lawyer draw up papers in the morning; then we can speak with Bedlow."

Jane wasn't sure what he thought they'd agreed upon, but clearly their expectations weren't united. Which was another good reason for something in writing.

"Mr. Lloyd—"

"Franklin. We're neighbors now."

Jane scowled. "Mr. Lloyd, we seem to have a misunder-standing. I shall rent the land to you, after I pay the debt that I owe you. Otherwise, aren't you really renting land from yourself?"

He released a heavy breath. "Have you always been this stubborn, or is it a recent occurrence?"

"Always." She shrugged. Stubbornness wasn't her best quality, Jane knew that. But sometimes a woman had to stand her ground in order to take care of herself. And in this case she had Danny and the baby to worry about too.

"Then what if we agree upon a rental price, and each month I will take that amount off the debt until it is paid in full."

The thought brought a glimmer of hope to Jane's weary heart. That wouldn't feel like charity, would it? She would still be paying him, only in trade. Barter was a perfectly acceptable manner of currency, especially when times were tough. Mama Rose had taught her that.

"I believe I can agree to that, sir."

The light in Mr. Lloyd's eyes could only be pure happiness and maybe a bit of relief. "Tomorrow we'll go together and tell Trent you're not leaving with the freighters when they go." He gazed down at her as though he wanted to hug her but held back. "Will that be acceptable?"

Jane suddenly felt shy. She nodded and swallowed hard. Her mind asked questions she didn't have the nerve to ask. Such as, "When, oh when can we go home?"

Thankfully, he answered for her. "Give me a few days to wrap up some business, and I'll take you back to your homestead. I can get settled in and have my house built over the summer."

"Too good for a soddy?" Jane smiled. The soddy had served her well over the past four years, but her heart longed for the feel of plank floors beneath her feet.

"I have no need to live in a soddy. A home is what I want, and I am financially capable of getting what I want. As a matter of fact, when you're finished paying the debt from the rent, we can start designing a home for you, if you like."

The thought was such a distant dream in her heart that Jane had never really considered the possibility. "I suppose it's something to think about." Although she had the children's future to consider too. If Danny were to build his own herd, he would need money to get started. So saving money should be her first priority. Of course as the children grew, the soddy would become too cramped for them.

It was too much to take in when she was so weary from the weeks on the trail. With a soft sigh, she walked to the wing chair and sat. Her dress pulled tight around her belly. She looked up to find Mr. Lloyd staring at her middle with a frown. "You're—?"

Before she could answer, the door opened, and one of the servants entered. "Telegram, Mr. Lloyd, sir." The man wore long braids in his shiny black hair. He spoke little English from what Jane had surmised thus far. She'd never seen a Chinese man or woman before today but was thrilled to see this one walk in the door at that moment and divert Mr. Lloyd's attention from her bulging stomach.

"Thank you, Huan."

The servant bowed and left the room without the slightest hint of a sound.

Reading the telegram, Mr. Lloyd's eyebrows drew up in horror.

"What is it?" Jane asked. "It isn't Bess or one of the children?"

He inhaled a ragged breath. "It's my brother, Coop. He's been shot. There was a dispute over payroll."

Jane gasped and stood as quickly as her pregnancy would

allow. "Oh, Franklin, I'm so sorry. Is he—is he okay? Or..." How did one know how to ask the first question that came to mind without tearing open a wound?

He shook his head. "I don't know. The telegram was brief. *Coop shot. Payroll dispute. Come home.* Listen, Jane, I must ride out faster than a wagon would allow, and I couldn't ask you and Danny to keep the pace I'll be forced to take. Will you wait for me here? Make yourself at home. The servants' names are Shen Huan and Shen Cheng. They're brothers. Cheng works in the kitchen. I usually just call him Cookie. Shen is their last name. That's how they do it in China. Last name first. I will tell them to serve you as they'd serve me, and when I return, I'll take you home."

"But I can—"

"No." He took her hands. His were ice cold. "You mustn't try to go home alone. It's too dangerous, especially for a woman." She opened her mouth to protest, but he gave her no opportunity. "Even a capable woman, such as yourself. Promise me?"

"All right. I will wait for you. But please don't instruct the servants to serve us. We have always cared for our own needs."

He smiled. "Cookie won't let you near the kitchen, and Huan is adamant about how the house should be cleaned. Believe me, it's for your own protection."

Jane returned his smile. She could only guess how much the effort had cost him, given the situation at home. "Then

I suppose I will have to be a lady of leisure for the next few weeks."

"You deserve it."

Embarrassed, she glanced at the floor. "When will you go?"

"Before daybreak. Do you feel like you can go to Bedlow alone?"

Jane gave a short laugh. On one hand, it felt good to have a man care about her enough to want to protect her. On the other hand, it was a bit insulting. "I am not a child, Franklin. I've been fighting my own battles for quite some time."

"All right, then. But be careful. He's vermin and will not be glad that you are leaving him."

"I'll be careful."

He nodded. "If you'll excuse me, I'll say good night." He lifted her hand, which he still held, and briefly pressed her knuckles to his lips. "Good-bye for now. Tell Danny good-bye."

"I will."

Jane couldn't pull her gaze away as he walked purposefully toward the door. When he got there, he turned with a smile. "I like the way you say my name."

Heat poured into her cheeks as he left. She listened to the thump of his boots on the wooden floor until they were out of earshot.

With a sigh, she dropped into her seat and lifted her knuckles to her cheek. This was the first time she'd ever been the recipient of such a gallant gesture. She closed her eyes, savoring the memory.

* * * * *

Deadwood bustled with activity as Jane and Danny made their way through the throng and headed toward Mr. Bedlow's General Store. Despite the rushing and yelling and bodies hurrying to purchase supplies, for Jane it felt as sullen as a graveyard without Franklin's presence. He had already been gone when she awoke to a bright morning sun streaming in her window. A curious disappointment twisted her stomach. She had to admit to herself that perhaps her feelings for him were more than just mere friendship.

Even Danny had missed him. She had told her son that they would be staying in the enormous house and that Mr. Lloyd wouldn't be back for a few weeks. Danny seemed glad they would eventually be going home to the homestead. But he was fascinated with Mr. Lloyd's Chinese helpers, and she had a suspicion the feelings were mutual. Even Cookie had allowed Danny in the kitchen while he cooked breakfast. He listened to Danny's incessant questions and valiantly tried to answer a few of them in his broken English.

To her relief, Mr. Bedlow was at the general store when she arrived. She had suspected he might be in the saloon. The store was dusty and looked as though it hadn't been tidied in a while. Nothing like Franklin's spit-spot mercantile.

Mr. Bedlow stood behind the register. He pushed in the drawer as she walked across the room. She smiled, although her palms were damp with nervous energy.

"Good morning, Mrs. Albright." His face was solemn.

"Just the person I needed to see. Please, come with me into the office." Without waiting for an answer, he walked toward the door at the back of the store.

Jane held tightly to Danny's hand and followed.

Bedlow looked at Danny just before they went inside the office. "How about staying out here with Craig? He'll give you a peppermint stick."

Danny grinned at the mention of the sugary treat. "Thank you, sir!"

"Oh, but I'd rather he stays with me," Jane objected.

"Trust me." Mr. Bedlow took her arm, smiling all the while. "It would be better if he didn't hear what I have to say to you."

Alarm seized her stomach. "I don't understand."

"You will, shortly."

She turned and caught a glimpse of Danny being swung up onto Craig's massive shoulders as Mr. Bedlow pulled her into the office and closed the door.

"Sir, what is this all about?" she asked, her frustration over his callous disregard for her wishes bolstering her courage. "I demand you bring my son back to me."

"Sit down, Jane."

His hard tone and commanding demeanor bade her obey, so she did, slowly lowering herself onto a hard, wood chair. "What is this about?" Fear chased away any semblance of bravery she might have felt a moment ago.

"I'm disappointed in you, Jane, dear."

"Please address me as Mrs. Albright. It truly is improper for you to keep speaking in such a familiar tone."

He kept his eyes, dark and glittering, on her as he lifted a cigar from a silver box, identical to the one in the freight office in Sidney. He bit off the end and spat it on the floor. The silence seemed deafening. Seconds ticked off as though they were minutes. Finally he lit the cigar, puffed a few times, and pointed at her with the cigar between his fingers. "As I said, I am disappointed in you, Jane."

Realizing propriety was the last thing he cared about, she concentrated on his words. "What have I done to disappoint you, Mr. Bedlow?"

"I thought you were an experienced freighter."

"No, sir. I never implied such a thing."

"So you say. But there are four men back in Sidney who will testify to your bragging in an unladylike manner."

A gasp left her throat. "Why, that's not true. What did they say I bragged about?"

"That you were the best freighter in the Black Hills."

"But sir, I never said any such thing. As a matter of fact, Uncle Nathan had to teach me to use the whip that very morning of our departure. I distinctly remember apologizing to Bob and Andy before we left and several times along the way."

"I'm afraid that they distinctly remember it differently."

"But—"

He raised a silencing palm. "If only you had been honest,

we might have avoided the unfortunate destruction of my valuable property."

Nausea rose to her throat, and Jane forced herself not to run for the exit. "I'm sure I don't know what you mean."

"Every item you hauled is broken."

Shock nearly overwhelmed her, and her head spun. "Mr. Bedlow, I don't understand. I inspected the supplies after arriving. Your man—Craig, the one out there with my son—did as well. He told me everything looked good, and I was free to go."

He leaned back in his chair and leveled his gaze at her. "That isn't what he told me."

"Then he is lying. Ask Franklin. He was with me."

Anger flashed in the man's dark eyes. "Franklin? You two have gotten chummy? I heard you stayed with him last night. I must say I was surprised."

Drawing herself up to her full height in the chair, she glared at his implication. "Sir, I will thank you not to create a scenario that did not exist. I simply could not stay in a saloon, and Mr. Lloyd graciously allowed me a place to sleep."

A short, ugly laugh left his lips. "I'm sure he did."

She stomped the floor. "There was nothing improper, and Mr. Lloyd's servants were there as chaperones."

As though bored with the subject, Mr. Bedlow waved his hand over the desk. "No matter. Back to the situation at hand. I'm afraid your neglect has cost me several hundred dollars, and I must insist you remit the cost."

Bile rose to Jane's throat. "But that's not possible. I am

innocent of what you are accusing me of. And your man…
ask him…"

"I already have. He told me the items are not salvageable."

"I do not know how I can pay you, sir. I have only fifty
dollars."

He shook his head regretfully. "Then I'm afraid there's
nothing for me to do but find a place for you in one of my
establishments in Deadwood and allow you to earn the
money you owe."

"I don't understand. Are you suggesting that I work in a
saloon?"

"Yes." His clipped tone and amused expression were all
the insult she would allow.

Jane shot to her feet too fast, and the blood rushed to her
head. She swayed. Mr. Bedlow was at her side in a flash. He
took hold of her as she fought past the faintness. She knew he
was holding her too close, pulling her against him as though
in an embrace, but she was too weak to fight.

"You're even more lovely than I imagined," he whispered
against her ear.

"Wh–what?"

"I could be persuaded to forgive the debt without a dime
of repayment." She felt his lips press against her cheek.

"Stop it. What are you doing?"

She tried to move from his grip, but he held her tighter.
"Listen to me. Stop being so stubborn." He kept her close but
moved his head back so he could look into her eyes.

Jane saw a vulnerability there she had yet to observe during their brief acquaintance. But she sensed that that might not be positive.

"What are you trying to say, Mr. Bedlow?"

"Come live with me. In my house."

A frown creased her brow, and she pushed against his rock-hard chest. "Do you mean as your housekeeper or cook?"

A short laugh blew from his lips, and his smoky breath made her queasy. "As my mistress."

Outrage flooded over her, and she pushed against him to no avail. Finally she lifted her boot and slammed the pointed toe hard against his shin.

With a howl of pain and a vile obscenity, he turned her loose. He raised his arm and brought the back of his hand hard on her mouth. Her head felt rattled, and the murky taste of blood filled her mouth.

She knew her mouth was swelling. It was a sensation she wasn't altogether unfamiliar with, only she had thought with Tom's death she'd never have to endure violence at the hands of another man.

Mr. Bedlow reached into his jacket and retrieved a white handkerchief. He handed it to her. "I'll consider that kick a result of your surprise."

She took the cloth and pressed it to her mouth. Anger burned. Hatred, even, as she stared silently.

"Perhaps you want to consider the invitation?"

"There's nothing to consider." She winced as the pain intensified. Speaking always made it worse. "I will not work in your saloon, and I will not be your mistress. Furthermore, I do not owe you a cent. However, it's obvious you are fabricating the story to keep me here. Why you would want me here, I can't imagine, since you don't even know me."

"The heart knows what it wants. And I've wanted you since I laid eyes on you the first time. Can't you just be flattered that a man finds you so compelling he would ask you to live in his home? As the first woman who has ever been invited to live in my home other than servants?"

"Be that as it may, my answer remains the same." She glared at him, feeling anything but affection. "However, I will work for you. Right here. In your general store. But I will never step foot inside that filthy saloon."

He drew a heavy breath and released it. "I'm afraid you've left me no choice, then."

Waiting for him to elaborate, she forced herself to stare at him without flinching. But she knew she wouldn't sell herself in either a brothel or a fine home to one man. Nothing was worth such a thing.

Bedlow leaned against his desk and folded his arms across his chest. "Craig has taken Danny to my home."

Jane's heart began to race. A surge of heat rushed through her body, settling in her chest. Her hands shook as she recognized the enormity of his blackmail. "You can't take my son."

"I already have." He bent and cupped her chin. "He'll be there waiting for you when you agree to being my mistress."

Tears formed in her eyes as she faced the inevitable situation. She had never felt such hopelessness. How could she stand under the weight of knowing she wasn't capable of protecting her son?

"Why? What on earth do you want from me that you can't get from dozens of women in Deadwood?"

"Would you believe me if I said 'love'? 'Respectability'? I need the sort of woman you are presiding over my home so I can include distinguished guests at my dinner parties."

She stared at him, fighting the urge to laugh as hysteria rose in her. "Love? Respectability?"

"You don't believe someone like me can want love?" He looked pained. "Perhaps it is a futile hope, but if you come live with me, we can be a family. If it works out, maybe we'll get married when a preacher comes through. Our name, Bedlow, that is, would be another well-known, respected name in Deadwood."

Was he completely insane? "Mr. Bedlow, I'm not going to be your mistress. Even if I wanted to be anywhere near you, it's fornication. I don't believe in that outside of marriage."

"You would rather lose your son than share my bed?" A short laugh spurted from his lips. "I'm insulted." All amusement left his features as though wiped from his face.

Tears slipped down Jane's cheeks, stinging her cut lip. "Please, be good to my boy until I can procure employment and start paying you back the money you and I both know I don't owe you."

"No one in this town will employ you. I've made sure of it."

"What are you doing to me, Mr. Bedlow? I am twenty-five, a widow with a son and a baby on the way. That's right. A baby." Perhaps he would not continue with this cruelty if there was a baby involved. "I should have informed you of my condition before you hired me on, but I'm sure you can imagine why I wouldn't."

His lips twisted in a sardonic grin. "I can well imagine you would have been afraid I wouldn't hire you, and likely a gentleman wouldn't have. However, I knew about the baby. Even back in Sidney, I suspected you were pregnant. If you come to my house, I give you my word I will not touch you until the baby is born, and you are recovered."

Jane shoved back her modesty as he used such bold words. Even while she lived with Mama Rose, pregnancies were only to be whispered about. One rarely made even the tiniest reference to a lady's delicate condition and one never, ever used such a vulgar word as *pregnant*.

"How can you possibly believe I would agree to such madness? And how could you desire a woman carrying another man's child?"

"A dead man." He shrugged. "The heart isn't to be questioned. However, since you're too stubborn to accept my proposal—"

"You mean, your proposition?"

"Touché." He put his finger to his lips to shush her. "Since you are too stubborn to come to my house, you still owe me for the destroyed supplies. And since no one would dare go against me and hire you, I have decided to be generous."

"I won't work in the saloon."

Let him beat her. She folded her arms and watched for movement, waiting for the blows to begin. Instead he stared hard, his lips turned into a cold smile. "You will work in the saloon. I will carry you over my shoulder, if necessary. But you will work."

"I'll never do it willingly."

"I don't need your willingness, only your cooperation. And make no mistake, you will cooperate if you know what's good for your son's well-being."

Defeat filled her as clarity forced a hard truth into her mind. Dear God, he could force her to do anything he wanted her to do. If he forced her to be his mistress, she would be powerless against him. If he forced her to dress in the low-cut, shiny dresses and entertain miners, there would be nothing she could do about it. All he had to do was threaten to harm her son.

Chapter Eight

· · · · · · · · · · · · · ·

Mid-July

Franklin frowned at his watch again. Bedlow's wagons had rolled into town an hour ago. He expected Bedlow's men to walk past on their way to the saloon. He wanted to ask about Jane. He swung his legs off the desk and stood. He'd tried to keep his mind off her during his own long three-week ride, but in spite of his worry about Coop, his thoughts kept drifting back to her.

At least he'd been busy since he'd arrived in Sidney three weeks ago. Uncle Nathan had done his best, but they were behind in contracts and deliveries. Luckily, there had only been a couple of cancellations due to the delay. Uncle Nathan had been a mainstay in his and his brother's lives since they were small children and an important part of their freighting company. But he was getting older.

Thankfully, Coop's injury hadn't been as bad as originally thought. Doc said he'd be able to come back to work on Monday, if he'd take things slow for a while.

Outside, Franklin mounted his horse and headed toward the freight yards. A brisk wind had picked up while he was inside, and he could smell rain in the air. More rain would saturate the ground, swell the Platte River. He didn't need any more delays. He hoped to be back in Deadwood within the month. They would definitely need to hire someone to help Uncle Nathan in the office until Coop was back on his feet full-time.

A block down, he saw a couple of Bedlow's men walking toward the saloon. "Thacker!"

Thacker spun around, his hand reaching for his pistol. When he saw Franklin, he sneered. "What do you want, Lloyd?"

Franklin ignored the man's surly tone. "I'm just inquiring after Mrs. Albright."

The man cut his eyes at his companion, then worked his jaw around a chew of tobacco and spat. "She stayed in Deadwood."

Relief washed over Franklin. Then she had spoken to Trent after all. That was good. He imagined her in the library at his home, as he'd left her. He smiled at the men. "Well, you two try not to get too awful stupid drunk. If that's possible."

Thacker's mouth slid into an obscene grin, and he winked. "So it don't bother you, knowin' your gal took a shine to Bedlow?"

"What are you talking about, Thacker?" Franklin laughed. "The last person Mrs. Albright would take a shine to is Bedlow. She knows what a ball of filth he is."

Andy, eyes averted, had remained silent. Franklin knew

the man to be somewhat decent, even if he did work for Bedlow.

Thacker snickered. "Last time I seen your woman, she was in Bedlow's Saloon. Maybe you don't know her like you think you do."

Franklin's throat dried instantly. "Andy? Is there any truth to this fool's statements?"

"I saw her."

Andy looked as though he might elaborate, but Thacker shoved Franklin's shoulder. "Who you callin' a fool? Least I can keep a woman."

Franklin sized him up, tempted and frustrated enough to leave the man eating mud, but he needed more answers. Feeling like he'd been kicked in the gut, Franklin kneed his horse and rode the rest of the way to Solomon's. It couldn't be true. Thacker must be trying to get under his skin. Wagons stood in rows on the far side of the yard. Franklin dismounted and headed for the stable. He ran a practiced eye over the livestock there. His stomach knotted. They weren't here. He headed over to the clerk, who walked around, tallying the oxen that had arrived.

He wasn't even sure what he wanted to ask. The clerk looked up at him. "Can I help you, Mr. Lloyd?"

"I don't know. I came to ask about Mrs. Albright."

"You mean the woman freighter?"

Franklin nodded.

"Oh, Mr. Bedlow asked us to order several yards of white

silk and a veil. Oh, and a cradle. I guess it was possible for someone to snag the boss after all. None of us ever would have believed it."

Franklin winced and tightened his lips over his clenched teeth. How could he have been so wrong about her? She'd been horrified that he'd attended to her while she was ill. Had her modesty been an act?

No, if she were desperate enough to accept a proposal from Bedlow, she had either fallen in love, or been coerced. He couldn't imagine Jane being coerced into anything. And what could Bedlow have possibly tried to hold over her? His mind twisted here and there faster than a tornado until he had to admit that Bedlow must have courted her with enough flare that she had fallen for him.

He spun the horse around and headed back to the house, mentally kicking himself for not bringing her and Danny with him. As it turned out, another week on the trail wouldn't have hurt anything. He stormed through the front door, almost colliding with a young towheaded girl, who stumbled backwards.

"Becky, I'm so sorry." He bent down and patted her head, relieved to see a smile crease her face.

"It's all right, Uncle Franklin. I'm not hurt." She cocked her head to one side. "Why are you in such a hurry? You hungry? We already ate."

Bess entered the foyer from the kitchen, a damp curl falling across her forehead. "But maybe Cook and I saved something back for him, Becky. Come eat, Franklin."

"Thank you, but I'm not hungry. I want to look in on Coop, then I have some paperwork to take care of. I'll be down later." He turned and headed for the stairs.

"Franklin?" At Bess's puzzled tone, he turned back to her.

"What is it?" He couldn't keep the impatience from his voice.

"That's what I'd like to know." Her brow was puckered with worry.

His heart skipped a beat. That same expression used to cross Martha's lovely face whenever she was concerned about something. Usually him.

He cleared his throat. "What do you mean?"

She ignored his question. "Why are you so upset? Bedlow's wagons came into town. Is this about Jane Albright?"

He sighed and retraced his steps. He should know better than to try to hide anything from his sister-in-law. She knew him too well. "I really do have some work upstairs to take care of. Could you join me in the parlor in about an hour? We'll talk then."

"Of course. Call me when you're ready." She patted his arm, then took Becky by the hand. "Come on, dear. It's time for your reading lesson."

Franklin found his brother sitting by the window working on a harness.

"'Bout time you showed up. It's two hours past closing."

"Well, you're in a good mood," Franklin growled back. "Indoors getting to you?"

"Yeah, sorry. It'll be good to get back to work again. How is everything going?"

"Fine. So don't even think about getting up until Doc says you're ready to be on your feet."

"If you don't tell me more than just fine, I'm getting up right now."

Even though he knew Coop was still too wounded to do more than bluff, Franklin filled him in on the progress.

"We lost Rutledge's account?"

Franklin nodded. "The order got messed up, and he lost several hundred dollars."

"Uncle Nathan?"

"'Fraid so."

"I have to get back down there before we lose any more business."

"Don't blame the old man," Franklin said. "He might not be as sharp as he once was, but he's still better than most."

"Tell that to Mr. Rutledge." Coop rolled his eyes. "Don't worry. I won't hurt the old man's feelings."

"Good. Get some rest. I'll see you at dinner." He stood and walked toward the door.

"Hey, Frank," Coop called after him, "something wrong? I mean, other than me being a useless pile of skin and muscle?"

"You're not that. And nothing's wrong that anyone can do anything about. You get some rest."

Franklin left his brother and walked down the hall to his own room.

After Martha had died, he'd moved out of their suite of rooms and into a small room on the other side of the house. It was bare of everything but necessities. Bess insisted on keeping it for him even though he'd deeded the house over to her when he resettled in Deadwood. She'd also added a few homey touches to the room here and there. Bright rag rugs by the bed and in front of the wash stand. A patchwork quilt on the bed instead of the plain wool blanket he'd opted for. The blanket was stored in a trunk beneath the window for colder weather.

He shrugged out of his coat and laid it across the bed, then sat at the corner desk and worked on some letters he'd been putting off.

When he went downstairs, Bess was already in the parlor. A tray with a pot of coffee and sandwiches sat on a small table.

"There you are. You really need to eat a little something, Frank. It's a long time till supper." Not sure he could swallow past the tightness in his throat, he nevertheless reached for a sandwich.

Bess handed him a cup of coffee then sat back in her chair. "Now tell me why Jane isn't here."

"She stayed in Deadwood."

Confusion washed over her face.

Franklin blamed himself for her confusion. After all, he could have told her in the first place that Jane was quitting Mr. Bedlow and coming home to pay the rest of the debt by renting the land, but things had escalated once he'd gotten home and he'd put in long hours at the freight office.

"Whatever for?"

First things first. "I never got around to telling you that Jane wasn't going to haul freight after all. She was going to rent most of her homestead land to me except for a couple of acres for her own use. That way she can pay off the debt, I can use the grazing land, and she gets to go back home with Danny."

"Why that's brilliant! We should have thought of that in the first place."

"I wish I had." He shook his head, disgusted with himself for hand-delivering Jane Albright into Bedlow's lair.

"What do you mean? You sound worried."

"Apparently Bedlow made her a better offer, or she just prefers his company to ours." His stomach tightened as he spoke. "She must have taken a liking to him."

"What? You aren't serious. Why would you say such a thing?"

"One of Bedlow's men told me the news. I was rather surprised myself at first, but of course, we don't really know Mrs. Albright that well, do we?" Not like he thought he had anyway. The bitter thought settled in his brain, and he had to bite his tongue to keep from exploding with angry words. "She has evidently accepted a proposal from Bedlow and has even been seen in his saloons."

Bess gasped. "Nonsense!" She leaned forward, and he ducked back to keep from getting a waving finger in his eye. "I cannot believe you would fall for such an untruth. Why, that dear girl would die before she'd take to the likes of Bedlow or sink to his level. The man is flat out lying."

A glimmer of hope washed over him. "But what reason would he have to lie about it?"

"Why indeed? I suggest you find out. And I'll warrant that whatever it is, Bedlow's behind it." Her eyes widened. "That poor girl could be in danger. And here you are wasting time nursing your ego. Shame on you!"

The worry Franklin had held at bay hit him full force. Was it possible Bess was right? Something had been bothering him ever since he heard the news. It just didn't ring true. Regardless of any question about her morals or character, he knew Jane loved her boy, and the homestead was important to her. That much he'd bet on.

He tossed the rest of the sandwich onto the tray and stood. "You may be right. I'm going to find Thacker and get to the bottom of this."

Bess's hand clutched his sleeve. "Be careful, Franklin. Bedlow's men are ruthless. Don't take chances."

Franklin gave a wry grin "And just a moment ago you were scolding me and my ego." He patted her hand. "Don't worry. I won't do anything foolish."

* * * * *

A clap of thunder rent the air. Franklin pulled on the reins to control the skittish horse. A few raindrops settled on the dusty street as he rode through town. He tied the horse to the hitching post in front of the saloon, where he suspected he'd find Thacker.

Pushing through the swinging doors, he stopped just inside to get his bearings. He hadn't been inside a saloon since he'd dragged his young apprentice, Casey Sparks, out, dunked him in the horse trough, and taken him home, kicking and sputtering, to his worried mother. The boy thanked him the next day. Even though, a year later, his mother, also an employee of Franklin's, had succumbed to illness, Casey had stayed with him and become a loyal employee.

The smoke-filled room reeked of tobacco, alcohol, and unwashed bodies. Striding through the rowdy crowd, he made his way to the bar.

Clyde, the bartender, gave him a surprised look. "What'll it be, Parson? Haven't seen you around in a while."

"Clyde, you know I'm not a preacher anymore." When would everyone get that through their heads? "I'm looking for Bob Thacker. Is he still in here?"

Clyde scratched his beard and glanced toward the stairs. "Uh, I 'spect he's a mite busy right now."

Frustrated, Franklin glanced around the room. He spotted Andy Armor, the man who'd been with Thacker earlier, sitting at a corner table alone. "Okay, thanks," Franklin told Clyde.

He walked through the crowd again, pushing aside bodies that stumbled into his way, until he reached Armor's table.

The man held a cigar between two of the three fingers on his right hand and cupped a glass of beer in the other. He glanced up, startled.

"What can I do for you, Lloyd?" Armor's voice shook slightly. Franklin didn't know if he was nervous or drunk.

"I was looking for Thacker, but he doesn't appear to be available. I need something cleared up, and I guess you're going to have to do."

Armor glanced around the room, then said in a low voice, "Not here. Go outside and around back. I'll meet you there in a few minutes."

Taken aback that the man had agreed so quickly, Franklin went back through the swinging doors and mounted his horse. He rode around to the back of the saloon, staying mounted just in case Armor had ambush on his mind. The man didn't seem like the type, but you never knew. After all, he was employed by Bedlow.

After a few minutes he heard stealthy footsteps, and Armor came around the building.

Franklin waited a minute to make sure he was alone, then dismounted Tryst, holding the reins.

"I guess you want to know about Miz Albright."

"That's right. What can you tell me?"

"Well, first of all, I can tell you Bob was lying to you. Miz Albright is a real Christian lady, and that stuff he said was hogwash."

"What do you mean? She wasn't in the saloon?" Rain

began to pour down in a torrent, but Franklin ignored it except to adjust his hat.

"No, she was in the saloon all righty. But I ain't sure how much choice she had." He peered into the darkness, as though someone might overhear.

Franklin's stomach tightened, and his mouth felt like cotton. "Tell me what you know."

"Well, sir, when Bedlow went to her wagon to check on his supplies, pert near everything was smashed or ruined in some way."

"What? But how could that be?" He'd heard of entire loads being lost like that, but it was usually because of a wagon turning over or outlaws shooting things up.

Armor shrugged. "I dunno. May have been damaged somehow on the trail, but that don't seem too likely. I watched her when she packed up and battened everything down. She did a right good job too. And she double-checked everything when we stopped at night. Still…" He swallowed.

"So what about Mrs. Albright? What did she do?" Franklin could hear his own voice shake.

"She told me she had to find a way to work off what she owed Bedlow. But that varmint had everyone too scared to hire her on."

"Why would she tell you?" Was this man feeding him lies too?

"Well, you see, I think she kinda took a liking to me. On account of the music."

"The music?" What was the man rambling on about? Couldn't he get to the point?

"I played the harmonica every night on the trail, and one night I played 'Amazing Grace' for her." A strange expression crossed his face. "She thanked me real sweet and Christian-like. I'd a-played it for her every night if Bob hadn't thrown such a fit."

"All right, Armor, so what exactly did she say to you about Bedlow?" Franklin had never been one to panic, but he was getting pretty near it now.

"Seems he told her she had to work off what she owed him for the damaged freight."

"Work it off, how? How did he want her to work it off?" Franklin grabbed the man by the front of his shirt, then realizing what he'd done, turned loose, fighting to hold back overwhelming nausea.

"Mr. Lloyd." The man's eyes blazed into Franklin's. "Like I said, Miz Albright is a real lady. But Bedlow ain't no gentleman. There's no telling what he has in mind. But it ain't nothing good. If I was you, I wouldn't waste any time getting there."

Coldness crept up Franklin's body and his face felt like stone. He returned the man's gaze. "Thank you, Mr. Armor. I believe you're right. I'll leave today."

Relief lit the other man's eyes. "Good. And I'd be obliged if you'd call me Andy."

"Thanks, Andy." He mounted Tryst. "If you find yourself in need of a change of jobs, come see me. I'll hire you on the spot."

"That so?"

Franklin nodded. "You have my word."

"Thank you, sir. I just might do that."

Franklin waited for Andy to get back around the building before he nudged Tryst forward. If Thacker knew Andy had talked to him, he'd probably kill him. Franklin didn't want that on his conscience.

He hated to leave Uncle Nathan and Coop to play catch-up without him, but they'd just have to hire a couple of good hands. Actually, Andy would be a good choice. He'd have to be sure and mention it to Coop and Nathan.

His mind flew back to Jane, and a shudder ran through his body. He headed back to the house to pack his saddlebags. Bess was sitting in the parlor embroidering. By the expectant look she gave him as he walked in, he knew she'd been waiting for him.

She patted the sofa next to her, and he sank down. "I can tell by your face you don't have good news."

"I'm afraid not." Leaning over, he put his face in his hands for a moment, then sat up straight, taking a deep breath.

"Don't try to spare me, Franklin. Just tell me."

He didn't hold back. By the time he'd relayed to her what Andy had told him, her face was white and her lips pinched.

"You're going to get her." It wasn't a question.

"Yes, I'll only take what can fit into my saddlebags. I'll be riding hard."

She nodded and stood. "I'll make you some sandwiches

and pack up some jerky for the trail. They won't take much space."

He nodded. "Not too much, though. There will be small game. I won't go hungry."

"I know." She started to speak, then bit her lip and headed to the kitchen.

He went upstairs to talk to Uncle Nathan and Coop and pack the few belongings he'd take with him.

An hour later, he stood in the hallway. He'd already strapped his gear to the horse. Now to say good-bye...

"I'll be praying." Bess's eyes swam with tears.

"I know." He smiled and kissed her on the cheek. "I'll get word to you as soon as I know anything."

She nodded. "She'll be all right, Franklin. God is watching over her. But hurry."

He nodded and forced himself to smile as he shut the door behind him. Before mounting, he checked the saddle and harness.

Thankfully, the rain had blown over, and dusk was settling as he rode out of Sidney. He waved at the sentry and headed toward Deadwood.

Was God watching over her? He wished he could believe it. But what about Martha? Was God watching over Martha when—coldness gripped his heart. If anyone was going to rescue Jane Albright, it would have to be him.

Chapter Nine

. . . .

Mid-July

Bedlow's Saloon never closed. Consequently, the saloon girls took shifts sleeping. Though she'd only been working for Bedlow for six weeks, Jane felt like she hadn't slept in years. Her eyes burned from lack of sleep. Her body felt bruised and battered.

Still, she was thankful. For all of his innuendo and cruelty, Bedlow had not forced her to entertain the men or prostitute herself. Instead, she was forced to clean the filthy, spit-spattered floors and walls, the vomit when the men exceeded their limits, and the blood from the inevitable fights that broke out each night. And she did it with thanks, knowing the alternative was serving the way poor Molly had been forced to pay back her so-called debt. The difference was that Bedlow fancied himself in love with Jane, though she couldn't fathom why. There was no hiding her pregnancy now. The last time she'd passed the mirror, she looked much less than her best.

The backbreaking, constant work left her little time for rest on the narrow cot Bedlow had provided for her in the storeroom. He refused to put a lock on the door, so she was in constant fear that one of the men might find his way in there and try to use her.

Carrying her bucket of soapy water, she tapped on Vera's door. The woman was off her shift, so Jane knew she would be in her room. The problem with trying to clean the girls' rooms was that while they worked, they needed the rooms, and when they weren't working, they were sleeping. There was never a good time. Most of them complained but knew she had no choice. But Vera's complaining had escalated into abuse. She never missed an opportunity to berate Jane. She had tripped her, slapped her, and "accidentally" knocked into Jane's stomach. She was the oldest by far of the women—perhaps thirty years old. Vulgar and experienced, she was still a favorite with the men. But for some reason, she delighted in testing Jane.

Jane tapped again. Today was wash day, and she needed to change Vera's sheets. No matter how stubborn the woman was, Jane would have to be even more. She knocked hard. "Vera!"

The door jerked open. Vera stood looking out at Jane with eyes that appeared evil, as though there was something unnatural inhabiting her. "What do you want, Ignoramus? You know I'm trying to sleep."

Of all the words the woman could have used, "ignoramus" was the least offensive. She'd certainly called Jane much worse—and did so on a regular basis. "Vera, you know Tuesday is the day I launder the bedding. I need to change your sheet and take the dirty one."

A sneer came over her still-stained red lips. "You're pathetic, you know that?"

Jane tensed but refused to engage in the woman's twisted games. "So you keep telling me."

Vera pushed the door open and stood while Jane walked by her. Jane held her breath, expecting to be tripped or pushed or worse. "I know you're tired, but I'll have this bed changed in a minute and be out of your way."

"You make me sick." Vera sat at her vanity, swinging her crossed leg while she watched Jane. "How can you bear to clean up after other people?"

Jane set the bucket of water on the floor and took a deep breath. She stripped the bed and unfolded the fresh sheet. "I suppose the alternative is less bearable."

Vera's eyes flashed anger, and she shifted. "So you're saying you'd rather clean up other people's filth than be like me?"

Jane refused to give in to the other woman's baiting. She continued to tuck the new sheet around the edges of the feather mattress. But Vera's leg was swinging harder, and Jane knew she was growing angrier. "Lord, protect me and the baby, please," she whispered.

"What did you say?"

"Just a simple prayer, Vera. Nothing more."

Vera's volatile nature had unleashed on Jane more than once. The confrontational woman seemed to enjoy physical fights. Jane had never known a woman with such a mean streak. She avoided her when she could, but laundry day she had no choice but to endure the insults and pray Vera would prefer to let Jane finish up and leave quickly.

This time pain slammed into her head, and a heavy silver hairbrush crashed to the floor. Jane's legs buckled. She sat hard on the bed, attempting to make sense of the pain and the sudden wetness on her forehead.

"Vera! You've split her head open." Molly shot through the open door. "Why are you so cruel?"

Vera stood nonchalantly and crawled into her bed. "Get her out of here before she gets blood all over my clean bed."

Blood? Jane reached up and touched the painful spot. Her hand came away sticky. Unwilling to give Vera the satisfaction of seeing her cry, she swallowed back tears. Perhaps that was pride, and she knew God looked unfavorably on the sin, but Vera was cruel, unjust, and unremorseful for her wickedness. At least Molly and some of the others were only prostituting themselves until they paid off debts to Bedlow. Or because he forced them into it.

Her head was beginning to spin.

"Come on," Molly said gently. "Let's get you cleaned up." She led Jane into her bedroom. "Here, honey," Molly said, "sit on my bed."

"I don't want to get blood on your clean sheets."

She always changed Molly's first. Her heart turned over for the girl. Bedlow should be horsewhipped for forcing girls to work for him. She longed for a real sheriff to report him to. But as Franklin had implied, the sheriff looked the other way and pretended all the women were there because they wanted to be. Ridiculous.

Closing her eyes against the pain, she felt herself starting to fade. "I need to lie down."

"All right, but don't go to sleep. This cut is deep. I'm going to call for Doc White. He'll have to sew it up, I think."

Jane shook her head. She wished she could open her eyes, but they were so very heavy. From what felt like a large distance, Jane heard the door fling open. "What is going on?" Bedlow's voice echoed through the room.

Molly wet the towel again and dabbed at Jane's forehead. "Vera threw a hairbrush at her."

"Why'd she do that?"

"No good reason. She hates Jane."

"I'll put an end to this. You take care of her, or so help me, you'll regret it."

Jane felt herself losing consciousness pretty quickly and forced her eyes open. Even if Vera's cruelty had brought about her own inevitable consequences at Bedlow's hands, Jane didn't want to be the cause of it. Barely able to move without throwing up, she reached out for Bedlow and caught his hand.

He turned around, his eyebrows shooting up in surprise. He sat on the edge of the bed and pressed her hand to his heart. "What is it, honey?"

Honey? How could he be so presumptuous when he was forcing her to scrub floors and empty slop buckets and take abuse from prostitutes? She shoved aside her anger. "Vera—"

"Don't worry. I'll make her pay for what she did to you."

"Please."

Bedlow kissed her fingers, and Jane's mind went to another man who had kissed her knuckles. *Franklin.* She had dreams that he would come and rescue her. Futile, when she never awoke from the very real nightmare of Bedlow. "I promise she'll never hurt you again."

"Please don't harm her. I don't want to be the cause—"

"Shh. The doctor will be here soon to take care of you. You let me worry about Vera." He set her hand down on her stomach, and she felt the bed shift as he stood up. "Keep her in bed and see that no one comes in here except you and the doctor. And get that blood stopped before she bleeds out. I swear, I'm going to kill Vera."

Kill her. "No." Jane knew her voice was barely loud enough for anyone to hear, but she had to get through to him. "Trent?"

She heard his sharp intake of breath at the use of his first name. She had never given him the satisfaction, though he had tried to coax, coerce, and bully her into giving up use of his formal name in favor of the more intimate use of Trent.

"What is it, Jane?"

"Trent, please, I'm begging you not to beat Vera."

"She needs to be punished for what she's done to you." He spoke as an adult to a child. "Doesn't your Bible say something about an eye for an eye?"

"Vengeance belongs to the Lord. Don't harm her. Please?"

"You just concentrate on getting well."

She couldn't hold her eyes open any longer. Inside, she screamed for him not to harm the other woman. But she couldn't voice it anymore. Her head swam, even lying down, and she was nauseated, but that wasn't an unusual occurrence these days. How could Bedlow be so vicious one day, and so kind and compassionate another?

She felt the cool cloth on her forehead again and Molly's gentle touch. "Thank you, Molly."

"You're welcome," she said. "You know Vera only hates you because she's jealous?"

"Whatever for?" Instinctively, Jane knew Molly was keeping her talking until the doctor got there. And it was probably just as well. She could have something seriously wrong with her head as a result of Vera's heavy silver brush slamming right into the middle of her forehead.

"Don't you know?" Molly wiped at the blood again.

"I have no idea."

Molly chuckled, but the effort sounded insincere. "You're too naïve for your own good. Bedlow used to treat Vera like a mistress. Even though she worked and entertained the men, she always felt like she was a special one, and for the most part, she was. She lorded it over the rest of us. Bedlow seemed pretty crazy about her. She was sort of his right-hand girl— until you showed up."

"Me? I'm anything but a 'right-hand girl.' He forces me to work a filthy job—one, by the way, that she constantly mocks. Why would she possibly think this is Bedlow caring about me? She has nothing to be jealous of."

"Vera is coarse and mean and vulgar. Men enjoy playing with a woman like that, but even men like Bedlow want a good woman to come home to at night. Vera wanted to be that woman. The mistress in Bedlow's big house."

"Maybe she still will be. The two of them are well-suited."

Molly shook her head. "Never. Everyone knows he asked you, and you refused him." She glanced toward the door, then leaned in close. "People don't refuse Bedlow. He always gives an option, but if he doesn't like the choice made, he forces the issue. If it's a business deal, he shoots the person holding out of the deal. If it's a woman, he won't hesitate to force himself on her. That's why everyone was so surprised when you ended up scrubbing and dumping buckets. We think he must love you because if he didn't, he would have raped you and prob-ably locked you up in that house."

The vivid mental images Molly conjured caused Jane to shudder. She knew God had been protecting her, but she had no idea just how much. Bedlow disgusted and terrified her, but she had to be kind to him in order to keep Danny safe.

"I'll never be his mistress. And as soon as I work off my debt, I'm going home. You can come with me, Molly."

The door opened. Finally, the doctor had arrived with

Bedlow. The bed dipped as Doc White sat next to Jane. "Open your eyes," he softly commanded.

She obeyed. He was an older man, probably fifty, and his face and eyes looked hard. Jane instantly took a disliking to him.

"Well, looks like you got quite the injury."

"Yes, sir."

"How far gone is your pregnancy?"

"Seven and a half months."

Glancing up at Bedlow, he heaved a sigh. "It's too late to do anything about it now. It would kill her."

Jane didn't like the look that passed between the two men. "What do you mean by that?" She tried to sit up, but dizziness and the doctor's firm hand pressed her back to the pillow. "Take your hands off me." She turned her gaze to Bedlow. "What did he mean?"

"Nothing, honey. He just forgot that you aren't like the rest of the girls."

"I don't understand. Why would that have anything to do with how far along I am in my pregnancy?" Her muddled brain refused to put pieces together.

"Drink this," the doctor commanded.

"What is it?"

"Laudanum." He put the cup to her lips.

"I don't need it. What are you doing?"

"I'm going to have to sew up that gash in your forehead. You will likely have a scar."

She didn't care about a scar. Why should she?

She sipped, forcing the bitter medicine down and trying hard not to let it come back up her throat.

"Shall I tend Vera when I'm done here?" she heard the doctor ask through a hazy, faraway tunnel.

"I guess you better." Bedlow's voice sounded cold even in her drug-induced haze. "No sense losing money. Actually, wait a day. Come back tomorrow for Vera."

Horror filled Jane, but there was no fighting the medicine she'd received. She muttered, "Vera," even as she drifted into a cozy, fuzzy sleep.

Over the next two days, she drifted in and out of sleep, woke to the sound of a gentle voice and broth being forced down her throat. Her head ached constantly and when she tried to open her eyes, her stomach recoiled, sending her over the edge of the bed, retching.

"It be okay, honey. Mam's here to take care of you now. You jus' gwine back to sleep and let de good Lawd whisper love songs in your ears."

Lazily, Jane smiled without opening her eyes. Peace filled her as the soft Negro tones soothed her and lulled her back to sleep.

On day three, she woke, lucid, but her head pounded, and her eyes didn't quite focus. The room smelled of fresh bread and perfume.

Molly helped her sit up.

"Thank you," she murmured. "I'm still in your bed?"

"Yes. Mr. Bedlow gave me Vera's room. I've been promoted to head hostess because Doc White said if I hadn't staunched the blood flow, you might have bled out and died. Bedlow is in my debt." She laughed.

"There was an old Negro woman. Was I dreaming?"

"I ain't so old, honey." Jane looked toward the corner where the voice had come from. The woman sitting in a wooden rocker gave a chuckle. "But I suppose I am, compared to you."

Jane smiled. "So you weren't just a dream. I've never seen you around here before."

"Mistah Trent tole me he needed me to come. So I did. We best take a look at them dressings." She stood and stretched her back. "Whooee, I am surely not as young as I once was."

"Why does it smell like bread?"

The old woman cackled. "I bakes and delivers bread to most of the general stores and one restaurant."

Molly laughed. "Mam is the best baker in the world. Apples are beginning to come in season, or they will be soon. Just wait until she makes some apple tarts."

The woman's face beamed. Clearly she relished every word of praise.

"You said Mam. Do you mean Mammy?"

"I do."

"I take it Trent used to be your master before the end of the war?"

She had been free for many years. So why was she still

with such a monster? "I'm his mammy. He came home from the war and worked his fingers to the bone to take care of us. I ain't leavin' him now."

"Us?"

"My boy."

"Big George," Molly offered.

Jane smiled. "Big George is your son? He's a fine one." And he was. The enormous man didn't use his size as a weapon, intimidating the girls. Rather, he did his best to keep them from being harmed by the men.

"Yes'm," Mam said, her eyes shining. "That's him all right."

Molly refilled the basin with clean water and handed Mam fresh bandages. "Jane has taken quite a liking to Big George, and he has to her too. She makes sure he gets enough to eat, and he watches over her especially." She smiled. "He doesn't let the men anywhere near her."

"He's a fine son." Mam went to work on the bandages. When she was finished, she left the room, carrying the wash basin and the soiled bandages.

"Mr. Bedlow has been going crazy since you got sick. He checks in here a dozen times a day."

"I can't imagine why. I've never given him a moment of encouragement. I have no intention of staying. Once my debt is paid, I will be leaving Deadwood for good."

Molly reached forward and took her hand. "Did you really mean what you said about me coming home with you and Danny?"

A burst of hope filled Jane. "Of course. Will you?"

Molly's face lit up and she nodded, then her expression turned cautious. "But let's keep it between us until the right time."

"I understand."

"Are you hungry?"

Surprisingly, Jane's stomach gurgled in response to the question. "I am ravenous, to be honest."

"Good. Doc White says you can eat lightly for a few days. So I'll run down and ask the kitchen to dish up some soup and bread."

"Could I have some of Mam's bread and some milk too? For the baby?"

Molly stood, jostling the bed and reminding Jane that her body ached. "I'll be back in a little while. Is there anything else you'd like?"

"My Bible?"

Molly smiled. "I thought you might want that. I already brought it in case you woke up." She walked to her bureau and removed the book from her top drawer. "Here you go."

Jane clutched the treasure to her. "Thank you."

"I'll be back."

Molly left in a swish of bright satin skirts.

Having her Bible close meant everything to Jane during these wretched days when she was held prisoner by Danny's kidnapping. The words of the Psalms offered her hope, the only hope in her world. Waking up to such a gloomy outlook, she had to hang on to the memory that God loved Danny even more than she did. He loved this new baby, and somehow God would work everything out for her good, for Danny's good, for the baby's good. Somehow.

She only hoped God's plan included a speedy reconciliation with her boy. Her arms ached to hold his warm little body close. Her ears strained for the sound of his laughter. And even in this place where it seemed like God couldn't possibly live, she reminded herself that God was always with her and that He would be with her son as well.

She tried to let the thought sink in and bring her peace, but the combination of her headache, hunger, pregnancy discomfort, and loneliness mocked her efforts.

When even the Psalms didn't help, she closed the Bible and stared at the wall, fighting against the tears and the growing despair. When would she ever see her son again?

Chapter Ten

. . . .

Late July

Franklin entered Deadwood on horseback at three in the morning. Even late in July the overnight air sank through his shirt and chilled his skin. He knew the saloon business was waning this time of morning, and he was tempted to head straight for Bedlow's Saloon, but it would be better during the day when even fewer men hung around. Miners were busy panning for gold during the day, although most of the mines had been gutted after four years of continuous streams of hopefuls. He hadn't seen much except for a few flakes of gold dust here and there.

He headed for his house. By the time he had Tryst brushed down, fed, and put up for the night, Huan had somehow discovered his presence and greeted him at the door.

"Good be home," he said, bowing in his characteristically Chinese way.

Franklin knew it was a sign of respect, knew it was the Chinese way, but tonight it irritated him. "Please, stop bowing like I'm some kind of king of England or something."

"So solly, Mistah Lloyd."

Franklin sighed. "What are you doing up so late?"

"You home."

"Okay, okay. Go back to bed. I'll take care of myself for tonight."

Huan hesitated.

"Shen Huan, I mean it. Go to sleep. You don't have to take care of me in the middle of the night."

Three weeks alone on the trail had given Franklin plenty of time to think. And one of the things he'd discovered during that time was that as much as he hated the idea of Bedlow forcing people to work for him, he was often no better. He treated his two servants like slaves. Paying small wages, which was the reason he had originally hired Chinese servants, and expecting their service every moment of the day or night.

"Huan."

The servant was just about out the door. He stopped and turned.

"I want to hire three more servants to help you and Cookie. Do you know more needing jobs?"

"We have one brother," he said in marginally better English than his brother Cheng. "He work saloon." He scowled. "Bad place."

Franklin nodded. "All right. Bring him to help you. And more?"

"Cheng have wife. She do laundry. Clean house. She not like mean white woman."

"Cheng's married, and they don't live together?"

Huan shook his head. "Cheng live here." It was a simple statement of fact, with no emotion.

Franklin sat on his bed and tugged wearily at his boots that had grown tight during the long ride. He had pushed especially hard today, knowing he could make it home.

In a flash, Huan was by his side. He reached for the boots. "I help."

"Thanks."

Huan grunted as he tugged on the boot.

"Do you have a god, Huan?"

Huan glanced up with a frown. "God?"

"Yeah. Do the Chinese have a god?"

"Some worship ancestors."

"How about you?"

"I serve Christian God."

"You mean *the* God?"

Huan nodded and tugged harder. Finally the boot came loose. He stumbled and righted himself. He set it down and reached for the second. "In beginning God created heaven and earth."

"From Genesis."

"Yes. Bible."

This boot came off easier. Huan set it down next to the other and hesitated, waiting for Franklin to finish.

"Do you read English?"

Solemnly, Huan shook his head. "Not read at all. Cheng."

All this time the brothers had been working for him,

Franklin had never thought to ask about their families or religion or really cared about anything except for their service to him.

Huan quietly left him to his maudlin thoughts and twenty minutes later returned with a bucket of warm water for him to wash. "Thank you, Huan. Please go to bed now, and don't get up early. As a matter of fact, take tomorrow as a holiday."

"Ho-li-day?"

"In other words, I don't want to see you working tomorrow."

Huan frowned. "I have not pleased Mr. Lloyd?"

"You're the best servant in Deadwood." Franklin smiled and put a hand on the young man's shoulder. "So enjoy a day off and let me fend for myself."

Confused and probably a little offended, Huan left Franklin's room. Sliding into bed, Franklin's thoughts turned to Jane Albright. He didn't know for sure why she was with Bedlow. But he would discover the reason tomorrow.

Knowing he would need all of his strength tomorrow, he closed his eyes, but sleep remained elusive. Finally he drifted, but no more than two hours later, he rose, washed in the cool water left over from Huan's bucket, dressed, and left the house without coffee or breakfast.

He hitched the horse to a buggy that had come with the house. He'd never used it, but it seemed more comfortable than the wagon and one horse could pull it, taking less time to prepare.

By eight o'clock, he pulled the horse to a stop, set the brake on the buggy, and walked inside the saloon.

A handful of miners sat nursing beer. Several were passed out on tables or the floor, and in the corner an all-night card game continued. He was just about to call out for Jane, when a pretty young girl who looked too innocent and fresh-faced to be in the profession her low-cut, tight outfit suggested, said, "Mr. Lloyd, I'm Molly. A friend of Jane's. I assume you've come to see her."

"I have." He averted his gaze and forced himself to look at the stairs.

"Come with me. And please, act like you're coming upstairs for a reason."

"I am coming upstairs for a reason, and you know it's not for *that*."

"Yes, but if you don't pretend it is, you'll be stopped." She glanced over her shoulder. "I hope you have ten dollars. Because that's what it's going to cost you to get past Big George there at the top of the stairs."

Franklin glanced up to find an enormous black man with arms the size of cannonballs. He dug into his pocket, found the bill, and handed it over to the girl, who slapped it in the bodyguard's hand.

He had no idea how he would get Jane past the guard. He would have to think about that when the time came. "Where is she?" he whispered.

"Shh." She pressed herself back against the wall and pulled him in. Franklin knew she was playing a game and went along. Pressing his face into the hollow of her neck, he wondered exactly what they were doing and how this would get him close to Jane. Molly's too-strong perfume nearly gagged him and robbed him of any desire he might have felt being this close to an ill-clad woman after so many years. He realized what she was doing when another pair breezed past them without a second look. Molly pushed him away, took his hand, and resumed her walk down the hall. She stopped in front of a door. Looking back and forth, she went inside and pulled him after her.

Franklin's heart nearly stopped. Jane lay in the bed, her eyes closed. A bandage covered her entire forehead and both eyes were black. Outraged, he swung around. "What happened to her? Did Bedlow do that?"

Reaching out, Molly gave his arm a hard pinch. "Shut up, you imbecile. Do you want Big George to come in here and knock you senseless? I've seen him do it with one hit. And you aren't that big."

"What happened?"

"A jealous woman threw something at her and cut her head open. The doctor had to stitch it up, but she's still dizzy and hurt."

"When did this happen?"

"Four days. The doc says she'll be in bed for a week."

He moved closer to the bed and knelt at her side. He could see under the covers that her condition was as he suspected before he left Deadwood. "When will her baby come?"

"She thinks about a month." Molly drew in a breath and

released it slowly. "But I wouldn't be surprised if it came early, the way she works."

"What sort of work is Bedlow forcing on her?"

"Well, she's not a prostitute, if that's what you're worried about."

"It was one of the things I was worried about. It would kill Jane to be forced to do something against her moral convictions."

"Yes." Molly touched his shoulder. "Let me wake her up, so she doesn't become afraid."

He moved out of the way. Molly sat down on the bed next to Jane.

"Jane," she whispered, "time to wake up."

A moan escaped Jane's lips.

"Jane, Franklin's come to see you. Hurry and open your eyes before someone finds him in here instead of my room."

Jane opened her eyes. "Why are you wearing Vera's dress?"

"Because her things are up for grabs." She moved the bed-clothes. "You need to get up."

"Wait. Why are Vera's things up for grabs?"

"Why do you think?"

"I don't know."

Molly slowed down her pace and took a breath. "She was beaten badly. Almost died. Bedlow gave us all her clothes. When she's better, she'll be stripped back down to a chemise and pantalettes."

"But I asked Trent not to harm her."

"Don't be naïve, Jane. Do you really think he wouldn't beat her just because you asked him? He beat her and locked her away in your little room and gave me hers. No one has seen or heard from her in days. Cook isn't even allowed to take her food."

Franklin stepped forward. "Jane."

She turned to him, as though just registering that Molly had said he was here. As soon as their eyes met, tears filled hers. Those beautiful blue eyes that now had black and purple bruises around them. "Franklin," she whispered.

That was all he needed to hear. He nudged Molly out of the way and bent forward. He wrapped her in the quilt that was placed over her and lifted. "I'm getting you out of here."

"Franklin, wait."

"I don't care why you're here. I know you don't love Bedlow." She was so light he barely registered the weight. He could feel her bones. He pressed kisses to her cheeks, chin, careful to avoid her forehead. "Sweetheart, we need to get you out of here."

Tears slid down her cheeks. "I can't go."

"I know all about that so-called debt you supposedly owe. Don't worry. I'll pay it even though you don't owe it." He walked through the door and to the hall. "Don't speak."

Big George turned. He stared at them. "Where you takin' Miss Jane?"

Franklin sized him up. There was no way he was any sort of match for the massive man. So he prayed a simple, *God help me.* "She doesn't belong in a place like this. I'm taking her home with me. I care about her."

"I can't let you take her. She Mr. Bedlow's woman."

Franklin tensed, and his mind filled with questions he wasn't sure he wanted to know the answers to.

Molly had come behind him. "George, I'm sorry I lied about him. But he loves Jane, and you know how good she is. How many times has she brought you extra food? And remember when she helped you read that letter from your Sienna back in Texas? Let her go."

"Miss Jane, you want to go with this fella?"

"I can't, George." Jane looked up at him. "Franklin, please put me down. I can't go."

From the corner of his eye, Franklin saw movement coming up the steps. Instinctively, he knew it was Bedlow.

"Yes, Frank. Put Jane down." Bedlow reached the top of the steps.

"Why, Jane?"

"Mr. Bedlow and I have an arrangement. I—I work here when I'm not so ill."

She pushed against him and Frank set her on the ornately carpeted hallway. Bedlow stepped forward and slipped an arm possessively about her waist, drawing her close. Closer than a mere employer had any business doing.

Hot jealousy burned in Franklin. "What sort of work do you do for this vermin?"

"Careful, Frank." Bedlow smiled, but his eyes were hard,

his voice cold. "It's impolite to insult a man in his own establishment. Didn't we cover this lesson already back in Sidney? I seem to remember you insulting me there too."

Franklin swallowed down the anger and leveled his gaze at Bedlow, keenly aware that Big George stood only a few feet away. "I will settle her debt with you. With interest."

"Tempting, but I'll have to decline."

"Keeping her here against her will is slavery, Bedlow." Franklin felt Big George shift, and he knew he'd struck a chord. "It's illegal."

"I'm offended you would think me capable of such a thing." Bedlow shook his head and turned to Jane. "Honey, do you feel as though I'm keeping you against your will?"

Jane actually smiled up at Bedlow, albeit a wan smile. "Of course not. I have a debt to pay, and it's my responsibility to pay it."

Panic rose inside Franklin. "But I can take care of it for you."

"What difference does it make to whom I owe the debt, Mr. Lloyd? You, or Mr. Bedlow? Either way, I am indentured."

"No, because you won't work for me. All you have to do is let me rent the land."

"No, Franklin." Shaking her head, she stared at him. He tried to read the depths of that look. Flesh out the meaning. She was pleading with him to follow her wishes.

She drew a breath, her face growing pale. Franklin stepped forward, ready to grab her before she fainted. But Big George moved first. Agile for a giant of a man, he blocked Franklin while Bedlow swung her into his arms. "If you'll excuse us now, Frank, Mrs. Albright has said her piece. She will be staying with me." Jane slumped against him, her head resting on Bedlow's shoulder as though she were a bride.

It was more than Franklin could bear. "I'm leaving."

Big George walked him to the top of the steps. "If you know what be good for ya, you'll leave Miss Jane alone."

Franklin turned to him. "Miss Jane is in some sort of trouble. I know she says she'd rather stay, but that's not the truth. And you are a smart man, George. You know she wants to get away from here."

George grabbed him by the arm and started down the stairs, half dragging, half leading Franklin. Franklin's heart sank. He had hoped that George would be something of an ally for Jane after Molly had implied that Jane had been good to him, but obviously the man was loyal to Mr. Bedlow.

With an arm like a vise, he held Franklin, opened the door with the other, and flung Franklin outside. "Don't come back here. She's safer if you stay away."

Franklin stared at the closed door. As he walked back to the buggy, he felt complete and utter defeat.

* * * * *

Jane allowed Bedlow to lay her gently back in her bed. "Just lay there and get your strength back." He sat on the bed. Too close for Jane's comfort, but she forced a smile.

"Thank you."

"Now do you want to tell me why Frank Lloyd felt he could carry you away from me?"

Oh, Lord. How did she explain without revealing too much of her heart? "My husband left me deeply indebted to him." She smiled. "That's what brought me to you in the first place."

Emotion flashed across his face, and he lifted her hand with one of his and covered it with the other.

"He wanted to pay my train fare and Danny's to go away and leave him with my land." Speaking Danny's name nearly brought her to tears, but she swallowed back her weakness, knowing Bedlow would not be moved by it right now. "But I refused. More than once."

Knowing he would appreciate the larceny of the full story, she told about drugging him, taking the wagon, bartering with her dead husband's shirts to board the oxen, and then walking the town, trying to find someone who would hire her.

"You're a special woman. No wonder Frank's in love with you too."

His words sent a bittersweet rush through her. "He isn't in love. He just wants my land, and he can't have it. He gave me six months to pay Tom's debt, and I'm determined to try."

"If you come live with me, your children will have a home."

She closed her eyes, feigning the need to do so but quietly praying for the right words.

But Bedlow saved her the necessity. "Clearly, you are not ready to think about that again." He patted her thigh.

She nearly raged at the inappropriate touch but knew she had to remain calm. "Mr. Bedlow, please do not be so familiar when you touch me."

He frowned. "Oh, the leg. You proper women—I'll never understand why things like that matter to you."

"Well, it just does. I don't know how to explain it."

"Okay, for you, I'll try to be a gentleman."

Surprised, she felt heat rush to her face. "Why thank you, Trent."

"I enjoy when you call me by my given name. I hope you'll use it from now on."

She had never seen this type of gentleness from him, but she hoped he'd continue. She wanted to be kind without leading him on.

Molly stood in the corner. When Bedlow turned to her, the hardness returned to his face. He walked toward her. Fear shot to her eyes as he reached out and cupped her face, digging his fingers in. "How did Frank get past Big George?"

"He—he came upstairs as a customer."

"And you played along?"

"Please, Mr. Bedlow. I didn't know he was going to try to take her out."

Jane had to do something. Nothing she'd said had made a difference with Vera, but Molly—he couldn't hurt Molly.

"Trent," she said softly, "Molly tried to stop him."

Keeping his fingers closed around Molly's face, he turned, searching Jane's eyes for truth. Luckily, he was easy to fool.

"She told him he couldn't take me out of here. She didn't want me to get hurt. That's why she didn't call for help. She knew he'd have to get past Big George, and that wasn't going to be possible."

"I don't like it. How did he know which room you were in?"

Molly shook violently. "I told him," she said through distorted lips. "I knew she owed him a debt, and I didn't want him trying to call in the law."

"She was protecting you and me, Trent. There's no need to hurt Molly. She's stayed with you even when she could have left."

He stared hard. "All right." He let go, leaving deep imprints of his abuse. Anger flashed through Jane. He looked at Molly. "Go powder your face and get back to work."

Molly stumbled through the door. Bedlow turned to Jane. "Don't think you can sweet-talk me into changing my mind, Jane. I do care for you more than I have any other woman, but I'm not a fool to be toyed with. If you weren't pregnant, I'd have already gotten what I want from you, one way or another. And don't think you're going to get your debt to me paid off anytime soon. Trust me, you'll be here for a long time."

Leveling her gaze at him, Jane kept her tone even. "I know."

He nodded and walked toward the door. Fear clutched Jane's heart. Was he going to take the baby too? Taking Danny was torturous and cruel beyond reason, but taking both

Danny and the baby, who would need her, seemed more than she could bear. Would she be able to stand strong against his advances if he had both of her children?

Chapter Eleven

....

Early August

The clanging of the cowbell over the door was a welcome intrusion against the tedium of balancing his books. Franklin glanced up, squinting in the blinding glare of the sun. He blinked and made out a small figure hesitating in the doorway. Probably one of the miners' youngsters. Why folks would bring families to this godforsaken place was a mystery to him.

The little girl took a couple of steps, then stopped and stared at him from across the room. She looked to be around eleven or twelve. Blond hair hung in long braids in front of her shoulders.

She made no move to come any farther, so he smiled at her and motioned for her to come to the counter. "Hello, young lady. May I help you with something?"

"Would it be all right if I look around first?"

"Of course. You're a customer."

Her lip quivered and almost smiled, then she turned and began to move among the merchandise, not touching anything but stopping every now and then to look at an object.

She wrinkled her nose as she passed a shelf containing ammonia. Franklin chuckled under his breath. Suddenly, her eyes widened and she walked over to a ready-made dress hanging for display. It was blue with white lace trim on the sleeves and around the collar. Fascinated, he watched her reach out and touch it, then jerk her hand back, putting it behind her back. She stood staring at the garment, then glanced down at her own dress. For the first time, Franklin took notice of what she was wearing. Her faded calico dress was much too short, the hem grazing just below the knees—much too short for decency, especially for a girl who was soon to become a young lady. The bodice strained across a budding figure. Sympathy shot through Franklin, and he averted his eyes.

She swallowed and licked her lips, then began to look around the store again, her movements slow.

The bell rang, and a couple of roughnecks from the saloon shoved through the door. The girl ducked behind a tall pine chest and froze.

"Howdy. Need me a plug of tobacca." Charles Piper, one of the miners who spent more time in the saloon than working his claim, had obviously been drinking for some time by the slurring of his words. He and his friend staggered to the counter.

Franklin cut a plug of tobacco and handed it to the man, who struggled to reach into his pocket. Finally he dropped some coins on the counter, and both men stumbled out, to Franklin's relief.

The girl still stood behind the chest. What had she been through to put that kind of fear in her? Surely her father would have protected her from the rough miners they came across.

"They're gone now. You can come out."

She peeked around the chest, then slowly abandoned her hiding place, fear still on her face and her hands trembling.

"I think those two may have spent a little too much time celebrating, don't you?" he asked lightly.

She nodded and stepped up to the counter. "My pa sent me to get some coffee and cornmeal. You got any?"

"Sure do. Say, weren't you in here with your pa a few months ago?"

"Yes, sir. When we first came to town, we stocked up here." She cleared her throat nervously.

"Oh yes, I remember. Your pa's a miner, isn't he?" He remembered them clearly now. The tall, balding man, who watched his daughter closely through bespectacled eyes, as though afraid she'd vanish in front of his eyes. He'd looked more like a schoolteacher than a miner.

She nodded. "Could I have that cornmeal and coffee now? I need to get back to the claim."

He frowned. "You didn't come into town by yourself, did you?"

"Yes, sir. Pa struck gold and didn't want to leave the claim." A stricken look crossed her face. Franklin understood. Her pa had probably told her not to mention the strike. People had been murdered over gold strikes before.

"That was a very good idea. And don't worry, your secret is safe with me."

"Thank you, sir." Her voice sounded weak. She swayed, then righted herself.

"Hey, now, are you ill?" He hurried around the counter and took her by the arm, steadying her. As his hand brushed hers, he could feel the heat from her skin. He reached up and placed a hand on her forehead.

She jerked away. "I'm fine. Could I have those supp—" She swayed again, then fell against him.

"Casey!" he shouted. His apprentice ran out from the supply room. "Bring the buggy around front for me, then go fetch the doctor. Tell him I have a sick child at my house, then get back here and mind the store till I get back."

Casey stared at the girl, his mouth hanging open.

"Get going."

"Yes, sir." Casey ran towards the back door.

By the time Franklin had lifted the child in his arms and carried her out, the buggy was waiting, and Casey was headed down the street.

The girl stirred as he propped her up against the door of the buggy. He patted her shoulder. "It's okay. Lie back and rest." He hurried around and climbed in, flicking the reins.

Huan came running as Franklin pushed through the front door with the girl in his arms. For a moment, surprise crossed his face, then all emotion was erased, and he came forward to take the child from Franklin's arms.

"Put her in the blue room and bring some water."

Huan complied, and Franklin sat next to the bed, holding the girl's small hand in his. He hadn't realized how tiny she was until he'd lifted her in his arms at the store. Now he could feel the tiny, fragile bones in her hand.

He closed his eyes. *Lord, please don't let this be anything serious. She's so young.*

The front door slammed, and footsteps hurried across the hardwood floor of the foyer. Franklin jumped up as Doc White entered the room.

"What's this, Lloyd? Where'd you pick up this one?" The doctor stared down at the still form, impatience in his cold eyes. "A little young for you, isn't she?"

Sickened at the man's inference, Franklin took a deep breath. Everyone knew the doctor was another of Bedlow's toadies. It would be like him to refuse to treat her, if Franklin said anything. "The girl is one of the miner's daughters. She collapsed at the store."

"Hmm." He lifted the girl's limp wrist and felt her pulse, then reached for his bag. He moved the stethoscope across her chest, listening in several places.

Her eyes fluttered open, and she shot straight up. "What are you doing? Get away from me."

The stethoscope went flying and Doc White cursed.

Franklin shot him a look while turning to the girl. "Honey, you fainted at the store. This is Doctor White. He's just examining you to see what caused it."

Her eyes darted from Franklin to the doctor, and she dropped back against the pillows.

"How long since you've eaten, girl?" the doctor asked gruffly, placing his instruments back in the bag.

She licked her dry lips and ducked her head. "We ran out of flour a few days ago. There hasn't been much to eat 'ceptin' a little dried deer meat."

The doctor threw a bored glance at Franklin. "Well, there you have it. Feed her and let her rest a day or two."

"I can't stay here. Pa's expecting me back with the supplies." She sat up again, then moaned and lay back down.

The doctor shrugged. Franklin paid him quickly, and Huan ushered the man out of the room. He turned at the door and stared at the girl, his eyes narrowed. With a glance in Franklin's direction, he left.

Franklin turned his attention to the patient. "How about if I send Huan with the supplies and a message explaining what happened? Does your pa read?"

"Of course Pa can read." An indignant frown crossed her face. "My pa's about the smartest man from Denver to Deadwood."

"Sorry, I didn't mean to offend you." He held his hand out. "I'm Franklin Lloyd. And you are?"

She took his hand and shook it. "Jenny Ames. Nice to meet you."

"Well, Jenny Ames, how about if I write a letter to your pa, and you can add a few words at the end, if you feel up to it? Then, tomorrow or the next day, I'll take you home."

"Hey, where's my horse? Pa'd be real upset if anything happened to Canyon."

"Canyon is enjoying a nice meal in my stable with my horse, Tryst. And you need to do the same. How does chicken soup and a biscuit sound?"

"Really? I haven't had chicken since we left Denver." Her tongue darted across her lips.

Something stirred in Franklin. She looked so vulnerable lying there. He'd feed her all right. And maybe he could do a little more.

* * * * *

Jane sat in front of the vanity, staring critically at herself in the mirror. It had been over two weeks since the incident with Vera, and the bruises beneath her eyes had lightened to a light purple and green.

She looked and felt hideous. Still, Mr. Bedlow had ordered her out of bed and out of the room today. She knew she shouldn't feel guilty for even having a room instead of the storeroom, but thinking about Vera in pain and sleeping on the hard, narrow cot knotted her stomach.

A week after the beating, Vera had finally been allowed to emerge—her face swollen and bruised beyond recognition. She held her sides when she walked, and rumor had it that she had suffered several broken ribs. Her eyes still looked upon Jane with hatred, but she kept her thoughts to herself.

Jane stayed away from her. She saw no reason to encourage something that might get the other woman harmed again, but she had asked Big George to please keep an eye on Vera and make sure she was getting enough to eat. And to be extra careful not to allow customers that wouldn't care about her injuries, for Bedlow had put her back to work the day after Franklin had come to the saloon. The men didn't care about her face. They only cared about her body, and Vera did her best to pretend nothing had changed. But she could barely move. Jane could only imagine the pain she endured each night.

Bedlow was deaf to her pleas, and finally Jane accepted the inevitable. She would not be able to help Vera through Bedlow. But perhaps George could at least look out for her. And he had promised that he would.

Molly peeked in. "Are you ready? He's getting antsy."

"For heaven's sake, I'm coming. I vow, I've never seen a man so sadistic as to want to watch a woman scrub his filthy floors."

"Just hurry."

Jane walked to the door to find Mr. Bedlow at the top of the steps waiting for her. He smiled broadly. "It's good to see you back on your feet, Mrs. Albright."

Mrs. Albright? He hadn't called her that in a while. George grinned when he stepped aside. Bedlow offered his arm, which she took, and they walked down the steps and to the front door.

"Where are you taking me, Mr. Bedlow?"

"I thought you were going to call me Trent from now on."

"You called me Mrs. Albright. I thought we were back to propriety."

"I was merely trying to be gallant." He chuckled as they stepped out into the bright early July day. The morning breeze still carried a bit of cool with it, but Jane knew by midday, the sun would claim its rightful place high above Deadwood and beat down mercilessly.

"Where are we going?"

"Not far. You'll see." He led her across the street and stopped in front of the general store. "I have a surprise for you."

Dread rose, bitter in her mouth. Bedlow did no favors without demanding a high price in return. "Oh?"

"Don't look so frightened." By his wry tone she knew he had read her thoughts. Disconcerting. She wanted a man who would know her well. Someone who knew when she was hurting, angry, or needed to be held. Molly believed he had softened considerably since Jane's arrival at the saloon. The girls seemed less tense; they fought less.

"I'm not scared. It's just that I can't fathom what you might be thinking."

"I am sending you to the general store to work until your baby's born." He cut a glance to her. "In other words, no more scrubbing the saloon."

Jane wanted to respond properly. She knew responding improperly could mean he changed his mind. "Thank you."

The simple reply brought about a scowl. "Well, if I can't interest you in the general store, perhaps the playhouse."

The playhouse hosted bawdy shows with music and dancing around the clock. And Bedlow owned Bedlow's Playhouse as well. To the young women at the saloon, a move to the playhouse was a step up. But Bedlow knew Jane would be mortified with the move. And this wasn't the first time he'd brought it up.

She smiled. "I'm very happy to move from the saloon to the general store, Trent." She squeezed his arm. "Thank you."

Her efforts appeased him, and he covered her hand with his. "The general store needs a woman's touch. A good woman. If you ever come to your senses, part of this could be yours—and maybe Danny's someday."

"But our agreement is that I am working to pay off a debt." Jane's stomach clenched tightly. "Shouldn't that be paid soon?"

His eyebrows shot up as though he'd forgotten about her debt. She had suspected more than once that he had no intention of ever letting her go.

"I want you, Jane. How much clearer do I have to be?"

"You're quite clear. And how much clearer do I have to be that I'm not one of your saloon girls?"

"I never thought you were. You can come home with me today. My promise stands not to touch you until your baby is born and you're recovered."

"Please, Trent," she whispered. "I'm never going to willingly spend one night under your roof."

"You want your baby to live in a saloon?" He smiled, knowing what her answer would be.

Jane placed her hand on her stomach. It wouldn't be long

now before the new little life entered the world. She had no doubt that Trent would make good on his threat to take her to his home in order for her to "recover" from childbirth. And because he had Danny in his grip, she would go and pretend that he didn't have plans for her once her body healed.

"If you're waiting for Frank to come back and try to rescue you again, you might as well put that dream behind you. I hear he took your rejection to heart."

"I don't know what you're talking about." But she sensed he needed no encouragement to elaborate.

He gave a short laugh. "It seems the pure Mr. Franklin has moved a girl in with him."

Jane drew in a quick, cool breath. "I find that difficult to believe."

"You think I'm lying?" His eyebrow rose. "Honey, Doc White saw her with his own eyes. He was called out there to doctor her. Said Frank hovered over her like a brand-new bridegroom, only without the wedding. Lovesick."

Jane shoved aside the image but could do nothing about the slicing pain that bled her heart. "Well, I suppose it's a good thing there was never anything between us besides business." She ventured a tight smile at Bedlow. "Just like you and me. Only business."

Rather than be upset, he bent and his lips grazed her cheek, his moustache tickling her skin. "You might just change your mind." He opened the door and nudged her inside ahead of him.

"Don't count—"

In the middle of the floor stood Danny. "Oh," she said, her legs suddenly melting to nothing, her stomach turning over. She dropped to her knees and held out her arms.

"Ma!" Danny ran full force and practically tackled her, but she didn't care. She pulled him tight, even as his arms about her neck nearly strangled her.

He smelled of sunshine and summer. His face was tanned, so she knew he must have been allowed outdoors, which was so important for a little boy.

Pulling back, she studied him. "Let me look at you."

His little eyes perused her face, and he frowned. He reached out and touched her bruises. "What happened?"

Forcing a laugh, she ruffled his unruly hair. "Would you believe I got hit right in the forehead? I even had to get the doctor to sew up my head."

His eyes grew even wider. "Can I see?"

"Doc said I can't take the bandage off except once a day." But she didn't want to focus on herself. She wanted to savor every second of her time with Danny. "Stand up straight and let me take a look. My gracious, you've grown an inch."

"Another one?" His incredulous tone brought a smile to her lips.

"Almost. And look at how long your hair is."

"I'm not cutting it. Uncle Trent says I don't have to. All the Indians have long hair." He gave her a guilty, brown-eyed look. "Do I have to cut it off, Ma? I really want it long like Crazy Horse."

She cut her glance to Bedlow. He chuckled. "I didn't see any harm in letting his hair grow. It's for a good cause."

Trent had been good to Danny. But she knew Trent's goodness. It always came with a price.

Trying to get off the floor, she grunted, moving her awkward body. Trent held out his hand. "May I?"

She grudgingly accepted. "Thank you." Once on her feet, she looked down at her little boy. "Well, I don't suppose it will hurt for it to grow a little longer. For now. But, young man, you know Ma doesn't like long hair on little boys, so you shouldn't have asked Mr. Trent to let you keep it long."

He kicked at the floor. "Aw, Ma, I'm sorry." He flung himself at her again. She lifted him, surprised at how much heavier he had grown in just a few weeks. "You've been feeding him well." She squeezed him, then set him back down, admitting to herself that he was too heavy to hold in her condition.

"A growing boy needs to eat."

"Thank you for this, Trent."

On impulse, she reached up and gave him a quick hug. She knew the action was a mistake the second she followed the impulse, for he grabbed her and pulled her tight, turning a simple hug of gratitude into a lover's embrace.

"Trent," she whispered, "please."

"Why do you fight this?" he murmured against her cheek. "I always get what I want."

Relief washed over her as he let her go. She held out her

hand to Danny. "Come and tell me everything you've been doing."

"Guess what I have?"

"What do you have?" She was a little surprised that he seemed to love his temporary home. So far he hadn't asked her to take him away; he hadn't seemed upset or scared of Trent.

"A pony!" He yelled the information and jumped a little with each word.

"You have a pony? Oh my gracious. What is your pony's name?" And what would happen to the pony when she took her boy and left Deadwood forever?

"His name is Sioux. And I painted him and Simone braided his tail."

She had no idea who Simone was, but she had a feeling the woman had no business around a child.

Jane's lips tipped upward. "Now you have Cheyenne and Sioux."

The spark left his eyes. "Not Cheyenne."

"What do you mean?" Then she remembered. The day they had taken Danny from her, Cheyenne was still at Franklin's house.

"But I have a puppy. A new one."

"And what is his name?"

"Brown."

His choice of names said a lot about his feelings for the new puppy, but Jane wouldn't betray that for anything in the world. "Why Brown?"

"Because he's brown."

Yes. He didn't want another dog. Cheyenne had been the boy's constant companion and only friend since birth.

"All right, Danny," Bedlow called. "It's time for you to go now. Ma has work to do."

Danny's eyes slanted. "I don't want to go. I want to stay with my ma."

Jane's heart nearly failed her at the thought of letting him go again. She again slid to her knees, grabbed onto her little boy, and pulled him tightly against her. Closing her eyes, she drank in the feel of his chubby body. The sunshine and little boy smell. How could she let him go?

Tears filled her eyes, but she mustn't let Danny see how upset she was. It would only make their separation harder for him. He clutched tightly. "I don't want to go, Ma. Come with me."

"I can't, Baby."

He pulled back, still in her arms, and looked at her. "When is Mr. Lloyd taking us home?"

"Let's go, Danny." Bedlow strode with purpose across the room and pulled Danny's arms from Jane's neck.

"No! Ma!"

"Stop that yelling!" Bedlow commanded. "Remember I said you had to come peacefully or no riding Sioux the rest of the week."

Immediately, Danny's cries ceased.

Bedlow nodded. "That's better. Come. Victor is waiting to drive you back to the house."

"Good-bye, Danny," Jane called, her lips trembling. "I love you so much."

"I love you, Ma." Fat tears fell down his cheeks, but he didn't cause any more ruckus.

After the two left, Jane hid her face in her hands and wept. When Bedlow came back, she stood and even allowed him to put his arms around her and pull her close while she cried. When her tears were spent, he offered her a handkerchief. She dabbed her eyes, blew her nose, and thanked him.

"Would you care to list my duties at the general store, Mr. Bedlow, or was that nothing but a ruse to surprise me with my son?" She wouldn't put it past him to send her straight back to emptying slops and scrubbing vomit.

"I did enjoy surprising you. But rest assured, this is most definitely your new position."

Too raw and spent by Danny being ripped away from her arms to attempt politeness, she placed her hands on her hips and stared at him. "Well then, what are my duties?"

He showed her where the money was and how to count the money in the morning and balance it in the evening to be sure it all came out right. The enormity of the job hit her like a silver hairbrush in the middle of her forehead. If she messed up even once and over or under counted, he could keep indenturing her.

If he did that, she'd have no choice but to either allow Danny to stay in Trent's care, or completely disregard her morals, not to mention the Word of God, concerning fornication.

She made a mental note to get a system in place that would completely protect her from Mr. Bedlow. Otherwise, she would never leave Deadwood. And what if her baby were a girl? What sort of life would a girl child raised in this town have? The answer that came to mind left her weak.

Chapter Twelve

....

Mid-August

Franklin waved good-bye to Jenny as she rode away with Huan, who was taking her back to her pa. The girl had been with him for three days, and the color had returned to her face. He had promised to send Casey every few days with food so they didn't run out again.

He hoped her pa might realize that she needed a new dress. And as she had paid for their supplies with gold, it was obvious the man could afford to properly clothe his little girl.

Tryst stood saddled, stomping the ground, impatient, so Franklin mounted up and headed toward his mercantile. Franklin smiled as he thought about the Shen brothers. All three had come from China together after their parents were killed in a typhoon. Huan and Chao had never married, and Franklin guessed them to be in their late twenties, perhaps early thirties. Cheng's wife, Mai, had been so grateful to get away from her abusive employer and to at last be living with her husband, she kept finding little ways to do extra for Franklin. She rubbed his feet and brought him some sort of tea concoction. Though he preferred coffee, he took it to please her.

Coming home at night wasn't so lonely anymore with his four Chinese servants there to greet him at the end of the day. They had drawn him in to their close-knit family like an adopted child. He tried not to think about what life might have been like, had Jane kept to the original plan and gone back to her homestead and he had settled onto the adjoining homestead. But she had made her choice. Ridiculously stubborn, she refused to allow him to pay off her debt. He had to admit he was having a difficult time forgiving her. It was one thing to insist upon paying him, but to remain in a saloon, with Danny—at least he assumed Danny was there too, although in the brief moments he was there he hadn't thought to ask about the boy. He missed the lad. He'd hoped to one day teach him to ranch and run side-by-side herds.

At the thought of Danny, Franklin turned his horse around and went back to the house.

Shen Mai glanced up from scrubbing the dining room floor as he passed. She hopped to her feet and hurried to him with tiny steps. "You need?"

He shook his head. "I came to get the dog."

Frowning, she shook her head. "Good dog. Not take."

"I'm not taking him away for good. His owner is a little boy. I thought I'd take him for a visit."

Her face brightened, and she nodded big. "O-kay. You take. Bring back."

"Where is he?"

"With Cookie." She thought for a second. "In garden."

He started to take a shortcut through the dining room, but she let up a howl and shoved him back into the foyer, fussing at him in her native language. He grinned. "Okay, Mai. I'm sorry."

"You go. That way." She pointed in the direction of the longer way to the back yard where the garden was located, not far from the house.

"I'm going." He chuckled as he walked through his house. Amazing how fast a person could take ownership. He was glad she felt comfortable enough as housekeeper, under Huan of course, to fuss at him for walking on his own floor. Women in every culture were still women and wouldn't stand for a man dirtying up their handiwork.

He found Cheyenne lying in the grass next to Cheng as the cook weeded his garden.

Cheng rose to his feet effortlessly. "You need?"

"I came back for the dog." He pointed to Cheyenne. Of his four servants, Cheng had the hardest time speaking English. Franklin managed to convey his need for a rope to tie up the animal. A sheepdog was too big to carry on the horse; besides, he'd never sit for it. And if Franklin allowed him to run after him without restraint, he'd likely scare the fire out of Tryst.

Cheng brought him a rope, and together they looped it around the dog's neck.

"Missa Lloyd." Cheng rarely spoke to Franklin, more due to his poor command of English, Franklin had always assumed. He pulled a book from his shirt and passed it to Franklin.

Franklin took it. "The Bible?"

"You help?"

A knot formed instantly. "I'm busy right now. Going to town." He motioned to the dog. "I'll be back tonight."

"Tonight?" Cheng made the same "come back here" motion with his hand that Franklin had made. "O-kay. You help to-night." He patted Cheyenne on the head and turned away without saying good-bye.

"Okay, fine, fine. I help to-night," Franklin muttered as he led Cheyenne toward Tryst.

When he got to town, he stopped at Bedlow's Saloon, tied the dog to the hitching post away from any of the horses, and pushed through the swinging doors. Two painted women sashayed to him immediately. "Hi, honey."

He scowled at them, in no mood to be tempted or taunted. "I'm looking for Jane."

"Jane isn't here."

Glancing up at the voice, Franklin drew his breath. The woman moved carefully, holding onto the railing. The bruises on her face were fairly fresh and swollen. If she was once beautiful beneath the wounds, he couldn't imagine that she could ever be again.

"Are you all right, ma'am?" he asked, shaking off the women who clung to each arm. "Do you need help?"

She gave a short laugh and stopped at the bar. "Beer," she said. "What can I get you?"

"Nothing, thank you. Are you sure you don't need help?"

"Oh? Do you mean these bruises?" She drank down half the beer.

"You were beaten. No one deserves that. Not even—" Franklin winced at his poor choice of words.

"Women like me?" She laughed and drank more.

Franklin wondered if the alcohol dulled the pain from her injuries. "I apologize. That was unforgivable. But you do not deserve to be beaten."

"Let's just say these are the marks anyone must endure who does not approve of your lovely Jane."

"Jane did this?" Shock made him stupid. Of course she didn't. "No. She couldn't have. You're too battered. She doesn't even have the strength to do something like this."

"You're right. But she has fans who will do anything for her."

"Are you saying Jane asked someone to hurt you?"

"Well, I didn't hear it with my own ears." She laughed and sipped. "But there are rumors to that effect."

"Vera! Stop lying about Jane." Molly came over from the other side of the room. "If you only had heard her begging Trent not to hurt you, you would be ashamed of yourself." She turned to Franklin. "The reason she looks that way is because she's the one that split Jane's head wide open. Trent punished her. Jane, of course, would never be cruel. Even with blood gushing down her face, she was asking Trent not to hurt Vera."

Franklin went weak with relief. He scowled at Vera.

She laughed. "Still think I don't deserve this?"

"Leave him alone, you old cow." Molly took his arm and led him away from the bar. "What are you doing in here? Big George is going to toss you right out when he sees you. And he might not be as nice as he was last time."

"I want to see Jane and Danny. I brought Danny's dog. I figured he'd be missing that mutt by now."

She smiled. "That's so sweet. Jane's not here. Bedlow put her to work in the general store, so she spends every day there. She's got a real head for numbers. I think even Trent is surprised at how well she's done since she took over for Craig a couple of weeks ago."

At Craig's name, Franklin felt anger rise. That man's lies were what kept Jane in Deadwood, associating with people she should never have been forced to go anywhere near. "Jane is minding Bedlow's store. Good. That's better than working in a saloon. What about Danny? He's the one I've really come to see, anyway."

She averted her gaze, and her cheeks turned pink. He couldn't help but think that Molly would have been a lovely girl without all the paint marring her natural beauty.

"Well? Where is he?"

She pressed her hands to her hips. "Look, Mr. Lloyd. Danny's at Mr. Bedlow's house. He lives there. But I wouldn't try to go over there and make trouble. It's like a fort. And trying to get past his henchmen is near impossible."

Franklin grabbed hold of a chair next to a round table in order to steady himself. "What about Jane?"

"I can't talk about this anymore. Go across the street and get your answers from her."

Molly's hesitation was all he needed. Franklin stormed out of the saloon. So Jane had thrown her lot and Danny's in with Bedlow. The only thing he couldn't understand was why?

Stepping out into the bright summer day, he was tempted to storm across the street and demand answers from the woman he had thought he was beginning to fall in love with.

A wagon rattled to the store and pulled to a stop. He recognized Andy Armor. The man hopped down from the wagon just as Jane emerged from the building. Her pregnancy was so advanced now that she pressed on her back and moved from side to side as she walked forward. He couldn't take his eyes from her. She was still the loveliest thing he'd ever seen. All he wanted to do was go to her and beg her to come away with him.

She looked up, caught his gaze, and a beautiful smile flashed her dimple and curved her full lips—lips he'd wanted to kiss almost from the first moment he'd met her. It seemed like he had always known her. Her face softened as she continued to meet his gaze. He began to move toward her without giving thought to what he'd say once he reached her. Then he stopped short as another figure exited the general store.

Disappointment and confusion creased her face. As Bedlow stood next to her, draping his arm about her shoulders, she turned away. Bedlow held out his hand to Andy, then glanced up and noticed Franklin. His expression darkened. He slipped his arm around Jane's waist, as he had in the saloon the day Franklin had hoped to rescue her, and pulled her close. Jane turned and said something to him. He nodded, bent, and pressed a kiss to her cheek and allowed her to return to the general store. He turned back to Franklin, tipped his hat triumphantly, then dismissed him and began looking over inventory.

Franklin mounted Tryst and led Cheyenne away.

* * * * *

Jane stood on the other side of the large store window and watched between the painted letters as Franklin rode down the street, his shoulders squared. When he turned at the end of the street and headed toward his mercantile several blocks away, she had to swallow down her tears.

If only Trent didn't have Danny, she would throw off the weight of this town and run after Franklin, begging him to take her home. But somehow God had not answered her prayers, and Danny was still captive at Bedlow's home. Soon she would also be a captive there, as the baby made an appearance. Her body had shifted yet again, and she felt as though she could now breathe, but her entire lower body constantly hurt with the pressure of preparing to deliver a child.

The door opened, and the men began to bring in crates of goods. "Now you be careful with these," Trent teased. "Don't break anything."

The last couple of weeks since he had put her in charge of the general store, he had been acting odd. More light-hearted, familiar, as though they were sweethearts instead of what they were—captor and captive. But she knew how quickly he could go into a rage, so she measured his moods and tried to match him. If he was melancholy, she talked gently and soothed his ego. If he was joyful, she smiled a lot and laughed at his jokes.

To anyone who didn't know better, one would assume she was a woman in love, and they were courting. But Jane had come to understand that her best weapon right now was the fact that, for some reason, Bedlow believed himself to be in love with her. He was waiting to possess her. Once he did, things might change, so she had a few weeks at most to find out her true debt and how much she'd worked off.

So far she hadn't had the nerve to go into the locked office. Bedlow had forbade her to enter the room, and she had obeyed for the sake of her baby and Danny. If he grew too angry, he could do to her what he'd done to Vera. Betrayal wasn't tolerated. Disobedience was punished severely.

"What do you suppose Frank was doing at the saloon?"

Jane tensed at Bedlow's question. "I'm sure I don't know," she replied. "I was just as surprised as you were." She gave a sigh. "He brought Danny's dog, so I imagine he wants to be rid of us once and for all—including Cheyenne."

He reached out and cupped her chin. "Or maybe he was bringing the dog for Danny, so he could see you. And please you."

Praying for wisdom, she pressed a smile to her lips. "And

why would he want to see me? I made it clear last time that I wasn't leaving with him." That Franklin might think she *wanted* to be with Bedlow turned her stomach and sent a burst of reckless courage to her lips. "He doesn't know it's only because you kidnapped Danny."

"Otherwise you'd let him pay your debt and go with him?"

"I would take my son back to the home his father claimed for us, and let Mr. Lloyd rent my land for his cattle for as long as it takes to settle the debt I owe him."

His dark eyes searched her face. Then, as he had been doing far too much lately, he dipped his head and pressed a kiss to her lips. Usually he settled for a peck that was so fast she didn't have time to respond. This was different. More bold. He pulled her to him and tried to deepen this kiss.

Instinctively, she shoved him back, fury building within her. "How dare you! Don't *ever* do that again." Her chest heaved as she glared. She expected him to be angry, perhaps even lash out at her.

Instead he tossed back his head and laughed. "Oh, you can be sure I will be kissing you like that and better many, many times in the near future." He glanced at her belly. "It's not going to be long now." His face washed of amusement, and he stepped forward, towering above her. "Do not forget who I am, Jane. I love you, but my love, like everything else, has limits. Don't test me. And as far as Danny's father—"

The door opened. Jane let out a breath as Andy walked in. "This is the last of it, Mr. Bedlow."

"Fine," Trent snapped. "Set it anywhere, and get to the saloon. I'll settle up with you there."

"Yes, sir."

They remained silent as Andy did as he was told. When he left, he glanced over his shoulder, as though reluctant to leave. But he slapped on his hat and walked outside. Jane noted that he waited for a minute.

The respite had given Trent time to calm down. "There are gowns in the crates. Find a dark blue one. I ordered it with your eyes in mind. Wear it tonight. You're coming to dinner at my house."

He strode across the room, his boots thudding against the wooden floor. He didn't look back as he opened the door and made his way across the street.

Jane unpacked and finally found the dress. Blue, like he'd said, and beautiful. Expensive, and silk. The problem was, it would never fit her in her condition. She imagined how Trent might react if she walked out in her green dress that she wore practically every day. He would be angry. There was nothing to do but fix it so that it did fit her. She walked across the room to the wall shelves that held bolts of material, lace, and ribbons and studied the bolts of calico, cotton, wool, and flannel. All were serviceable materials, but nothing was suitable for a dinner or ball gown. She would have to speak to Trent about that. If he wanted to compete for women's business, he would need to think of women's needs. And not the type of women he was used to either.

But every day men moved to town and brought their families. There were still many more prostitutes and actresses than ladies, but the ladies were coming. Anyone could see it was only a matter of time.

Standing next to the bolts of fabric, she stared helplessly about the room. Perhaps she should close up the general store and walk to a mercantile—there were plenty of them in Deadwood. Someone surely had some material she could add to her dress to let it out.

She glanced through the window, across the street to the saloon. Her heart jumped as she made out Trent's form, standing, watching the store. A chill slithered up her spine. "Dear God," she whispered. "Will You save Danny and me?"

Shaking, she turned away and walked back to the crate of dresses. He would just have to understand that if the dress didn't fit, it didn't fit, and there was nothing she could do about it. With a sigh, she lifted the lovely gown with longing. Trent or no Trent, she would have loved to wear it. Another gown similar to this one caught her eye, and she lifted it from the crate. Her stomach dipped. This gown was virtually identical. Before she could change her mind, she began to rip the seams, thanking God all the while that Mama Rose had forced her to learn how to sew.

For the rest of the day, she waited on customers and reworked the dress at a furious pace so it would be finished in time. She had just put in the last stitches when the door opened, and Vera walked in.

"I told him that would never fit you, but he insisted." She walked over and snatched up the dress to examine it. Then she glanced, eyebrows raised, at Jane. "I'm impressed." Fingering the gown, she studied the stitching. "If not for the lace you added for the extra material and the added stitching, I'd have never known the dress didn't come this way. You're more than meets the eye, aren't you? More than any homesteading housewife. Where did you learn to do this?"

Jane shrugged. Why should she tell Vera anything? She had caused the bruises that were still smudged under Jane's eyes. Her head still hurt most of the time.

"Well, wherever it was, you're too good to be wasting time as a dowdy old general store clerk."

"I hear this used to be your job." Jane knew she sounded petty, but this woman brought her to it. "Maybe that's why you think my skills lie elsewhere."

Vera tossed her head. "Suit yourself. I only came to tell you Trent said you should lock up and get over there so you can have a bath and get dressed."

"All right. Thank you for letting me know. I'll have to clean up around here first."

"I was told I'm to do that." She took the scraps from Jane's hands. "You have a romantic night ahead of you. Pregnant and all. I'd be very surprised if you come back to the store or the saloon. Trent's finally taking you to his house. I doubt he'll bring you out."

Dread filled Jane. Was he not going to keep his promise?

"Isn't it funny?"

"No. Not even a little."

Vera scowled. "You don't even know what I was going to say."

Jane inhaled a deep breath and released it slowly. "I'm sorry. What's funny?"

"You have everything I would give anything to have, and you hate the very idea of all of it."

"I don't even know what you are talking about, Vera. What could I possibly have that you'd want? I have nothing except debts that keep me from my son and my home."

She gave a short laugh. "Never mind. You'd best get. Trent doesn't wait for anyone. Not even you—at least not for long."

Chapter Thirteen

With every minute that ticked by, Franklin had to fight with himself not to jump back on Tryst and ride to Bedlow's General Store, grab up Jane, and bring her back to his house.

Something didn't feel right, but he couldn't quite put his finger on just what it was. He had a suspicion that Jane was somehow being coerced into staying with Bedlow. Remembering those days at her homestead, he mentally berated himself for forcing her to do this thing. If he had not been so stubborn—if he had given in about the land. If only he had thought ahead to simply rent her land and let her keep her home, which was really what she cared about, this wouldn't have happened. She wouldn't be forced to endure the lower, baser ranks of humanity as she carried out her plan to pay off her debt to Bedlow and make her way home. But Franklin knew Bedlow. He would find a way to keep her indebted to him, especially as he seemed to be in love with her.

Love. Franklin snorted his disgust. Bedlow didn't have the first hint of an idea as to what that meant. He possessed. He conquered. Simply put, he pursued until he caught and then took what he wanted and discarded the rest. What would happen if Jane fell into his trap? What if he drew her in to his lies, and she believed him? What if he fooled her into caring for him? Would he take what he wanted from her, leaving her demoralized and empty?

As dusk was beginning to settle, he closed up shop and mounted Tryst, grabbed hold of Cheyenne's rope, and headed for home. His route home didn't exactly take him past Bedlow's, but he found himself on McKinley Street anyway. He drew in a breath as he passed the saloon. Jane walked out, looking beautiful in a blue gown, her hand tucked inside Bedlow's arm. He led her to a waiting buggy.

Franklin rode past without taking a second look. He cut down the alley and doubled back, headed toward his home. His stomach churned. The closer he got to home, the sicker he felt.

From a distance, he noticed something wasn't right at home. He kicked Tryst into a canter. The Shen family stood outside the house, their cries and wails rending the air. His heart tore when he saw Huan lying across the horse that just this morning he had been riding, with Jenny behind him, her little arms wrapped around him, trusting. "What happened?"

"He shot." Mai pointed. "Dead." Tears soaked her cheeks. Her swollen eyes were practically closed.

"Who did this? How did he get here?"

"Horse."

"Let's get him down and inside."

Cheng and Chao pulled Huan from the horse and took him into the parlor. Tears flowed down their cheeks.

Franklin pulled Cheng aside. "I'm going to the mining camp to try to find out what happened to Huan and to make sure Jenny and her pa are all right. I'm sorry for your loss. Huan was a good man, and I'll miss him."

Cheng nodded and gave Franklin's arm a pat. Franklin was almost sure the cook understood less than half of what he'd just told him, but he couldn't waste time trying to make him understand. The sun was giving way to dusk, and if he didn't hurry he'd be stuck out there after dark, which was dangerous.

By the time he got to the camp, the sun was almost completely gone. He stopped at the first claim and asked for Mr. Ames. But none knew who he was talking about. Finally, when the camps were settling down and lamps were lit, fires burning bright, he found what he had come after.

"Ames?" a grizzled old-timer shouted, as though hard of hearing. "Dern shame, what with that little girl and all. And the Chinaman got hisself kilt in the process."

"Ames was shot too? Did you see who did it?"

"Didn't see who it was." The miner shoveled a spoonful of beans into his mouth, then spoke as though his mouth wasn't filled to capacity. "Took the little girl, though. And all the gold Ames had hid away."

"He left his gold out here?" *Foolish! Foolish!* Franklin couldn't help but think. Ames should have cashed it in and deposited his money in the Deadwood Bank.

Nodding, the old-timer gave him a sad smile. "He was

a book-learned man but not smart in the ways of men. I buried him." He reached into his tent and came back with a burlap bag. "Nothing valuable here. Just books, some photographs. That's about it. If the girl ever gets found, she might want it."

"That was kind of you. You said they took Jenny?" Franklin held tightly to Tryst's reins. "Did you see which way they took her?"

The miner gave a regretful shake of his head. "Wish I knew. I'd go after that sweet gal. Ain't no tellin' what they got in mind for a pretty little thing like that."

Franklin wanted to believe that all men were essentially good and would do the right thing, but he'd seen too much to allow himself that supposition. Someone had taken that girl, and if he didn't find her, she could be in grave danger.

He thanked the old miner for his time and carefully headed back home. Normally, he would make camp rather than chance Tryst losing his footing in the dark and injuring himself, but he couldn't this time. Not with the Shens mourning Huan and Jenny Ames missing.

He guided Tryst slowly and methodically until they were out of the woods and close to Deadwood, then the full moon lit the road, and he pushed a little harder. He stopped in the sheriff's office. The deputy took his statement about Huan and Jenny.

"We'll ask around and find out what's to be done." He leaned back in his chair and folded his arms across his chest.

"But don't count on us ever finding that little girl. It's been hours. Almost a whole day. By the time we can get us a posse together, it will be a full day. There's just too many places for someone to hide."

"But you will go looking?"

"If the sheriff agrees it's the thing to do."

Frustrated, and without much hope that the so-called Deadwood law would lift a finger to find a lost orphan, Franklin headed back toward home. The Shens had laid Huan's body out respectfully. "When will you bury him?" Franklin asked Cheng.

"Tomorrow. We read Bi-ble. You help?"

"Yes." The least he could do was help give Huan a Christian burial.

Mai came into the parlor. "Missa Lloyd, you eat. On table."

"Oh, Mai, don't serve me tonight. You should all be together. Please take the next few days off. I'll fend for myself."

Shaking her head, she tugged on Franklin's sleeve. "You eat. On table."

Franklin allowed himself to be led to the table. Allowed Mai to do what she clearly wanted to do. He sat thinking of Jenny Ames and wondered about her. Was she hurt? Afraid? Crying? It had been a long time since Franklin uttered a prayer. But as he imagined Jenny, hurting and scared, he lifted a silent plea to God.

* * * * *

Jane couldn't possibly eat another bite, and she told Trent so.

"You're pregnant. You're supposed to eat like a horse."

"Must you always say what is on your mind?" A twinge in her back had been nagging at her all evening, and she had to force herself not to squirm. But her irritation had risen with her discomfort.

"You are in a foul mood. I should have thought seeing Danny would have made you happy."

"It has. I apologize. I'm just not hungry tonight."

He gave a sharp laugh. "Maybe you won't have such a long time getting a pretty figure if you don't eat so much now."

Why couldn't he just hush? Everything in her wanted to give in to the frustration, to pick a fight. But he was not the sort of man a woman could safely fight with and walk away unscathed.

Squelching the irritation, she decided to focus on the beautiful, if perhaps a bit too ornate, home. In the dining room alone, the silver and china were worth much more than the debt she had to pay off. The thought irritated her further. The paintings on the wall were costly, and the curtains stitched by someone who most definitely knew how to work a needle and thread.

"Your home is lovely, Trent." She took another sip of her water.

"It could be our home, you know."

Jane didn't want to do anything to anger him, so she

determined to keep her voice level. "No, it couldn't. It couldn't be my house."

Danny burst into the room, his face painted, his hair even longer than it had been since the last time she had seen him. He had run back to his room to retrieve the bow and arrow Trent had purchased for him. Jane placed her arm about his shoulder and pulled him close. "I hope you thanked Mr. Bedlow."

His mouth dropped. He turned to Trent. "Thank you, Mr. Bedlow."

"I thought we agreed you would call me Uncle Trent."

"Uncle Trent." He grinned.

"Okay, Crazy Horse," Trent said, clapping his hands together, "bedtime for you."

Jane wanted to protest. She wanted to say, "How dare you decide when my son goes to bed." But she kept silent.

Standing, Trent reached his hand to her. "I thought you might like to tuck him into bed tonight."

"Yes, I would." She knew he was waiting for her to thank him. Inside she railed against the very idea. After all, why should she show gratitude for the man allowing her the privilege of tucking in her own son? She should be doing that very thing every night, and she would be, were it not for the fact that he had stolen Danny from her. How could anyone be so selfish and cruel?

In the end, she did take his hand. Another pain seized her back as she stood. And she sucked in a breath as Trent lifted

Danny to his shoulder, and they walked down the hall as though one family. As they passed a room a few doors down from Danny's, a woman exited.

Jane's head was turned toward the room, and she saw a figure on the bed. "Who is that?"

"I want my pa!" a child's voice called.

Before the woman could close and lock the door, Jane shoved her aside and pushed open the door. A young girl sat, knees to her chest and blond braids awry. Tears stained her cheeks, and a red handprint marred her face. A food tray sat untouched.

Jane wheeled on the woman, whose hair was as dark as her expression. Her brown eyes were cold, her lips and cheeks painted rosy, and she wore a low-cut, form-fitting gown. "Did you strike this child?" Jane demanded.

"That is none of your affair," the woman retorted, her nose wrinkled in a sneer.

"I'm making it my affair. Who is this girl, and why is she locked away in here?"

The question was directed at Trent, and he answered. "Her pa was found dead at the mining camp. The men who killed her pa took her, and my men intercepted them. They brought her to me."

"Why wouldn't they take her to the sheriff?" Suspicion shot immediately through Jane's mind. Bringing a little girl to Trent made no sense—until she thought of Molly. She had only been thirteen. But this girl seemed much younger—still several years from her first woman-time, surely. She turned to the child. "How old are you, sweetheart?"

"Eleven." Hiccups jerked her body. "Can I get out of here?"

"Where would you like to go?"

Hope widened her green eyes. "Could you take me to Mr. Franklin Lloyd? He owns the Lloyds' Mercantile and lives— somewhere. He took me to his house when I was sick, so I could get better. I was just going back to Pa when the men started shooting. They killed Shen Huan too."

"Who is Shen Huan?"

"Mr. Lloyd's servant. He cleans—cleaned."

Jane turned to Trent. "May I speak with you in private?"

"Of course."

She patted the girl. "We'll be right back. Would you try to eat something? You will get weak and sickly if you don't eat." She looked at Danny, who had been taking in the whole scene. "Sweetheart, will you do Mommy a big favor and stay right here with Jenny while she eats her supper?"

"Yes, Ma."

"Thank you, Baby." Jane glared at the woman as she walked past her. "You leave that child alone."

"I don't take orders from you, cow."

Trent reached out and grabbed the woman's wrist, twisting her arm. "You don't speak to her that way."

The woman gasped. Jane placed her hand on his arm. "Trent, don't hurt her. Just please keep her away from the child."

He let her go, and she stumbled into the hall, then righted herself. "Get your things and get out," he commanded.

She raised her chin. "Make no mistake about why he wants that little girl." She flung the words at Jane with a sneer.

Muttering a vile oath, Trent took a menacing step forward. The woman screeched, and he restrained himself. But the look he gave her left no room for doubt as to what he might do if she didn't leave his sight immediately. "Get out."

Jane turned to him. "I'd like to know what your plans are concerning that child."

His lips curved upward, but his smile didn't quite reach his eyes. He slipped his arms around her waist and pulled her close. "Don't listen to Simone."

So that was Simone. Had she ever struck Danny? The thought made Jane see red.

"Yes, but why did you bring the child into your home instead of contacting authorities?"

"Of course I am going to do so. I just thought she might like a few days to mourn her father before going to an orphanage."

Jane turned and looked in on the child. She was attempting to nibble on her food. Jane cringed at the thought in her head. She had no choice but to spend the night in this house. For the first time she wondered if perhaps this were the reason Danny had been brought to Trent's home. Perhaps these weeks had been for no other reason than to save this girl.

She was beginning to feel a bit smothered by Trent's closeness but forced herself to turn in his arms. "I am going to need my nightgown brought from the saloon." She tried to keep her face so he did not have easy access to her lips. Lately he never passed up the opportunity to kiss her.

"Oh?" His eyes brightened. "You've decided to stay with me?"

She shook her head and leveled her gaze at him so there was no room for him to mistake her intent. "I'm staying for Jenny's sake."

"I'll have the housekeeper get you a room ready."

"No thank you. I'll sleep in there with her. And I'd like for Danny to sleep in here with me. On a pallet."

When Jane recognized the refusal in his eyes, she rushed her words. "If it's all right with you, of course. Otherwise, she might be afraid. Think about it, Trent. Her pa was killed, probably in front of her eyes. Evil men rode off with her. And now she's in a strange home."

He scrutinized her, then nodded. "Probably a good idea. But Danny can stay in his own room. I don't need you getting any ideas about trying to run off."

So he knew her better than she thought he did. Frustration grew, but she pushed the feeling aside. Now was not the time to let her emotions rule her tongue or her expression. She smiled. "Thank you, Trent." Rising on her tiptoes, she forced herself to press a quick kiss to his cheek.

If she could keep him thinking about her, perhaps his

mind would stay away from Jenny.

He grabbed her hand, pulled her against him, and searched her face. "Don't play me for a fool, Jane."

Swallowing hard, she nodded. His eyes moved over her face again, and then he let her go. She stumbled back. Trent lunged forward, steadying her.

She stared at him.

He scowled. "Danny!" he called. "Let's go feed Sioux."

"Ma said stay with Jenny."

"It's okay, Danny," Jane said. "I'm coming to stay with her."

A minute later Trent swung Danny to his shoulders and their laughter rang down the hall.

Chapter Fourteen

Shen Huan was the first to be buried in the cemetery intended for family. But Franklin was beginning to doubt that the family of his dreams would ever grace his home. Instead, he had a family of four Chinese servants. Three now.

His hands shook as he took the Bible from Cheng's outstretched hand and read from Psalm 23. The words seemed to bring comfort to the others, even though they probably didn't understand half of them.

For him, the words meant nothing: *"He maketh me lie down in green pastures…. He restoreth my soul."* His soul felt empty.

He finished the psalm, handed the Bible back to Cheng, and left the family to grieve over their loved one.

Walking the five minutes from the cemetery to the house gave him the solitude to berate himself for causing Huan's death. He should never have gotten involved with Jenny Ames and her pa. When would he learn to mind his own business?

Look at what he'd done to a good woman like Jane Albright. If not his fault, whose? No matter. She would never raise the money to pay Tom's debt in just a couple more months. He entered through the back door, untying his tie as he walked through the kitchen and down the hall. As he turned to head upstairs to change his clothes, he heard a knock at the door.

When he opened the door, Andy Armor stood on the porch.

"Mr. Lloyd," he said, kneading the back of his neck. Then he took in Franklin's attire. "Did I catch you at a bad time? I can come back later."

Franklin shook his head and stepped out into the warm summer morning. "One of my employees was killed yesterday. We were having a service for him at the cemetery in back of the house."

"The Chinaman with the little girl?"

"What do you know about that?" Franklin's heartbeat rose, and he frowned at Andy. "Here—sit down and tell me about it."

They strode across the full-length porch and sat on the wooden rocking chairs Huan had insisted upon after seeing several of the homes in Denver with them.

Sitting with his elbows resting on his thighs, holding his hat between his knees, Andy let out a breath. "I'm probably going to get shot for this. But I can tell you it had something to do with Bedlow."

Franklin tightened his grip on the arms on the chair. "How do you mean?"

"He had a hankerin' for the fella's gold."

"His gold? How did he know about Mr. Ames' strike?"

"It ain't easy to keep something like that a secret these

days," Andy said. "Maybe three years ago when there weren't near as many people and lots more gold. But these days, any strike at all is mighty exciting."

What he said was true. The gold was nearly depleted, but somehow Mr. Ames had managed to find himself a viable mine. "So you're saying Mr. Bedlow somehow knew about the strike and sent his men to kill Mr. Ames? To what end?"

Andy shrugged. "Mr. Bedlow has his ways of getting around the law."

Such as buying off the local sheriff. There was no need to mention it. The most pressing issue still had not been discussed. "What about Jenny?"

"The little girl?" Misery clouded Andy's face. "I saw her."

"Where?" Any hope Franklin had carried that she might be found had fled by now. But once again possibility sprang up inside him.

"You ain't going to like it, and it ain't going to do no good to run off."

"Where, Andy?"

"Bedlow's house."

Franklin sprang to his feet. "Bedlow has Jenny?"

"Yeah, but your Mrs. Albright is making sure nothing happens to her."

His gut twisted at Andy's words, nauseating him. If Jane were keeping the girl safe, that meant she was also staying at Bedlow's home. The image was more than he could bear and impossible to shake from his mind. He'd lost her for good.

"How is she doing that?"

"Sleeping in the little girl's room."

Franklin gave a tight smile. So she had left Bedlow's bed to save the girl. That much was commendable. And typical of Jane to be stubborn. "What was your purpose in coming? Just to tell me this?" Franklin shrugged. "I don't know what I can do about it."

"The little girl asked for you."

"How'd you hear that?"

"Danny told me. I was in the barn last night when him and Bedlow came to feed his horse."

"What were you doing at Bedlow's?"

"Two of his men were shot. He needed me to help protect the place last night."

That was the problem with being a man like Bedlow. Too many enemies. Judging from Andy's presence on Franklin's porch, more enemies than Bedlow even knew he had.

"How is Danny? Is he being treated well?"

Andy nodded. "Nothing to worry about there. Bedlow treats him like a son."

The words twisted inside Franklin like a bowie knife. Even Danny. But he couldn't blame the boy. Children were trusting by nature—until the trust was crushed. "I suppose that's good. I guess I don't have to ask why Jenny was taken to Bedlow's?"

Andy scratched at his stubbled jaw. "I reckon you don't."

"She's nothing but a baby."

"Yeah. He won't use her for a while. He'll put her to work

pouring drinks or scrubbing floors. Get her used to the men and the goings on. But eventually someone will offer a price he can't pass up, and he'll sell her innocence."

"How do we get her out of there, then?"

"Mrs. Albright."

Franklin nodded. It was the only solution that made good sense. Jane would have to help them.

The sun beat down on the east part of the house now, and Franklin noticed Andy's forehead beginning to bead with sweat.

"How would you like to come inside?"

Andy shook his head. "I best get back."

"You're still working for Bedlow after all this?"

Andy leveled his gaze at Franklin and spoke earnestly. "Can you think of a better way to save that little girl? Bedlow hired another freighter. He only keeps men he trusts at the house, and I've been with him long enough that he trusts me. I'm working there now. Miss Jane is there. We'll get that little girl out soon."

Franklin nodded. "What about Miss Jane?" He cleared his throat. "You think we need to rescue her too?"

Swiping at his brow with the back of his sleeve, Andy shook his head. "I ain't got it all figured out, but she's staying with him, and he ain't exactly making her that I can see."

That's all Franklin needed to hear. Jane had made her decision. This was about more than paying off her debt to Bedlow. Something must have changed their relationship, and there was no room left for whatever possibilities there had been between Jane and Franklin.

An awkward silence settled between them.

Andy finally stood. "I best be getting back. I'll find a way to speak with Miss Jane, and I'll get word to you somehow."

Franklin nodded. "If it looks like Jenny is in any trouble sooner, you'll do whatever it takes, right?"

"As God is my witness."

"I'll expect to hear from you within a few days, then."

The two men shook hands, then Andy made his way down the steps and mounted his horse.

As Andy rode away, Franklin ruminated on their conversation. He had to push Jane out of his head and concentrate on Jenny. His anger burned toward Bedlow. Huan was dead because of him. Jenny's pa too, and now Jenny was in danger of losing her future to lust and greed.

He walked inside, slammed the door, then stormed upstairs, yanking at his tie and top buttons as he threw open his bedroom door.

Dropping to a chair, he yanked at his dressy boots. Frustration welled up when the boot refused to budge. He pulled as hard as he could until it slid off with a jerk. Then he threw the boot across the room. It crashed into the mirror over his shaving supplies. Dropping his head into his hands, Franklin released a breath. Jenny's image played across his mind. Innocent and sweet. But for how long?

He punched his thigh. Why did evil always win?

* * * * *

The pains were coming at regular intervals now. Thankfully, she'd slept well and had awakened to intermittent pains so she could concentrate on Jenny, wipe her tears.

Though Jenny grieved her pa, in true childlike resilience she had stopped crying and had been playing with Danny all day. She seemed to enjoy the boy, and he had even taken her to the stable to play. Only the knowledge that Andy Armor had been stationed to guard the part of the property that held the barn had given Jane the peace to allow the two to go.

Now she lay on the bed she'd shared with Jenny and closed her eyes to ward off the pain of another contraction. The other side of the bed dipped just as the pain eased. She opened her eyes to find Trent lying on his side, staring, with his head resting in his hand.

"You're in bed during the day?" he asked. "Are you ill?"

She breathed in—first, because he had the audacity to lie next to her, and second, because she knew she had no choice but to inform him of her situation. "The baby's coming."

His expression didn't change. "I'll call Doc White."

Jane reached out and took his hand. "Please don't. I'd rather have a midwife. Surely there's a woman in town—"

He shook his head insistently. "Doc knows how to care for you better. If something were to go wrong—"

"This isn't my first child. I delivered Danny alone in the soddy and cared for him for two weeks before Tom came home. So, you see, I am not in need of a doctor. I'm not scared."

"Be that as it may, I am not going to risk losing you." He covered her hand with his.

She didn't want to argue with him on today of all days. But she would not submit to Doc White's ministrations. The thought of that man coming anywhere near her child after he had implied that she might want to miscarry this baby…

"I won't allow him to touch me or my baby."

"There is only one midwife in town. If you haven't noticed, there aren't many married women in Deadwood."

"How often do you call on her?"

His mouth twisted. "She doesn't perform abortions, if that's what you're asking. Usually the girls don't tell me until it's too late to safely get rid of the baby."

Tears formed in her eyes as a contraction seized her. How on earth could he be so complacent about a life?

She squeezed Trent's hand until the pain eased. He slipped his hand from her grasp. "Okay, honey, I'm going for the midwife."

Relief flooded her. "Thank you."

By the time Mam Truman, the former slave woman, arrived, the pains had increased in intensity. Trent stood and sat respectively, pacing and fidgeting.

"For heaven's sake," Jane said to the midwife, "make him go away. He's driving me to distraction."

Mam Truman turned to him and nodded to the door. Jane

doubted anyone else could have induced obedience, but he reluctantly obeyed, pausing at the door to look back at Jane.

Mam gave him a shove out the door. "Gwine now! I'll come get you soon as we got a baby." She shook her head as she closed the door behind him. "Never saw him care about any baby. This ain't his baby, is it?"

"No, my husband's."

A scowl wrinkled her already wrinkled face. "Where's he?"

If Jane hadn't felt so miserable, she might have taken offense to the midwife's implication. "He's dead."

Mam worked a cool cloth across Jane's forehead. "The worst thing is when a man don't live to help raise his own childrens."

"Well, it's just as well he didn't." She looked up into Mam's wizened eyes. "He wasn't the sort of man I'd want raising my son or this new baby."

"And Mistah Bedlow is?"

"No, of course not. Mr. Bedlow believes I owe him a debt. I've been working in his general store to pay him back. As soon as I've settled my debt, my children and I will leave Deadwood forever."

"Is that whut you think?" Mam shook her head. "Honey, you is doin' nothin' but foolin' yourself. I ain't never seen Mr. Bedlow gwine so over a woman."

"I can't help that." A pain started low in her back, radiating to the front. "I. Never. Encouraged. Him. He. Knows. How. I. Feel."

Mam held her hand and spoke softly until the contraction reached its peak and subsided. Then she bent forward and met Jane's gaze. Her black eyes never wavered. "Mistah Bedlow don't care how you feel. Only how he feels. And he wants you. He think he love you, but a man without God don't know anything but lust and evil. He gwine take you no matter how you feel. And he gwine use these babies of yours against you."

Tears misted Jane's eyes. The old midwife spoke the truth. Jane had been fooling herself, biding her time until the baby was born so she could finish earning enough to pay off her so-called debt. She had to get out of here as soon as she could go.

"He's been keeping me at the saloon and my boy here," she admitted.

"It's what he does. He don't want you runnin' off."

"Do you know Franklin Lloyd?"

Recognition flashed in her eyes. "I knows him."

"After my baby is born, will you please take it to Mr. Lloyd?"

Mam's eyes narrowed. "Whut are you sayin'?"

"You can tell Mr. Bedlow the baby didn't survive."

"Honey, your baby need you." She patted Jane's shoulder. "Jesus is gwine make a way in de wilderness."

Despair filled her at the midwife's refusal. "Will you go to him and give him a message from me?"

Nodding, Mam wiped the cloth across Jane's forehead again. "I do that."

"Tell him I want him to pay off Bedlow's debt. Tell him the

only reason I didn't go with him before is because Bedlow had my son. Tell him about the baby and that Danny is here. Ask him to bring the sheriff and take me away from here."

"Oh, honey." Mam's eyes shone with pity. "I can tell him. But that trashy sheriff ain't gwine go against Mistah Bedlow."

Another pain began, stopping the conversation. Forty-five minutes later, another baby boy entered the world. Jane was too weary to even consider what to name him. So she left that for later. Mam set him in her arms while she cleaned Jane and applied herbs. Jane smiled as she looked at her new little boy. He looked exactly like Danny.

When Mam finished her task, she deftly changed the sheets with Jane still in the bed and gathered up the bloody sheets and clothes. "I'll be back to see you tomorrow," she promised.

"Thank you for everything."

"You're most welcome."

"Will you ask Mr. Bedlow to bring Danny so he can see his little brother? And Jenny too?"

She had dozed off when Danny crawled into bed beside her. "Ma," he whispered, "wake up." She smiled at his sweet voice.

"I'm awake." The slight weight of the baby cuddled next to her reminded her why Danny was there. She opened her eyes. "Did you see your new brother?"

Danny nodded. "What's his name?"

She shrugged. "He doesn't have one yet. What do you think we should call him?"

"Red Cloud?"

A chuckle at the door lifted her head. She smiled in spite of herself as Trent entered the room. "I'm sure Red Cloud's mother believed that to be a fine name. However, I was hoping for something a bit more traditional."

Trent walked forward. "May I hold him?"

The last thing she wanted in that moment was for Mr. Bedlow to lift her child in his arms. But there was no gracious way to refuse, and she didn't want to make him angry, so she nodded.

He frowned. "You don't want me to hold him?"

"Of course you are welcome to hold him. I'd be honored." She swallowed down the lie and forced a smile as he bent and lifted the baby from her arm.

"He's a handsome little lad, isn't he?"

Jane's stomach twisted as she remembered Mam's words. Would he try to use her baby the way he'd been using Danny? She watched him cuddling the infant. Of course he would. "Where's Jenny?" she asked. "I thought seeing the baby might make her feel better."

"She's gone," Danny said. He was on his knees next to her.

"Danny! Be careful with your ma," Trent fussed.

"Oh, he's not hurting me. I love having my boy with me." She slipped her arms around him and pulled him close.

Trent scowled but didn't object.

"What do you mean Jenny's gone?" Jane asked. "Where did she go?" Slowly she lifted her gaze to Trent. Her heart sank as she realized Trent had sent the girl away. "You didn't want her with me, did you?"

"My dear," he said. "You have nothing to worry about. No one will touch her until she's ready."

"You mean like Molly, who was thirteen years old when she came to you?"

Feeling Danny's weight in her arms, she stopped. "Danny, why don't you go to your room and play for a while? Ma needs to rest." She gathered him close, and he pressed his cheek to her shoulder. Jane smoothed his hair. "You look just like an Indian boy."

He grinned. "I am an Indian." Hopping from the bed he gave a war cry and galloped from the room like a brave on a pony.

Once he exited and Jane was sure he wouldn't hear, she turned her glare on Trent. "Where is she? Trent, you can't have her for your saloon."

Eyes hardening, he leaned over and set the baby in the cradle of her arm, but stayed close. So close she could smell the whiskey on his breath. "I'll make her a wedding gift to you."

"Trent, please. Why on earth would you want to marry me?"

"Because I love you." He pressed his lips to hers. The whiskey must have loosened his emotions, for his passion grew. He grabbed her face between his hands and deepened his kiss.

She turned her head. "Stop it!"

He pulled away, and dark anger flashed in his eyes. "Careful, darling. If not for your present condition, I wouldn't have allowed such an insult."

"How can you bargain with a child's innocence?"

The baby woke and started to squirm.

"You best feed him."

She turned more on her side. "Turn your head." When she was sure he had, she began feeding the baby and pulled the quilt so that it hid her without suffocating the baby. "What about Jenny? Will you be kind and bring her back to me?"

One of his eyebrows rose. "As a wedding gift."

Jane turned her head toward the window. There were no bars, but this house was a prison just the same. How on earth had she ever gotten herself into such a wretched position?

Chapter Fifteen

Franklin slung the scattered boxes out of his way and kicked at some loose garments scattered across the floor.

"Casey!" He lifted his foot from a sticky mess and noticed belatedly the molasses pouring from a punctured can.

"I'm right here, Mr. Lloyd." The boy's voice rang from across the messed-up storage room, then he appeared, panting, sweat dripping from his chin. He stopped short and blinked at the mess.

"What happened here?"

"I don't know, sir. It wasn't like this when I left last night. When I got here, the back door was wide open and the padlock's broken."

Franklin tightened his lips. "Bedlow," he muttered, scraping the molasses off his boot onto a piece of cardboard. He must have found out he was asking about the girl. Or maybe he had just done it out of spite. It didn't really seem like Bedlow's way of doing things, though. He'd be more likely to have him beaten up or shot.

The bell on the front door clanged. Great, he'd forgotten to lock the door behind him. Just what he needed. A customer before daylight.

Mam Truman stood inside the door, her wrinkled face still and calm.

Franklin forced a smile as he walked toward her. "Sorry, Mam, we're not open yet. Can you come back in an hour?"

Her eyes scanned his face. "Ain't wantin' to buy nothin' today. Miz Albright ast me to bring you a message."

"What's the message, Mam?"

"Miz Albright, she wants you to know she only with Bedlow 'cuz of her boy. He was keepin' them apart and threatenin' her if she didn't work for him."

Franklin inhaled sharply. He gave himself a mental kick. He should have known better than to think Jane would willingly stay with Bedlow. "Does she want me to come get her?"

"She had her baby just yesterday. Since you offered, she be wantin' you to pay off the debt and get her and the babies outta there, but—" Mam shook her head.

"But what? I'll go right now."

"Mistah Franklin, that ain't gwine be doin' you no good. Her neither. He done made up his mind to have that woman for his own one way or another, and paying off no debt ain't gwine change his mind."

"He can't just keep her there like a—"

"Slave?" The wizened woman smiled around toothless gums. "He been doin' that to those poor girls ever since we come to Deadwood."

"We?"

"I is free now. But I's still Massah Trent's Mam."

Franklin paced the floor. "Well, then I'll just have to break her out of there."

"How you 'spectin' to do that with all them men he got on the place?"

"I don't know. I'll think of something." Something in her eyes made him pause. "Mam, do you know a way?"

Fear flashed momentarily over her face, but just as soon as he saw it, it was gone.

"I don' know nothin' that won't get me whipped." She turned toward the door.

"Wait." Franklin laid his hand on her arm. "I need to get the girl, Jenny, away from him too."

"She ain't at the house no more. He done took that girl to the saloon."

"What?" The rage in Franklin's heart spilled over into his voice. "That depraved, lecherous—she's only eleven years old."

"Now wait a minute, Mistah Franklin." Mam straightened and frowned. "I knows Mistah Trent have some evil ways, and I grieve and pray over that boy day and night, but he wouldn't touch no one that young or make her do that kind of work for him. She gwine be servin' and cleanin' for now. That's all."

"You'd defend him, Mam?"

"Nawsir, I ain't defendin' him. I knows what he is. But I know where he draw the line."

Franklin watched her leave. Was she right? Maybe. But he didn't trust the man at all, and it was only a matter of time before Jenny would be forced to endure the same thing the rest of Bedlow's women endured. He had to get her out of there.

* * * * *

Darkness had fallen over Deadwood as Franklin slipped through the swinging doors of the saloon. He'd waited until the place was crowded, in hopes there might be a chance to slip out with Jenny unnoticed. If he could make it outside with her, they would have the cover of darkness and might have a chance to get away.

He moved swiftly away from the door, edging through the crowd, his glance sweeping the room.

"What are you doing here, Lloyd?" Craig Shewmate blocked his way.

Prepared for just such a contingency, Franklin met the man's stare. "Someone broke into my mercantile last night. I came to see if anyone here had seen anything."

"Well, I didn't see a thing." Craig addressed the crowded room. "Anyone here see who busted into Lloyd's store?" A chuckle or two lifted from among the patrons, but very few even bothered to look up from their drinks and cards. Craig shrugged. "Guess not. So if you ain't drinking, keeping company with the women, or playing cards, you best get on out of here."

His eyes fell on Jenny, dressed in a smaller version of the saloon girl dresses, cosmetics applied to her face, and his anger burned. Just then she glanced up and saw him, spilling the tray of drinks in her hand in her excitement.

She left the tray and darted through the indignant men, throwing herself into Franklin's arms. "Mr. Lloyd! You came for me."

"Of course I did, sweetheart." He lifted her in his arms and carried her toward the door.

"That's far enough, Lloyd." Two other men had joined Craig. They blocked the door, their guns pointed in his direction.

Franklin stopped. He couldn't risk a bullet hitting Jenny. "She's just a little girl. Let me take her out of here."

The man in the middle shook his head. "We heard you had her at your house for a while. Mr. Bedlow brung her here for her protection."

"What does he mean, Mr. Lloyd? Something bad?" Jenny asked.

"I'm afraid so, sweetheart." He kept his gaze fixed on the men. "These men have been around filth so long they don't understand decency."

Craig chuckled. "I'm touched, Lloyd."

"Don't any of you have sisters? Or maybe even daughters of your own? Look how young she is."

Laughter erupted from one of the others. "Don't worry. She'll grow up in a little while."

Craig cut a glance at Big George, who had come to investigate the disruption. "Big George, take the gal. I need to have a few words with our friend here."

The bouncer looked down at Franklin and shook his head. He released a heavy breath and held out his arms. "Give me the gal."

Of all the places for Jenny to be in that room, Franklin knew George's arms were the safest. Franklin handed Jenny over.

"No!" She reached for Franklin as the men grabbed him and hauled him out back.

A blow landed on the side of his head, and before he could defend himself, more blows landed from all sides. Pain speared throughout his entire body.

The last thing he felt was exploding agony on the back of his head, then everything went black....

* * * * *

"Mistah Lloyd, Mistah Lloyd, wake up." The voice penetrated the darkness of Franklin's mind and he began to rouse, then blacked out again.

When he came to, the pain was so excruciating, it took a minute to realize he was being carried. Nausea rose up, and he fought to keep it down. With difficulty, he opened his eyes. His vision blurred, and he squinted, finally making out Big George's face.

"Wh–what?"

"Mistah Lloyd, I wasn't sure if you was alive. We're 'bout to your house."

He felt himself being lowered and swayed as George set him on his feet. The back door of his house loomed before him.

"What happened?" Pain seared his lungs as he spoke.

"They beat you 'bout senseless, then came in to have another drink. I sashayed around back and found you. Thought I bettah get you out of there b'fore they decided to come back and finish the job."

"Where's Jenny?"

"Now Mr. Franklin, there ain't nothin' you can do for that little thing right now. Best you concentrate on gettin' yourself well."

"Where is she?"

George blew out a breath. "Molly took her upstairs. Said she ain't goin' downstairs the rest of the night."

That much was a relief anyway. "Thanks, George. Why didn't you just put me on my horse instead of carrying me all this way?"

"Horse was in front of the saloon. Didn't want to take no chances on bein' seen. I gotta get back." Without another word, Big George was gone.

Franklin leaned against the door and pounded as hard as he was able. He fell forward as the door swung open.

Cheng grabbed him before he hit the floor.

* * * * *

Jane stepped through the kitchen door that led to the back of Trent's home. She breathed in the smell of fresh air for the first time in two weeks. She felt strong and capable, but Trent insisted on carrying the baby as they walked down to the stables to see Danny ride his horse. The summer beauty of the hills all around the ranch house was breathtaking. "It's so nice to be outdoors."

"I still say it's too early to bring a baby outside. Two weeks old. What if he gets sick?"

She smiled in spite of herself. It was difficult not to have at least some affection for a man who cared about her child so much. And so far, he hadn't attempted to get too close. As a matter of fact, he'd kept his distance until Jane was beginning to wonder if he'd lost interest. She could only hope.

A cottage sat between the house and the stable, and Jane's curiosity got the better of her. "Who lives there?"

He adjusted the tiny bundle to his shoulder. "That's my mammy's little house."

"Mam?"

He nodded. "You seem surprised. Did you expect her to live in my house?"

"I didn't expect anything, to tell you the truth. I guess I just assumed that she lived in her own house with Big George."

He shook his head. "Big George has a back room at the saloon."

"He sleeps in the saloon?" Jane had lived there for weeks

and had no idea. "Why can't he have his own home, or at least a home he can share with Mam?"

He leaned toward Jane and gave her a patronizing smile. "You let me handle my own employees, okay? You have enough decisions of your own to make. For instance, what are you going to name your son? And when are you going to start sewing your wedding gown?"

So he hadn't lost interest after all.

She cleared her throat. "As far as the baby is concerned, I'll get around to that. Nothing seems quite right yet."

"It's a name. There are thousands of them. Just pick one."

"It's not so simple. A person is known by his name. He needs the one that tells who he is."

"I'm not trying to sway you, but I've always been partial to Solomon."

"Why is that?" Her curiosity got the better of her again. "Why is your business in Sidney named Solomon?"

He tweaked her nose. "That is my own affair."

Her cheeks warmed. "Fine. Then *when* I decide to name my son and *what* I decide to name him is my business."

He shrugged. "Fine, name him whatever you wish, my dear. I give in on that. But what about the other decision?"

She gave a sigh. "How can you force a woman to marry you by threatening a child?" All affection she'd felt a few minutes ago fled as she remembered Jenny. "It's unconscionable."

"Be that as it may, my offer stands. If you will marry me and give your sons my name, I will set Jenny free. You may adopt her and raise her as your own. Or, if you prefer, she may serve you as a sort of lady's maid. Or you may send her away, safe, from my evil clutches. It's up to you." He slipped his arm about her waist. "Her fate is in your hands."

Jane knew she had no real choice until Andy could find a way to rescue the girl and get her to Franklin, but even then, wouldn't Trent simply go and find the child? He would not allow himself to be bested—especially by Franklin.

The door to the cottage slammed behind them, and they turned to find Mam standing on her front porch, her slight body standing regally with her hands on her hips.

"What are you two jabbering about so seriously?"

"She won't set a date and marry me, Mam."

Mam shook her head and puckered her brow. "Well, who would want to marry a man who steals children?"

A shadow settled over his face as she leveled her gaze and stared him down.

"Easy, Mam."

She sniffed. "You can't do anything to me," she said bravely, but her hands visibly shook. "I am a free woman. I can leave here anytime I please."

"Where would you go?"

"I gots my plans. You don't know. You don't know everything you thinks you knows."

He smiled. "If you go, who is going to be mammy to my children?"

Watching the exchange between them, Jane knew he

had said the right thing. This woman had been with Trent his whole life. She knew he wasn't kind or good, but she loved him dearly all the same. The way a mother loves a child. If he were going to have children, she wasn't about to trust their raising to anyone but herself.

"Well, I ain't heard Miss Jane say she's gwine marry you anyway."

"Mam," Jane said, without responding to the last statement, "we're going down to the stable to watch Danny ride his pony. Would you like to come with us?"

Pleasure flashed across her face. "I'd surely love to, Miss Jane."

Trent strode back and extended his hand to help her negotiate the steps.

She glanced at Trent and scowled. "You best give ol' Mam that baby b'fore you drop him on his little head—and b'fore he even gets a name."

A chuckle rumbled in Trent's chest. "Here you go. Take good care of my boy. And please help his mother name him so we can stop calling him Boy, or Baby." He kissed Mam's wrinkled cheek and told Jane, "I will leave you in Mam's capable hands while I go on ahead and see that Danny's ready to show off his new skills."

They watched him walk away. Mam looked down at the sleeping baby's face. She smiled, tenderness shining from her brown eyes. "I's partial to the name Solomon."

Jane smiled. "Trent's already tried that one. I know he has a store with that name in Sidney, but I can't figure out why."

"That's for Mastah Trent to say."

"And he's already told me it's none of my affair."

Mam held the baby close to her breast, cradling him like a nursing mother. "Maybe I tell you." She let out a sigh and shook her head. "I'll leave it for another time."

"Mam?" Jane asked. "What makes a man become such a monster?"

"Oh, honey, he ain't no monster. He just gots the devil tuggin' on one side and goodness tuggin' on the other."

"Well, the goodness doesn't win very often."

"That be a sadness I can't rightly figure. His pa be a kind mastah. Died of dysentery durin' the war. Went to fight at the very end when all the young men be dead or wounded. They was askin' for all them too old and them too young."

"And what about his mother?"

"His ma, well, she died when Mistah was just a itty baby. He don't even remember."

"That's too bad."

"What about you? You got folks somewheres?"

"Not really." Jane shrugged. "I was orphaned and taken in by a strict woman who made me work a lot even as a child. I called her Mama Rose because it was expected, but never really felt as though she was my ma. Danny and the baby are my only family."

They reached the stable yard. Trent turned and grinned. He beckoned them to stand next to the wooden fence where he stood, resting his arms across the top of the fence and watching while Danny proudly rode astride. The trainer led the horse by a rope while Danny held the reins.

"He looks good up there, doesn't he?" Trent said proudly. "One of these days he'll race at the Kentucky Derby."

"Is that what Danny wants?" Jane asked with raised eyebrows. "I've never heard him say so. Although I know he adores Sioux."

"Well, we haven't brought it up yet. But if he goes on like he's doing, he's going to be a mighty fine horseman someday. It would be a shame to waste it."

Jane shook her head and laughed. But the sound was hollow even to her own ears. How could he be planning her son's future as though she had already agreed to marrying him? Did he assume so much that he couldn't fathom the possibility she might say no?

She planned to be home, on her homestead with both of her children, soon. It was a distant dream—but each day she sent up a silent prayer that God would come on His eagle's wings and take her and the children away from here. If God would grant her the prayer of her heart, she would go home. She only prayed that Trent would allow her to go and take Jenny with her. She wondered if Molly still planned to come with them. She hadn't seen her friend, except for brief glances across the street toward the saloon, for two weeks.

She wondered whether Molly was taking care of Jenny. She knew the answer. Of course Molly would. She must see herself in the little girl. That Jenny had Molly looking after her was the only ray of hope that kept Jane from total despair when her thoughts drifted to the girl.

Trent nudged her from her thoughts. "Watch—he's about to take his first jump."

"Is he ready for that? He's awfully little."

"I was jumping when I was his age."

"Mistah Trent, now you tell the truth."

Trent rolled his eyes. "Mam, when are you going to learn to keep your mouth shut?"

Giving a huff, she shook her head. "Too ol' to start doin' that now."

"Watch, Ma! I'm gonna jump!"

"Trent, I think it's too early for him to be jumping."

"It's too late to stop him now." Trent chuckled.

Danny had already taken his first jump over a low measuring bar. Relief flooded over Jane. The jump was nothing but a stick almost as low as the ground itself.

"Did you see that, Uncle Trent? I jumped over it, and I wasn't scared."

"Wonderful, Danny. I think that calls for a special celebration. How about if you get to stay up and eat with your mother and me in the dining room tonight, and I'll have Cook bake a cake to celebrate your victory?" He paused for a second to let the boy process the enormity of dinner with his mother and Trent. Then he continued, "And I think it's time that a valuable chief like you get a war bonnet."

Danny whooped.

"Careful, Danny, honey," Jane called. "You'll spook Sioux."

"I won't spook Sioux. He's a warrior. He's not scared of anything."

On the way back to the house, Trent took her hand, lacing his fingers with hers. "Are you feeling up to having dinner in the dining room? I suppose I should have made sure before asking the boy for a celebration dinner."

"Of course I'll be at the dinner. But you'll spoil him, Trent."

"Nonsense."

But it wasn't nonsense. Not to Jane. She never wanted to raise her sons to feel entitled. She wanted them to work for their land, for their rewards. "Don't you see," she told Trent, "if you reward him for all the small things, he'll never learn to reach for anything better. He'll expect to be rewarded. Or, at the very least, let the reward fit the accomplishment."

"And what, pray tell, is a fitting reward for the boy's first jump?"

"Certainly not a celebration dinner and a war bonnet."

He pulled her into his arms and bent to kiss her, but she turned her head, and his mouth landed on her cheek. He frowned but didn't belabor the issue. Instead he lifted his hand and rested it on Danny's shoulder. "Don't be silly. The boy is not even six years old and is smart enough and steady enough to jump. This deserves a celebration. Come on, Danny, let's see if the beans are ready to be pulled. If they are, maybe cook will boil them with a slab of bacon."

That was Danny's favorite, Jane knew—and so did Trent. She shook her head. "There's simply no point in trying to make you understand."

Perhaps he couldn't understand that sometimes one did things for the simple joy of doing them, and that joy was its own reward.

A valley lay between Trent's values and hers. Jane couldn't bear the thought of him sullying the simple goodness of her son, the simple pleasure that a hawk's feather and a bandana had brought him back at the homestead. She watched him walking next to Trent, both striding forward confidently as though they owned the world.

Her shoulders squared, and she lifted her chin toward the sky for support. She would not allow her son to grow up mimicking that man. For the first time, she considered how far she was willing to go to escape. And in a flash, she knew. If she had to kill Trent to get away, then she'd kill him.

Chapter Sixteen

....

Early September

Franklin's ribs were finally beginning to heal, and he was getting sick of being in bed. Without a doctor in town he could trust, he'd allowed Cheng to bring him a doctor from the Chinese community. He'd brought herbs, opium for the pain, and worked with gentle, deft hands, wrapping up Franklin's ribs.

The doctor had given Cheng strict instructions to keep Franklin confined to bed for at least two weeks. His injuries were severe. The blows to the head had taken a toll, and he had suffered a few days of memory fluctuations that, thankfully, had cleared up. But when he'd come to on the fourth day after his beating, Jenny and Jane weighed on him so heavily and with such a sense of urgency that he'd tried to get out of bed—until he realized it wasn't possible.

But Cheng had kept in touch with Andy, and Andy assured them that Jane was well at the house, and Molly was taking care of Jenny at the saloon. Rumor had it that Bedlow had threatened to shoot any man who came near Jenny or so much as asked her price.

So they had a short respite while Trent was running high on familial goodness. Clearly having Jane and her two children at his house had started him thinking like a family man. Franklin was grateful for that, for Jenny's sake, but he feared for Jane. He couldn't help but wonder how long she had before Bedlow would make demands that, if not fulfilled, would cause trouble for Jenny.

Franklin was already on edge by the time Cheng brought in his breakfast tray. And its contents didn't improve his foul mood. The tray held two eggs, two biscuits, and an orange.

"Cheng," he groused, "you know I hate oranges. How many times I got to tell you, they make my tongue itch? And what about gravy? Don't Chinamen know how to make gravy?"

"Fruit better. Make strong. Gravy. Bah. No good."

"Seems to me a man oughta be able to choose his own breakfast."

"You get well. You pick breakfast. You still sick. Cheng pick."

Cheng set his Bible on the table next to Franklin's bed and went about tidying up the room while Franklin ate. And just to get on the cook's nerves, Franklin ate as slowly as possible. Cheng kept turning to stare at him.

Finally, Franklin decided the cook had been punished enough. He laughed and set the tray aside. "All right. Bring it here."

Every day since he had been able to sit up and remain lucid, he had been true to his promise to Cheng that he would read the Bible to him since he couldn't read English and didn't own a Chinese Bible.

"Where are we today?"

"We read Luke."

"We read Luke yesterday."

"Luke."

Luke was Cheng's favorite account of the gospel. Franklin didn't know why. His had always been John. But this was the third day in a row Cheng had asked him to read Luke.

So he began reading—again—until Cheng interrupted.

"I don't know," Cheng said, his frown one of confusion, of frustration.

"What do you mean, you don't know? You mean you don't understand?"

Nodding, Cheng pointed to the Bible. "You read again."

Only because the servant had been so faithful and such a good friend did Franklin do as he asked. He read the passage again, then he started to explain. "The young man was spoiled and dissatisfied with working for his father and waiting for his inheritance. He wanted the good life. So his dad gave him everything, and he went out and squandered it by living in a town very much like Deadwood, I'd guess."

Cheng nodded.

"But when the young man ran out of money and became so desperate that he even fought pigs for their food, he went home. *Because,* he thought, *even the servants in my father's house are living better than I am.* So he went home, and his father welcomed him back."

"Why?" Cheng asked.

"It's like this, Cheng. Jesus was telling this story to try to get the people to understand something about God's nature. In other words, how God is on the inside. In his heart."

"This story? Not true?" Cheng's face fell.

"The Bible itself is true. And it's true so far as Jesus told the story, but it was for a reason. He wanted the people to see that God forgives sin. No matter how far you go or how horrible you've been, God will always forgive."

If he hadn't known better, he'd have thought Cheng set him up by making him explain the story of the Prodigal Son like that. But the cook didn't understand enough English to try to be duplicitous.

Cheng sat in silence, then finally nodded. "O-kay. We read different now."

Thirty minutes later they were finally on to the Gospel of John.

The door opened. Franklin glanced up and saw his brother, Coop, filling the doorway with his six-foot, two-inch frame.

Coop's laughter practically shook the room. "Look at you, Big Brother. Reading the Bible and telling it like it is. When did you start preaching again, Frank?"

"I'm not. When did you get here? And why didn't you tell me you were coming?"

Coop stayed in the doorway, grinning. "Oh, we decided to make it a surprise."

"We?"

"Me and my bride." Coop took one step into the room.

Frank grinned back. "Who in the world did you find dumb or desperate enough to marry the likes of you?"

"I like that!" Bess peeked around the corner with her hand over her eyes.

"Bess! I knew it would be you."

Her hands were still on her eyes. "Are you decent?"

"I'm covered up. Get in here, you two, and tell me how this happened."

Cheng stood and took the Bible from Franklin.

Bess shook her head. "Don't stop on our account. You have no idea how long I've waited for you to preach again."

"I'm not exactly preaching. Just helping him understand what we're reading."

Coop laughed. "The way I see it, that's preaching."

"Cheng," Franklin said, "I want you to meet my brother, Cooper. And this beautiful woman, Bess, who is much too good for him, is apparently now his wife." Franklin turned to Coop and Bess. "This is Shen Cheng. He and his wife, Mai, and his brother, Shen Chao, work for me here."

Coop reached out his hand, and Cheng took it. He bowed to Bess. "Lovely woman. I send Mai. Take care of you. Bath. Tea. Massage."

Bess shook her head. "Oh, please don't go to any trouble."

"No trouble. No trouble. Mai come. Soon." He motioned to the blue and gold settee. "Both sit."

Franklin eyed Bess. "Don't bother arguing. Cheng runs the place. What he says goes."

"Well, all right then. But only at her convenience."

"Cheng," Franklin said, "can I trouble you for a special meal tonight in honor of this visit and the occasion?"

"Yes. Good meal. I make special." His face beamed. "Good family. Brother. Sister. Good."

He left so happy, Franklin thought the loyal friend might burst into tears on his way back to the kitchen.

Focusing his attention back on the newlyweds, Franklin shook his head. "How did this happen?" he demanded.

Bess tossed back her head and laughed. "I told you I was waiting for my husband to catch me."

Coop slung his arm along the back of the settee. "And I tried for years."

"But he didn't love the Lord like I do, so I never gave him a second glance."

"You did too." Cooper touched her cheek with his knuckles, and Bess ducked her head.

"Well, I guess I did look, but not so as to encourage you."

Coop cradled her shoulder and pulled her closer to him on the settee. "A revival minister came through Sidney awhile back, and Uncle Nathan nagged me until I decided to go. I felt something I never had before." He met Franklin's gaze directly. "You know, I never felt nothing about church—even when Ma tried to make us go."

Franklin nodded. "Yes."

"Anyway, I figured if God could love me enough to make me feel sorry for some of the things I've done, He must be real, as you used to say He is."

Bess chuckled. "Then he came straight to me and pro-posed the next day."

"And she turned me down."

She looked deep into his eyes. "Only because I wanted to be sure it was real before I gave myself over to a man."

His gaze never left her face. Franklin was starting to get uncomfortable in the middle of the love and attraction between the two. "She made me wait a month, then finally gave in. We got married the next day. This is our honeymoon."

"Deadwood for a honeymoon?"

Bess nodded. "That's what Coop said. But I wanted to see you—and to check on Jane too. The last I heard you were worried about her working in the saloon for Bedlow. That rotten snake."

"He's worse than a rotten snake." Franklin's body grew tense, and his ribs began to ache.

"What happened?" Bess asked. "Has something happened to Jane?"

Franklin told them everything.

"How can you sit there in bed when Jane's being held prisoner at Bedlow's? I wouldn't let a woman I loved—"

Bess pinched the back of Cooper's hand. "Settle down. Look at your brother. Do you think he's just lying in bed because he's lazy? He went after Jane or Jenny or both and got himself nearly killed in the process."

Franklin finished the story with the details of his attempt to take Jenny from the saloon.

"They ganged up three to one?" Coop nearly exploded with anger. He jumped to his feet. "I'm going after that little girl, and then I'm going after Jane Albright."

Bess tugged on his sleeve. "Cooper Lloyd, you sit yourself right back down. I am not about to become a widow before I even have the honor of motherhood. Be rational."

"Women," he growled.

"Men! You'd all be dead of stupidity if not for women."

Cheng returned with coffee and Mai. "Very pleased to meet you, Mizzuz," Mai said. "You come with me?"

Franklin waited until he and Coop were the only two left in the room. He looked at his brother. "I'm relieved you're here. We're working on a plan to get them all out of there."

He told him about Andy. "He keeps us informed about Jane and the children's well-being. He's been a godsend."

Coop's face hardened. "When are you going to be back in the saddle?"

"Another week. If I try before then, I won't be much help."

Coop nodded. "So long as Jane and Jenny are both reported safe, we can gather some men we can trust, make a plan, and storm the house and saloon. Bedlow won't know what hit him until it's too late."

The two men talked for hours. By the time Bess reappeared, looking relaxed and lovely, there was no doubt in the mind of either men that the plan would work.

This time next week Bedlow would lose his grip on the woman Franklin loved.

* * * * *

Mid-September

Jane gently laid the satisfied baby in his cradle and buttoned the front of her dress. His eyes drooped as he smiled his sleepy, three-week-old smile. Her heart lurched.

When she stood up, arms encircled her from behind. Trent was becoming more and more aggressive over the past week since Danny's jump. She feared he soon would stop giving her a choice and demand she come to his bed. She prayed every night for mercy. If he insisted, she would have no choice but to surrender to him. There was too much at stake.

"You look beautiful this evening," he murmured against her neck.

"Thank you." She tried to move away, but he held her tighter.

He kissed her earlobe. Her stomach tightened and threatened to rebel.

"Do you like the gowns?"

He had purchased her several gowns after noting that her own was threadbare at best. She had worn trousers on the trail and had only packed the dress she'd worn to Sidney the day she'd put the laudanum in Franklin's coffee and hightailed it for Sidney with Danny and the oxen and wagon.

She stood completely still as he nuzzled her cheek. "The

LOVE FINDS YOU IN DEADWOOD, SOUTH DAKOTA

gowns are lovely, but I only took one. I don't have time to pay you back anymore."

He swiftly turned her to face him. "My wife doesn't have to pay me for anything. I gladly provide her needs. Including beautiful gowns that make her eyes shine like sapphires."

Jane cringed inside. How foolish she'd been to choose this gown to replace the one that was too large for her now that her pregnancy had ended. Her vanity had caused her to choose the gown that would flatter her eyes the most. And now look what that pride had gotten her.

"I'm sure your wife will be a very blessed woman." She nearly tripped over the words as they left her mouth. "But I'm not going to be that woman."

His eyes darkened. "Don't say what you know isn't true, Jane. I'm doing you honor by offering to marry you before I take you into my bed."

"And yet you first demanded I become your mistress to pay my debt to you."

"You don't need to worry about that. I've changed my mind." He cupped her head in his hands and kissed her with such intensity that Jane was left breathless, her mouth bruised.

He pulled away, his eyes so full of emotion it scared Jane. "I want you, but I can wait a little longer, because I don't want you to come to me without marriage. I know you'd never forgive yourself or me."

Relief nearly overwhelmed her. "I appreciate that. But I

don't want to marry you, Trent. I want to go home with my children and live on our homestead."

"Well, that is not going to be possible, so just get it out of that head of yours."

He released her and paced the room. "Why are you being so stubborn?"

And then it hit her. Trent Bedlow was that child she'd been worried Danny would become. Expecting to receive whatever the lust of the eye, the lust of the flesh, and the pride of life offered him.

"Is this about money? Do you want a settlement? A promise in writing that your children will receive an inheritance? What is it you are holding out for? You needn't worry about that. I have already started the process of adoption. And my lawyer is remaking my will so that even if there are children born of our union, Danny and the baby—you really do need to name that baby, Jane—Danny and the baby will be cared for as though they were mine by blood."

A gasp tore at her throat. Why, though, should she be surprised after all this time? How could anything shock her anymore? She turned her back.

Behind her she heard him release a breath. "Let's not fight anymore. I've brought you a surprise. Not that you deserve one."

Dread moved through her. She hated his surprises. They usually consisted of jewelry or fine foods he'd ordered. But this time she turned around and squealed with delight. "Jenny! Is it really you?"

The child rushed into her arms and clung so tightly, Jane felt she might squeeze the breath from her.

"Shh," Jane said. "It's okay. You're here with me now."

Remembering that Trent was still there, she looked over Jenny's shoulder. "Thank you for bringing her, Trent. It was a good thing to do, and I appreciate it."

He gave a short laugh. "I'm going to Sidney in the morning. I will be taking Danny with me. I won't be at dinner, as I'll be getting things ready for the trip. I'll bring Danny in to say good-bye in the morning before we leave." He left her staring at him as he turned and left the room with long, confident strides.

Jane disentangled herself from Jenny's arms. "Stay here and watch over the baby."

She followed Trent into the hall. "Wait. What do you mean you're taking Danny?"

"Precisely what I said."

She stomped her foot. "No. You can't take my boy."

"I can do as I choose." He cupped her chin. "This is my assurance that you won't run away and take the children while I'm gone. I thought about taking Jenny, but I wasn't quite sure if Jenny would be enough incentive to keep you here. But I know Danny is."

Jane's eyes filled with tears. "Please don't take him. Don't you think you've kept me from him long enough?"

"All you have to do is say the word. You can come along too. But the baby stays with Mam."

She stared him down. "No."

"I didn't think so. You will have six weeks to think about things. Danny will have a good time. I won't let any harm come to him. And when I return, I expect that wedding gown to be made and you to be ready to put it on and marry me. But either way, we will be sharing the same bed."

"Oh, Trent. This lunacy must stop. Who do you think you are?" She could hear her voice rising, on the verge of hysteria. "You play with people's life to suit your own."

"Tread carefully, Jane," he warned.

But Jane was beyond the point of treading carefully. She was on the verge of losing too much. "Jenny is a little girl. She needs a mother and a father. Not to live in a filthy saloon while a disgusting pack of men wait for her to get a little older. And Danny. He needs to be playing on the homestead his father built. It's his legacy. It's not much. Definitely not the sort of inheritance he would get if you raised him as your son, but a heritage nonetheless, and I want him to have it. And that's what I want for him." She swallowed hard, trying to regain her composure as she stared up at him, chest heaving.

"Who do I think I am?" He towered over her, his hands gripping her arms as he forced her gaze. "I think I am the one with the cards. *All* of them. You are a card. Jenny is a card. Danny and the baby are cards. Your precious Frank is a card. All of you cards in my game. And I hold all of you. I decide who I play today and who can wait." He leaned in close. "And honey, I decide who gets thrown away." He reached out and snatched her by her hair, pulling her painfully. "I could take you right now, and there would be nothing you could do about it. I could ride away with Danny, and you might never see him again."

"Trent, let go, please," she gasped. "You're hurting me."

"Do you think I want to hurt you, Jane? Do you think I want to separate you from your son and use a little girl to keep you in line?" He shook his head and turned loose of her hair. "I don't want to do those things. I want you to love me, to want me. To let me love you. Don't you understand that? I have never loved a woman like this before."

When he stopped speaking, he breathed heavily, as though just completing a race. His eyes held hers, and she knew he was waiting for a response.

"I'm sorry, Trent. I can't give you what you want. I can't love you." Jane said it quietly, calmly. She closed her eyes and waited for the blow that she was sure would come. She could feel his breath, hot on her face. Could feel his hands on her arms, the heat seeping through the silk sleeves—but not a blow.

"Open your eyes," he commanded, his voice so eerily calm that her insides began to quake.

She met his gaze.

"I poured my heart out to you just now. I've never done that. I told you I love you, and I want you to love me."

She nodded.

"Tell me you love me."

"What?"

"Tell. Me. You. Love. Me."

"But Trent, I just told you—"

"So help me, Jane, I need you to say it."

"If I say it, it will be a lie."

"Then tell me a lie or, so help me, I'll kill you."

"I love you, Trent."

His body relaxed. Leaning forward, he pressed a kiss to her forehead. "That's all I wanted to hear."

Chapter Seventeen

....

Through the store window, Franklin recognized Mam Truman's wagon rattling to a stop in front of his store. The old nag she used to pull the cart looked about on her last leg. But that was the least of Franklin's concerns.

He hurried out to meet her, smelling the yeast and baked dough even before he reached the back of the wagon. She was already standing there with the gate down, rummaging through the crates for his order. "Mam," he scolded, "why don't you ever wait for me to help you down from that wagon?"

"Good Lord gave me two strong, sturdy legs and a will to do all I can." Her eyes squinted in the predawn light as she scanned his face. "Glad to see you is well, Mistah Franklin."

"Thank you, Mam." He reached into the wagon and lifted the crate piled with baked goods. "I've been craving the taste of that twisty cinnamon bread." He smiled at her and headed into the store, allowing her to hold open the door. "We'll settle up at the counter," he said.

Mam craned her neck, clearly looking for someone or something.

"Casey isn't here yet," Franklin said. "If that's who you're looking for."

The early morning rush of customers wouldn't begin for another two hours at least—until right after sunup. Most of Mam's sweetbreads would sell within an hour.

He opened his metal money box and lifted out a few bills.

Mam counted them and handed two back. "That be too much, Mistah Franklin, and you knows it. I don't take what I don't earns."

Franklin smiled at the old woman. "All right, Mam. I didn't mean to insult you."

She gathered her shawl around her frail shoulders. "Take a lot more'n that to insult me. Now let me say what I gots to say b'fore your boy gets here." Mam dropped her voice to hushed tones. "Mastah Trent is leavin' today and gwine to Sidney to check on his businesses there."

Franklin's heart jumped. "How many men is he taking with him?"

"Not enough for you to waltz into his house and take Miss Jane, if that's whut you thinkin'." She shook her head as though he were the biggest fool. "He takin' little Danny with him to keep Miss Jane in line."

Anger welled up inside Franklin. "Have you seen Jenny lately? And Andy? I haven't heard from Andy in days."

"Mistah Andy been busy with helpin' Mastah Trent get ready for the trip. But I thinks Andy be stayin'." She leaned in close. "Miss Jane is 'bout at the end of her rope and so is

Mastah Trent. He say she marryin' him when he gets back and that be all there is to it."

"Why are you telling me this, Mam, unless you have a plan?"

She smiled around toothless gums. "I gots a plan. Yes, I do."

"Now, Mam, don't get yourself in trouble."

"Honey, I's had trouble all my life. Jesus never said otherwise. You be watchin' your house this mornin'."

"I'm working. Why so mysterious?"

"Let your boy work. You gwine home."

"What's this all about?"

The old woman shook her head. "You just do as ol' Mam says. Gwine home. Yessir, I gots me a plan."

* * * * *

"It won't work!" Franklin said, pacing the library as he listened to Coop's hairbrained scheme. He shook his head vehemently.

Coop sat in the leather wingback, confident as a prince. "I know we can make it work."

"He'll have too many men with him, Coop," Franklin said. "There aren't enough in this town who aren't loyal to Bedlow. I have ten men I can honestly say I'd count on to keep the secret and follow through with the plan without backing out in fear."

"Then we will have to appeal to the husbands and fathers. The men who don't frequent the saloons."

A short, bitter laugh left Franklin. "You're looking at him."

"There have to be more men in Deadwood. A few years ago, this place was a sight more rowdy than it is now. I bet if we go to the mines or to where the tracks are being laid, we'll be able to appeal to men who might see their own daughters in Jenny."

He made sense. Mining these days was hard labor with little reward, and most of the drifters and single men out to make it rich quick had moved on. The men left were the ones looking not for a big strike but enough to feed and clothe their families. They might be persuaded to ride with him. He wasn't a rich man compared to Bedlow, but he could pay for men to ride with him. "If we go in after Jenny, we take Jane and the baby also. She'll be in danger otherwise. And we'll have a fight on our hands because Bedlow is taking Danny with him to Sidney as a form of insurance that Jane will be there when he gets back."

Coop nodded. "She'll just have to come with us and trust that we'll get Danny too as soon as Trent gets back to town."

"Why not stop him on the trail?"

Coop shook his head. "Too much like we're trying to steal from him. We don't want to get hanged for outlaws."

Franklin huffed out a frustrated breath. "Then what's to be done about it? This is the right opportunity to make our move while his men are split in numbers. Part with him and part at home to protect his property."

"There's got to be an answer," Coop said. "We just have to think harder."

The door opened, and the men turned to find Cheng. "We don't need anything," Franklin said.

"Got visitor," Cheng replied.

"It's a little early for company, isn't it? If it's a salesman, Cheng, please tell him to go away. I've told you over and over I don't want to see them."

Cheng scowled. "Not salesman. You come."

Franklin followed Cheng to the kitchen and through the back door. On the ground, leaning against the house, were two small figures, lying side by side.

Coop sucked in a breath. "I take it those two are—"

"Jenny and Danny," Franklin provided.

Jenny's body lay curled around Danny's, and her arm covered him like a wing.

Reaching down, Franklin gently pressed her shoulder. "Jenny," he whispered, so as not to startle her. "Wake up, honey."

Jenny gave a scream as she awoke and jumped to her feet, raising a stick that Franklin hadn't noticed. It must have been lying between the two children.

"It's me, Jenny." Franklin reached forward. "Give me the stick."

She turned it over to him, and relief washed across her

face. "We got away." She shook the boy next to her. "Danny, wake up. We made it to Mr. Lloyd's house."

The little boy opened an eye and grinned, giving a little chubby-handed wave. "Hi, Mr. Lloyd." Then he frowned. "We ran away from Uncle Trent. He wanted to take me away from Ma again."

"Well, let's get you inside and warmed up. You can eat some breakfast."

Jenny waited for Danny, placing her hand on his shoulder as they preceded Franklin inside.

Coop gave a long, slow whistle. "Well, now, this changes everything, doesn't it?"

* * * * *

An explosion of pain awakened Jane. She opened her eyes as Trent grabbed her by her arms. The fury in his eyes was terrifying. She'd never seen him angry to this extent.

"Where are they?" he demanded.

"What are you talking about? Who?"

Raring back, he slapped her hard across her face. She tasted blood. "Don't play me for the fool, Jane. I've warned you about that. I want to know where Danny and Jenny are, and I want to know now."

Fear scrambled inside her, and she tried to make sense of what he was saying. "Do you mean Danny and Jenny ran away? But how would they have gotten past all the men?"

"That's what you're going to tell me." He yanked her from the bed, dragging her through the room.

"Trent, for heaven's sake, stop!"

He ignored her. His fingers bit into her soft, fleshy upper arms, and she fought back tears of pain. "I don't know what you are talking about."

His chest heaved with anger and exertion as he stared down at her on the floor. "You know. I know you do."

"Think about what you're saying. Would I be sound asleep in my bed if I had knowledge that my son and Jenny had gone in the night?"

"You might have sent them away."

"With whom?" she asked, incredulous. "Every single man, woman, and child on this ranch is loyal to you. If I had the power to send Danny and Jenny away, I would have left myself."

He dropped to the floor next to her, reached inside his jacket, and produced a handkerchief. "You're bleeding."

She took the cloth without a thank you and wiped at the blood that had already begun dripping onto her nightgown. "Have you begun a search yet, or did you come straight from discovering they were gone to my bedroom?"

"Here." His dark eyes flashed. "I shouldn't have listened to you about Jenny. I should have put her straight to work in the saloon. And when I catch her, that's exactly what I intend to do."

"Then I pray to God she gets away. How can you hold a child responsible for wanting to run away from her source of pain?"

"Pain? I didn't lay a hand on her, and neither did anyone else."

"You've imprisoned her, Trent." Jane just didn't care anymore. She was so tired of the threats and pretense. "You kept her at the saloon through fear and bullying. Of course she wants to get away from you."

"But she wasn't even going with me. She was going to be with you for six weeks."

"Maybe Danny didn't want to go."

He gazed thoughtfully at her. "You know something more than you're saying." Standing, he walked to the cradle and lifted the baby.

Fear gripped her stomach, and she scrambled to her feet. "What are you doing with him, Trent?"

"I suppose I could take him." His expression left no doubt in Jane's mind that Trent Bedlow was evil.

"Give me the baby and go look for Danny." She leveled her gaze at him and fought for control. "I had nothing to do with his escape. What if he's out there somewhere hurt or scared, or what if one of your enemies kidnapped him?"

A light flashed in his eyes. "Enemies?" To her vast relief, he had obviously considered a new thought and had grown tired of tormenting her with the baby. He handed the bundle over. "There's only one enemy I can think of who might have my son! And we both know who that is. Get yourself cleaned up before I get back. You're going with me."

"Going where?"

"Just be ready."

She watched him stride out the door and headed over to the window, watching as he went outside and spoke to two of his men. They mounted their horses and rode away. Rather than coming back to the house, Trent walked toward the direction of the stables. Did he wonder if Danny had taken his pony?

The baby began to squirm and search, so she sat in her chair and unbuttoned her gown. The door opened, and a wary Mam stepped inside and closed the door.

"Mam? What are you doing?"

"Listen, Miss Jane. I gots to tell you whut I done and whut we gonna do."

"Is this about Danny?"

Mam came close and nodded.

"What happened?"

"I was bakin' in my kitchen, and I seen those two headed toward the stable. So I goes after them, and they tell me they's leavin 'cause Mistah Danny don't want to go away from his ma." A soft sigh left her. "A boy loves his mama." A far-off look settled in the old eyes until Jane gently nudged her.

"Mam, what happened next?"

"So I ask them, 'How ya'll think you gonna run off without being caught?'" She shook her head. "They was gonna take that pony."

And they would have been found easily. Jane nodded. "Go on."

"So, Mistah Andy turn that pony loose so they think the children go on horseback. And I bring them back to my house to wait until my bread done bakin'."

"Mam! They could have been caught."

"Caught by who, honey? No one bothers ol' Mam in her kitchen. 'Sides, if I'd left on my delivery b'fore I usually do, Mistah Trent'd knowed it was me."

She had a point, but it was difficult to think of all the precious time lost.

"So when my breads and buns was done, I loaded them up and loaded them kids up under the sheet. We drove right past all Mistah Trent's men." She cackled. "I give 'em all a cinnamon bun and waved sweet as you please."

"Where did you take them, Mam?"

"Where they was goin' in the first place."

"Franklin?" Where else would they go?

"That's right. I delivered them b'fore the mornin' light and went about my business, deliverin' my goods."

Jane rubbed the baby's silky head as he nursed. Relief covered her, knowing Danny and Jenny were safe in Franklin's care.

"Thank you for letting me know, Mam."

Mam nodded. "Now we gots to figure out how to get you and that baby out the same way."

Hope flared, but she shook her head. "I don't see how that will be possible now. If I assumed Danny was with Franklin, so will Trent. He's not a fool. He won't let me make a move without his knowledge, and there are plenty of his men to make sure I don't run off."

Mam exhaled a breath. "I reckon you is right." She patted her and was just about to stand when the door opened.

"What are you doing here?" Trent demanded.

Jane noticed her hands tremble, but you'd never know it by the way her chin shot up when she stared back at Trent. "I came to see my baby boy, of course." She lifted her brow in curiosity. "Thought you was leavin' today. Why you still here?"

He glared at Jane. "You mean she didn't tell you all about it?"

Mam feigned innocence, so Jane decided it best to play along.

"Why would she tell me anything?" Mam asked.

"Danny and Jenny ran away." He dropped to the end of the bed, and Mam went to him, pressed his ear to her chest, and stroked his head. "It feels like I've lost Solomon all over again."

Curiosity filled Jane, but she didn't pry. Not now, when Mam was doing such a masterful job of soothing him. The baby had drifted to sleep, so she deftly got him situated and buttoned her nightdress.

"Did they take the pony?" Jane ventured to ask. She needed to know which trail he was following.

Trent raised his head from Mam's embrace. He stood and walked to Jane. She tensed, but he took her hands in his and captured her gaze. Bending, he pressed a gentle kiss to her swollen lip. "I'm sorry, Jane. When I saw him gone, I thought you had taken him. I never expected to find you in bed. I thought you would be gone."

Did he honestly believe she would still be here if she thought there was any hope of escape? "I knew nothing about it."

"I believe you." His gaze raked over her, but for once, no desire sprang to his eyes. Letting go of her hands, he stepped back. "I'll let you get dressed and then meet me in the dining room, please. Perhaps you wouldn't mind having breakfast with me today."

As though he hadn't ripped her out of bed, slapped her, and threatened to put Jenny straight to work entertaining the men. But what choice did she have? "I'll only be a few minutes."

He nodded and turned to Mam. "I need Big George. Will you go to the saloon and fetch him for me?"

"Of course I will, honey."

They closed the door behind them. A sense of foreboding shivered over Jane as she heard them speaking in hushed tones in the hallway. She prayed a prayer as she dressed. That Danny and Jenny would be safe at Franklin's home, that Mam would be safe, and that she and the baby could somehow leave this place and find their way to safety.

Chapter Eighteen

As he knew would happen, Bedlow sent two men to Franklin's home—Craig Shewmate and Bob Thacker. Franklin stood on the porch, hand on his six-shooter while they remained on their horses.

"Mr. Bedlow says you got something that belongs to him," Shewmate called.

"Are you calling me a thief?" Franklin challenged.

Shewmate's smile didn't reach his eyes. He leaned forward, resting his forearm on the saddle horn. "I'm calling you stupid if you mess with Bedlow."

Coop fingered his shotgun. "I say we send this Bedlow back a token of our esteem."

Shewmate's face drained of color, but he remained stoic. Not the best poker face Franklin had ever seen, but he had to give the man props for not falling apart under Coop's bluff.

"Don't look so worried," Franklin said. "We're not the murderers here."

The relief on the man's face was unmistakable. He rallied quickly, and his hard edge returned. "Bedlow wants his boy back."

Franklin's stomach tightened at the description of Danny as Bedlow's boy. "I don't know what you're talking about.

Bedlow's boy isn't here. As a matter of fact, I wasn't aware he had a boy."

"Now isn't the time to play dumb, Frank. I'm telling you, Bedlow thinks of that boy as his own son. As a matter of fact, he said to tell you there's going to be a wedding at his home in a week. And we'll be getting Danny back one way or another before then."

Franklin could feel Coop's cool perusal, gauging his response to the news. Franklin knew Jane wasn't going to willingly marry Bedlow. But whether or not he had worn her down enough to agree, he couldn't say without speaking with her.

"Mr. Bedlow is willing to make a concession." Shewmate shifted in the saddle.

"What kind of concession is that?"

"He'll let you keep the girl, Jenny, but you have to hand Danny over today."

Franklin took a step forward. Thacker reached toward his belt. Coop shouldered the shotgun. "Easy there, Trigger-finger," he said to Thacker. The two men had tussled before over a card game in Sidney—before Coop's conversion. But this sort of situation was enough to make a man forget he had gotten religion.

"Tell Bedlow once and for all that I didn't bring Danny here. He can threaten and bargain as much as he likes, but I'm not playing his games."

"I reckon there's nothing else to say, then." Shewmate shook his head. "Never took you for such a fool, Frank. All this over a woman and a couple of kids. You know there's not one man in Deadwood that's gonna go against Bedlow. The man owns just about every business in Deadwood and Sidney. You don't tussle with a man like that and walk away without a face full of dirt."

"Thanks for the advice. But I think I'll have to take my chances."

"It's your funeral." Shewmate squared his gaze at Coop. "Yours too, if you stand with him. I'll take Bedlow the message."

The two men cantered away, sitting straight and alert in the saddles. Coop set down the rifle as Bess opened the door and flung herself into her husband's arms.

Franklin couldn't help but watch them, remembering his Martha. She and Bess were so close in appearance that at times they were difficult to tell apart. But seeing Bess in Coop's arms left no doubt that he was in love with his wife and no other.

"I'm sorry you two had to get into the middle of this."

Bess turned in Coop's arms. "If you're in trouble, this is exactly where we need to be. We're family. We stick together."

Coop grinned. "You see why she's always been the only woman for me?"

"Yes." A smile touched his lips. He did see how two people fit together so perfectly. The way he and Jane had from those first moments in her soddy when she'd come to the door in bare feet and flour on her cheek. His stomach ached at the thought of Bedlow forcing her to marry him. At least Franklin had Danny and Jenny tucked away safe. The house had been built with an underground room. From the library, under the rug, a latch opened from the inside out. The original owner had designed it in case of Indian attacks. Built with rocks to keep it fireproof, the room served as a cellar for Cheng. He stored all of the winter's preserves and herbs down there.

It wouldn't fool anyone who was looking with any amount of diligence. Not for long, anyway. But it might buy them some time if Bedlow's men ambushed the house.

"We'd best put our plan into action."

Coop nodded. "I'll go now." He turned to Bess. "Don't do anything foolish, like go off alone today. I'd like for you to stay inside or on the porch."

Franklin grinned at the nurturing. It only took falling in love for a man to shove down his pride and act mushy in front of another man. Coop whipped around. "What are you looking at?"

"Nothing."

"That's right, nothing." Coop huffed.

Franklin chuckled and couldn't help but tease. "Nothing but a big, soft puppy dog."

"I've seen you act that way a time or two since we was youngsters."

"Fair enough."

Bess rolled her eyes. "Honestly, you two. When you get together, you revert to childhood all over again."

Coop bent and kissed her hard. "I'm not a child. Don't forget it." He winked as her face blossomed. "Do as I say, and stay close. There's no telling what Bedlow intends to do. But you can be sure he has a plan. We just need to get ours in place before he comes calling again."

Bess lifted his collar against the early autumn chill. Rising on her toes, she kissed him again. "Be careful."

* * * * *

It was a risky move to bring the men to Franklin's barn for the meeting, but there seemed to be no other place where they could be sure no one would overhear. The miners left their mines when Coop told them about Jenny. Most of them knew Mr. Ames, Jenny's pa, and to learn he'd been murdered by someone they could finger sent a river of anger through the men. Mr. Ames might have been unsuitable for the mines, he might have been scholarly, but he had taught several of them to read, and Jenny had become the symbol of their own little girls left at home while the men came looking for a way to make a living.

To Franklin's surprise, word had spread through the mining camp above Deadwood, and over thirty men had shown up. They might not be skilled with a gun like the thugs on Bedlow's payroll, but the sheer force of their numbers would help drive home the point they were trying to make. He hoped.

The buzz in the room softened to a hum, and then the barn grew silent as Franklin stepped up onto an overturned trough, the makeshift platform. "Thank you for coming, men."

"Just tell us where that snake Bedlow is, and we'll go take care of him."

"Now wait." Franklin raised his arms to calm the storm that rose from that comment. "We want to avoid violence and bloodshed if possible. It's justice we want."

"Only justice men like Bedlow and his band of thieves know is found at the end of a gun."

Franklin shook his head. "Bedlow has three times the men working for him than we have right here. If you want a fight, you can have one. But it will end badly for us, and then where would we be? Worse off than we started, plus Bedlow can come back in here, take Jenny and Danny, and the woman he's keeping prisoner will never be free."

The men remained quiet and allowed Franklin to share his plan. Only one man spoke up and asked, "What's in it for us? It's not my kids or my woman."

Coop stepped up. "What's in it for you?" He stared the miner down. "How much dust have you cleared from your mine this week? I haven't heard of anyone cashing in dust or nuggets in town." He turned to Franklin. "Have you?"

Franklin shook his head. "Not lately." Typically word got around whenever a miner got a strike. But that hadn't happened in a long time. Months. "I'm offering you a fair day's wages to ride with us. We need strong men who can keep from firing off their gun unless the signal is given. But more than that, it's time to soften Deadwood's edges. Every time decent folks move in, they end up leaving because the town is bawdy and corrupt. How about some decent men, who want to raise their families in a decent town, stand up and let Bedlow and his lot know that we aren't going to stand for his kind of law anymore?"

"Okay. What's the plan?"

* * * * *

Third week of September

With Big George watching her every move, Jane pulled out the white, silk material Trent had sent for from back East and continued the process of cutting out the pattern and sewing the stitches. One week. Now he'd given her just one week. With the children gone and his trip to Fort Sidney closed, Trent had informed her there was no need to wait. She would have no choice but to marry him unless Franklin came through. She hated feeling helpless. She, Jane Albright, had always taken care of herself. She had Mama Rose to thank for that. The cantankerous old sow had taught her that any man worth his salt will kiss the ground a strong woman walks on. If he wants a weakling, he's not a real man.

Mama Rose had taught her a lot of those things. Now, if only Jane had her bottle of laudanum, she'd sneak into the cook shack out back and dump the whole bottle in for the men. But there was no sense in thinking about things that were never going to come true. She had to focus on what was important for now—keeping herself and the baby safe and finding a way to get out of here before the wedding.

Trent had only one person left with which to blackmail her, and she had no doubt that he would stoop to threatening a baby to get his way.

Mam had taken over duties as nurse for the baby while Jane sewed. And, as if summoned by Jane's thoughts, the old woman carried the baby into the dining room, where the dress pieces were all laid out across the sleek mahogany table. Jane felt her milk let down at the sight of the baby.

"He is hungry as a little baby bear wantin' his mama."

"I'm ready for him."

She turned her back to Big George, who had turned away anyhow. For all the debauchery he saw from day to day, she had to wonder why he was so good. "Big George? I want to ask you a question."

"Yes, Miz Jane?"

"Why do you stay with Trent? The war has been over almost fifteen years. I know you don't like doing the things he makes you do."

He released a long breath. "Miz Jane, you got no business askin' stuff like that. It's my business."

Mam clicked her tongue against her gums. "Oh, George, you knows you can trust Miz Jane with the truth."

"You tells her if you wants, Mama. I reckon I got nothin' to say."

Jane turned to Mam. "I didn't mean to pry. Please forget I asked. I'm sorry, George. I won't bring it up ever again."

"Now see whut you done," Mam admonished him. "You gone and made Miz Jane sad. Don't she got enough sorrow these days?"

"Aw, Mama."

"No, please. Don't think any more about it. I'm terribly nosy."

Mam fingered the folds of silk. "Sure is beautiful, ain't it?"

"Yes." Jane gave a bittersweet smile. "The sort of gown every bride dreams of wearing. Silk and lace."

"Beautiful gown that brings only a life of misery."

"I'm afraid so."

"Once upon a time, Mistah Bedlow wanted another gal. Almost as much as he wants you, Miz Jane."

"Oh? What happened to her?"

"She dead."

The sadness in her eyes nearly broke Jane's heart. She reached out her fingers and pressed the dear lady's hand. Mam clutched her hand tightly. "My Tish. He loved her."

"That's enough, Mam." Trent strode with purpose into the room. He glanced at the table. "How's the dress coming along?"

"It's coming along beautifully." Jane captured his gaze. "Have you heard anything about Danny?" She had to keep up the ruse. If he even suspected that she knew anything, or that his beloved Mam would be anything but completely loyal to him, he wouldn't hesitate to kill them both.

The muscle along his jaw clenched. A telltale sign he knew something.

"Trent? Is everything okay? Danny isn't hurt?"

His eyes searched hers, then traveled to her lips, her neck. Jane covered herself more fully with the shawl. Even knowing he couldn't see any part of her covered skin, she still felt exposed.

He gave a short laugh. "I haven't heard anything about Danny. But I am confident he will be here for the wedding."

Mam's head jerked up. Trent gave a little frown, and she averted her eyes quickly.

Jane felt a rush of fear. She had to say something. "I pray he is able to attend."

"That's quite a different attitude."

Jane nodded to the folds of silk. "There's something about sewing a wedding gown that gives a woman romantic notions."

He bent and pressed a hard kiss to her lips, stinging the cut from yesterday's brutality. "Just see that those romantic notions are turned toward me and none other."

Jane gave him an innocent smile. "Who else?"

"Who else indeed?"

Her face warmed under his scrutiny. He two-fingered her chin. "You won't remember him for long."

"If you mean Mr. Lloyd," Jane said lightly, "he's long since left my mind. If he loved me, he would have taken me from your clutches long ago."

Despite the implication that she needed rescuing from him, Trent laughed. The sound of his own levity left an unsettled feeling in Jane throughout the rest of the day.

By dinnertime the gown, from neck to waist, was complete. She gathered up her work, walked into her bedroom, and put things away. Then she made her way the few steps to the nursery, where Mam sat rocking and singing.

"When you gwine give this little lamb a name, Miss Jane?"

"I'll tell you a secret if you promise not to tell."

The old woman's eyes crackled with conspiracy. "Not a soul. The Lawd is my witness."

Jane leaned in close, so not a soul could hear as she breathed her son's name for the first time. "Franklin John."

Mam's eyes grew instantly bright. "I'm honored to know you, little Mastah Franklin."

Jane knelt on the floor at Mam's feet as she rocked the sleepy baby. "Mam, you have no master but God. I want you to remember that. I trust that God can pull me out of this lion's mouth if He chooses, but even if His purposes are better served for me to marry Trent and live here the rest of my days, my children are not to be called Master. How can I teach them that all men are created equal like the Bible says, if you, a free woman, call them master?"

"I's been a slave all my life, Miz Jane. Before the war, a slave be beat for not addressin' a white person proper. Even little bitty ones like Little Mas—Franklin, here. But I am gwine help you raise them childrens right."

"Thank you." Jane reached out and touched the wrinkled arm, giving it a tender caress.

"But if I forgets ever once in a while, you won't be cross with ol' Mam, wills you?"

"Oh, Mam. I don't think that would be possible."

"Will you finish telling me what you were telling me earlier? About why you and George stay with Trent? About your daughter, Tish?"

She nodded, and instant pain formed in her dark eyes. "Tish was just a little bitty thing, about Miss Jenny's age, when Mistah Trent went away to the war. He never give her a thought. Him and George. They went off together. One night while they be in a battle, a big, white Yankee soldier come screamin' toward my George with his bay-o-net. George didn't have time to raise his own gun. But Mistah Trent sees it. He out of bullets in his gun, but he don't care. He run right at that Yankee, knocks the bay-o-net from his hands with the empty gun. Then he beat that Yankee dead."

"So George feels a debt of gratitude."

"Yes, Miz Jane. A man feel beholden to the man whut saved his life." She shrugged. "It just be the way of things."

Jane nodded. "I suppose you're right. But if Big George has his own life to pursue—a woman he loves, for instance— why shouldn't he go and make a life for himself? Raise a family? He's such a good man."

Pride spread wide over her dark face. The kind of mother-pride that shines and refuses to be hidden. "He is, ain't he?"

Jane nodded. "Tell me about Tish. You said Trent loved her?"

Such sorrow returned to the old eyes that Jane almost wished she hadn't brought it up.

"My baby girl. She like that white silk."

Jane gave her a gentle smile. "Pure and good?"

Mam's head shook from side to side, and for a second Jane wondered if the old woman had misunderstood her words. "My baby only look good on the outside. But inside, the devil make her black. She sashayed herself around Mistah Trent until she like to drove him mad. She lay with him in sin and bore his child, but she never give him the time of day after that. He about went mad with longing for her. She run off with a white cavalry officer."

"I'm so sorry." Jane noted that the woman had begun to tremble. "Here, Mam, let me take the baby."

Mam nodded and handed Baby Franklin over to Jane. Jane sat back on the floor. "Tish ran away with an officer? Did you ever find her?"

"Mistah Trent did."

A twister of emotion hit Jane full in the stomach. If Trent went after her…

"He took George with him, and when they find her, she…"

"What, Mam?"

"She sellin' herself like them girls in the saloon."

"What happened to her soldier?"

"He done left her."

"Mam, she must have been desperate to go to a saloon for work. I know these girls—Trent's girls—many of them have no choice."

She shook her head. "Tish could have come home. Mistah Trent and my George begged her. But the devil had hold of her soul. She like whut she doin'. So Mistah Trent sat down with the owner of that saloon and won her back in a hand of poker. Then she be workin' for him. And he make her stop. Locked her up and kept her for himself." She shook her head and pressed her fists to her chest. "My Tish couldn't stand to be locked away. One night she hanged herself in his saloon."

"Oh, Mam, I'm so sorry." Jane shuddered at the similarity —Trent's so-called love for her, his determination to keep her locked away until they married.

"You don't need to be sorry, honey. You need to be careful."

"You said Tish bore him a child."

The old woman rocked and nodded, tears flowing down her cheeks. "Mistah Trent loved that boy. He rocked him and didn't care a bit that he wasn't white. The boy was about eight years old when we started hearin' 'bout gold in the Black Hills. Trent didn't care nothin' about gold. He said whiskey and women were gonna make him richer than any gold strike could."

"He was right for the most part, wasn't he?" Jane had never doubted Trent's shrewdness and intelligence. "But at what cost to his heart and soul?"

Mam nodded. "A dear cost. To all of us."

"I take it the little boy's name was Solomon?"

"Yes."

"What happened to him?" The baby was starting to wake up and fuss. Jane unbuttoned her dress and offered her breast. The baby latched on, drinking and cooing. Jane couldn't imagine losing either of her children. But something had happened to Trent's boy.

Trent stood in the doorway, his legs and arms crossed. "I'll tell you the rest, since Mam has already revealed so much."

"I's sorry, Mistah Trent."

"Oh, Mam, don't be." He sat on the wing chair against the wall and looked at Jane. "It had turned extremely hot. For days the temperature was sweltering, and I promised Solomon we'd go swimming. I didn't let him go alone because, at that time, Deadwood was a filthy mining camp with the worst of people."

She didn't say what she wanted to say, but Trent smiled. He must have read her face. "These days Deadwood is a fine city compared to just five years ago."

Jane nodded. "I'll have to take your word for that."

His gaze slipped over the baby's head. Jane's face warmed, and she grabbed the shawl from the arm of the rocking chair.

A short laugh escaped him as she covered herself. "Why bother?"

"You are not my husband yet, sir." And pray God he never became her husband. "Solomon wanted to go swimming?"

His eyes took on a far-off expression. "I promised and broke the promise—and promised again the next day and broke it."

Jane began to understand even before Trent said the inevitable.

"So he decided to go alone. The current was swift, and he wasn't a strong swimmer."

"He drowned?"

Trent nodded, his Adam's apple moving up and down as he attempted to swallow down the tears. "And now you see why I can't allow anyone to take Danny from me. For all intents and purposes, he's become my son. I love him." He stared hard at her. "I will find him, you and I will be married, and the four of us will be a family."

Jane nodded.

Unless God worked a miracle, she was about to walk into the lion's den.

Chapter Nineteen

. . . .

Franklin made a stealthy trek out the back door and to the side of the steps.

"Mistah Franklin," Mam called to him with a hissing noise, "I's over here."

He met her next to the back of the house. "I can't thank you enough for getting Danny and Jenny to me." He wanted to reach out and hug the old treasure but refrained for fear of embarrassing her.

"They doin' good?"

He nodded. "Danny misses Jane, but he understands we're doing all we can to get her out of there."

"Mistah Franklin, you gots to get her outta there quick."

"Is she okay?" Franklin stared down into the old lady's eyes. "She isn't hurt, is she?"

"Nawsir, but she done got her weddin' dress finished, and Mistah Trent say tomorrow they's gettin' married. He planned a whole big party." She grabbed onto his arm. "But Miz Jane made up her mind. She be leavin' tonight."

Franklin's heart nearly exploded with joy. "What can I do?"

"Meet us in the woods two miles from Mistah Trent's barn." She pressed her fingers to her temple as though trying to remember where. "Down by the creek. Three o'clock in the mawnin'."

"I'll be there."

He watched her slip away and went back into the house to talk to Coop about the new development.

"I'll get some of the men ready," Coop said.

Franklin shook his head. "We can't do that. We have to be as still as possible. I'm going alone."

"No, you're not."

"I have to. Bedlow's men patrol those woods."

"All the more reason for backup," Coop said, stubbornly holding his ground.

"I am not taking any chances with Jane's life." Franklin put his hand on Coop's shoulder. "You know what it is to love a woman. Well, I know what it is to love one and lose her, then finally fall in love again, only to lose her. This is my opportunity to get her back. If you go in there with me for my protection, you'll jeopardize hers."

Coop was quiet for a minute. "Okay. But if you're not back here by four, I'm coming after you."

Franklin grinned. "Deal."

* * * * *

Jane's heart nearly burst from its chest as she walked the footpath between the main house and Mam's cottage. The day had dragged on, and the evening had slowed to one hour for each minute. She had forced herself to remain up, working on her veil in the sitting room, where Trent had been going over figures in his books all evening. Finally a little past time when she normally retired, she faked a yawn and said good night.

She hadn't slept a wink but watched the clock as the minutes ticked away so slowly. Finally the time had come. She gathered up the baby, hiding extra diapers but nothing else, inside his blanket. She could replace his clothing and blankets after she got away from Trent.

The aroma of bread filled her senses before she'd gotten halfway to the cottage.

"Where are you going, ma'am?"

Jane's stomach curled as Shewmate unfolded from the shadows and towered above her.

"Not that it's any of your business," Jane retorted, "but the baby is suffering from colic. I'm going down to Mam for a remedy."

"I'll come with you." He grabbed her arm, too tightly, and moved in close.

"Turn loose of me. How dare you?"

"Come on, Jane. Be nice to me, and I'll help you get away from Bedlow."

She gasped, her legs trembling. How much did he know? Had he heard her talking to Mam yesterday? Had he seen Mam return from Franklin's?

"Perhaps I don't want to get away from him," she said.

He gave a short laugh. "Do you think I'm a fool? You're desperate to get to Frank. You hate Bedlow as much as the rest of us."

Raising herself to full height, Jane lifted her chin. "You're wrong. I care for him very much." She choked out the words. "He's been good to my son, and we are going to be a family."

Shewmate snickered. "Don't be stupid. You'll be dead in five years if you marry him."

"I think you best let me go before I scream."

A branch cracked behind them, and Craig turned as Trent came into view. "No screaming is necessary, darling. I'm here."

Relief combined with dread washed over her. She knew that expression in Trent's eyes and didn't want to be the cause of Craig's death. The baby began to cry. "I was going to Mam's for something to help the baby's colic. Craig kindly offered to escort me."

"Don't waste your breath, Jane. I heard the entire conversation."

"Trent, you know what to expect hiring thugs and out-laws. They have no loyalty. Don't kill him, please. Not over me. He is just being who he is."

Trent frowned. "You expect me to let him go after the things he said to you? After he put his hands on you?"

Jane nodded. "Please. I don't want to start our marriage off this way."

His face softened as he stared at her. He turned back to

Craig. "Get out of here, and thank your lucky stars that my bride is not only beautiful but an angel as well."

Craig hurried away toward the bunkhouse, presumably for his things.

Jane smiled at Trent as he stepped toward her. "Thank you."

"Did you mean those things you said?"

"I do care for you, Trent."

"I suppose that's a start." He slid his arm around her. "What are you naming that boy?"

"I'll tell you tomorrow. On our wedding day."

"You mean today. It's already morning."

"And I haven't slept a wink."

"Here, I'll take the baby to Mam for the remedy. And you go rest." He leaned over and kissed her lightly on the lips as he took the baby.

Panic welled up. "Oh, Trent, you don't have to do this."

"My bride needs her beauty rest."

She had no choice but to surrender the baby and allow Trent to take him.

"Don't worry about him. When he gets hungry, I'll bring him to you. Otherwise, we'll take care of him all day while you sleep and then get ready."

Surrender was the only choice she had. Bitter disappointment threatened to choke her. There would be myriad people at the house tomorrow between the gawdy women and pretentious men out to celebrate the wedding of one of

Deadwood's most prestigious men. Trent had planned the ceremony for afternoon, then an enormous dinner followed by dancing. Now it appeared she would have no choice.

* * * * *

A branch cracked, and Franklin turned just in time to see the butt of a rifle coming at him. Pain exploded in his head, and the ground rose to meet him as he fell from Tryst....

Franklin awoke as water splashed across his face. He gasped loudly, trying to catch his breath.

"Oh, good. You're awake."

Opening his eyes, he found himself staring into the dark, flashing eyes of Trent Bedlow. He tried to move, but he was tied to a chair, his arms behind him. Even his feet were bound. Craig stood to the side, his arms folded across his chest. George looked on as well. But in the big man's eyes, Franklin could see regret.

Between the two men, standing directly in front of Franklin, Trent looked down, his face twisted with anger. "What were you doing in the woods?"

"Hunting."

Pain thundered across Franklin's face as Bedlow's fist crashed into his cheekbone. "What were you doing in the woods?"

Catching his breath, Franklin repeated his answer and the same response from Trent followed. "You're a fool, Frank.

I'll never let her go—even if she came to you, even if she loves you and not me. Even if she fights me every night for the rest of our lives, I will not give Jane up."

Franklin shook his head. "Then that makes you a pathetic creature, doesn't it?"

"What were you doing?" Trent's control was beginning to lessen, and Franklin could see he had to tread lightly to prevent himself from getting a bullet in his head.

"I was hunting. One of my men told me they saw a herd of deer. I tracked them too far on your land."

When Trent's eyes narrowed, it was obvious he was trying to decide if Franklin were telling the truth.

"Don't believe him, Boss," Craig said. "He wasn't tracking. He was waiting. I watched him for a good ten minutes."

"Okay, we'll give you a minute on that one. Where's Danny?"

"The boy ran away from you. Why would you think I know where he is?"

"I'll tell you a secret about women. When their children are missing, they become frantic. Unless they already know where those children are. Or that child, in this case."

There would be no fooling Trent. Even if Franklin kept up the pretense, Bedlow was right. Jane would have been beside herself every minute of every day. She would have been inconsolable.

He shook his head. "The boy stays. It's what his mother wants."

Bedlow sneered. "What his mother wants? His mother will do as she is told."

A short laugh erupted from Franklin's swollen lips. "Then you clearly don't know Jane."

Trent's fist came down hard, and Franklin heard his nose snap. Blood gushed.

"I want my son back," Trent roared.

"Danny isn't your son. But if you want him, you'll have to come get him."

Big George stepped in and said something low in Trent's ear.

Trent looked at his watch and nodded. "Excuse me. My bride is waiting for me. Time to become a married man." He chuckled. "Keep him here, Big George. Craig, come with me if you want to earn your way back into my good graces."

The door closed behind Trent and Craig, and Franklin slumped, surrounded by darkness.

* * * * *

"You surely is beautiful, Miz Jane."

Jane looked at Mam through the vanity mirror. Sadness engulfed her, and the tears she had been fighting all day began to win the battle.

"Shh," Mam said, pulling her into a warm embrace. Jane rested her head against Mam's small, comforting chest. "The Lawd might change all this yet."

"Yes, He might." But at this late time, Jane couldn't imagine how He would. She wondered what Franklin must think of her after she left him alone in the woods. She hoped that somehow he knew she had been detained.

They heard a light tap at the door, and Mam and Jane exchanged glances. Mam went to the door. "Mr. Bedlow would like to see Jane. He has a surprise for her."

Mam snorted. "You tell him any surprise he has can wait. He ain't seein' his bride before the weddin'. It's bad luck."

"I'm sorry, Mam. There's no choice. Mr. Bedlow's orders."

"It's all right, Mam." Jane stood and walked to the door. Surprise flooded through her as she saw Craig standing at the door. She frowned.

He chuckled. "Let's go."

"Go where?" His fingers bit into her arm, and he pulled her so fast she had to take two steps to every one of his. "This is my wedding day. Why would Trent ask me to leave the house?" She waved at all the wedding decorations as he pulled her down the steps she was supposed to use as an aisle, past the flowers and decorations in the foyer and dining room, to the door.

The autumn-cool air slid across her bare shoulders. As he helped her into the waiting buggy and climbed in beside her, she said, "You must have blackmailed Trent, or he would never have let you back on the ranch. And after I saved your hide too."

"Thank you for that, by the way. I thought I was as good as dead."

"What is this all about?"

He breathed out hard and turned to her. "Listen, I am trying to get back in good graces with Bedlow. The only reason he sent me to get you is that he knows I'm not going to take a chance on disappointing him again."

"At least tell me where we're going."

"The saloon."

"But whatever for?"

The wagon rolled over a deep rut in the road, and she swayed toward Craig, then righted herself just as quickly. "You'll just have to wait and find out."

She knew there was no point in pushing any further. Silently she turned her gaze to the horizon. What appeared to be black smoke billowed up from Deadwood. "Craig, what is that?"

He adjusted his gaze to where she pointed. "I don't know." He flicked the reins, and the horses quickened their steps.

As they drew closer, they could see that there was much more than just an isolated spot or two of smoke. Flames licked up from several buildings.

"Is the saloon on fire?" Jane asked.

"It doesn't look like the fire has reached that part of town yet."

Craig's words proved true as they pulled the buggy to a stop in front of the saloon. Not even the smell of smoke had reached them yet, but Jane could see it was only a matter of time.

"What is this all about?" she asked as Craig offered his hand. He was being extra respectful, so she had a feeling part of getting back into Trent's good graces meant he'd better not step out of line with her.

"You'll find out soon. Bedlow's waiting for you inside."

She pushed through the saloon door, her white silk gown, full and flowing, dragging along the dusty saloon floor. Molly's was the first familiar face she saw. She started to greet her, but Molly's eyes bore into her. "Where's Trent?" she asked Molly.

"He's over there, Jane," she said, softly nodding toward a table in the back. "Be careful. Something's not right."

"Thank you." She squeezed Molly's cold hand.

The saloon atmosphere seemed to come to a stop as she moved with slow, deliberate steps through the room. As the crowd parted, she saw Trent, sitting straight and strong, as though holding court. Vera was draped across him, her arms wrapped around his neck as she sat on his lap, whispering into his ear, nibbling his neck. The sight sickened Jane.

She continued her walk. "If it isn't my lovely bride, walking the aisle to meet her bridegroom."

"What is this, Trent?" Thankfully, her voice remained steady. No one would have guessed that beneath the yards and yards of billowing silk her shaky legs barely kept her upright.

As though her world weren't turning upside down before her eyes, someone burst into the saloon. "Fire! The town's on fire! Get your buckets. We're starting a line."

The saloon emptied of nearly every customer in a couple of minutes.

"Well, that's convenient," Trent said. His eyes traveled over her, stopping at her bare shoulders. "You're lovely."

"Thank you."

Vera remained planted on his lap. "Lovely." She gave a short laugh and downed a shot of whiskey from the table.

Trent shoved her off his lap and she crashed to the floor, flinging a curse at him.

Jane glared at Trent and reached a hand down to the woman whose body had clearly not recovered fully from the beating she'd received.

Vera slapped her hand away and cursed her as well. She labored to her feet, stumbling drunk, and swayed as she headed for the stairs.

Outside the saloon, the shouts were getting louder. "Someone check on that ruckus," Trent ordered.

His chair scraped the floor as he got up. He reached for her. "This way, my dear. There's something I want you to see."

She knew not to press, not to demand, not to do anything but follow instructions. There was a time to fight back, but this wasn't that time.

He tapped on the door to the storeroom where she'd kept her cot the first weeks in Deadwood. She fought the strong urge to run.

Trent stepped aside. "After you, my darling." His voice was eerie, icy.

She stepped into the room and gave a cry. "Franklin!"

Hands and feet tied to a chair, he was barely recognizable. His face was battered and bloody. She rushed forward, mindless of Trent or Big George in the room. Kneeling in front of him, she took his head in her hands. "Franklin, it's Jane."

Anger boiled as she spun around to Big George. "Shame on you for allowing this to happen!"

The black man's eyebrows shot up. "But Miz Jane—"

"No. Don't even 'but Miss Jane' me. You're twice the size of any man in this place. You know this is wrong, and you have the power to do something about it."

Trent clapped George on the shoulder, chuckling. "Don't fret, George. You know women. They have to blame someone."

Franklin opened his eyes. "Jane?"

"Yes, I'm here."

"Danny's fine. He's with me."

"I know. Don't try to talk."

"By all means, say everything you have to say now," Trent said. "This is the last time you'll see Jane."

Someone tapped on the door. Trent motioned to George, and he opened the door.

Craig Shewmate stood there. "Mr. Bedlow, I thought I'd better tell you. The fire is spreading pretty fast. And it's coming this way."

"What about the bucket line?" Trent asked.

Craig shook his head. "They can't keep up with the fire. The Gem's been destroyed."

"The Gem Theatre is gone?" For the first time, Trent seemed to be caught by the seriousness of the fire.

"Yes, sir. They're saying it started in the Bakery. There ain't much hope for this place neither. The roof already caught."

The room was beginning to fill with smoke, burning her nose.

Jane found her voice. "Trent, we have to get out of here." She reached for the ropes, but the knots were tied too tightly to free Franklin.

Trent yanked her up by her arm. "Let's go."

"What about Franklin? You can't just leave him here to die."

Trent steadied a gaze at George and nodded.

As Jane began to realize what he meant to do, she began to thrash and fight for all she was worth. "No! Trent! No! This is your chance to try goodness. To be merciful. Please. Please, Trent. Don't do this." He pulled her through the saloon, yanking her each time she pulled away from him. She didn't care that the rafters were blazing. Or that somewhere in the back of the place the wood gave way. The saloon was burning down around them, and she didn't care.

A gun blast shook the place, coming from the storeroom. Jane stopped short, in shock.

"It's over," Trent said. He turned her to face him and held his mouth inches from her, so that puffs of breath blew at her tendrils of hair. The heat of the fire was growing close, and smoke had filled her lungs. "Don't ever try to leave me again."

Without waiting for an answer, he rushed them outside to the waiting buggy. Big George ran out the door just as the place toppled.

"Murderer!" Jane called as Big George grabbed the reins of his horse and rode away. "You're nothing but a murderer."

"Stop it, Jane," Trent ordered. "It's over now. Instead of crying over a dead man, you might consider your own status."

"I couldn't care less. If you think I would marry you now, you're insane."

"Oh, I believe you will." He leaned close. "My men are retrieving Jenny and Danny as we speak, and we'll take the baby and head to Sidney for now. Once Deadwood is rebuilt, and believe me, it will be, we'll return and raise our family here."

"You truly are insane."

"Turn around, dear. And watch Deadwood go up in flames. Remember this is the day you learned your place."

"Riders up ahead, Mr. Bedlow."

Jane sucked in a cool breath as a group of riders galloped toward them. She had a moment of hope that perhaps she would be rescued until she recognized Andy Armor in the bunch.

She sat back and looked down. Her hands were caked with dried blood from Franklin's face. She began softly weeping.

The twenty or so men pulled up their horses, and Craig pulled the wagon to a halt. "What's going on, Andy?" Craig asked. "You're a turncoat?"

Jane looked up. One of the other men seemed familiar, but she couldn't place where she had seen him before. He gave her a bold wink. She averted her gaze.

Trent stared at the riders. "If you're looking for someone to rob, you've chosen the wrong day. Everything I own just burned to the ground."

The man who looked familiar cantered forward. "Bedlow, I presume?"

"That's right." Trent peered closer, and his face blanched. "Coop Lloyd."

"We are going to relieve you of your passenger now," Coop said. Then he turned toward her. "Jane, honey," he said as though they'd known each other their whole lives, "get down and come climb up behind me." He peered harder, staring at the bloodstains on her gown. "You all right?"

She nodded. "It's not my blood." She couldn't tell him whose blood it was. Not yet. She stood.

Trent grabbed her and yanked her back until she landed hard in the seat beside him. "You're not going anywhere."

"Let her go, Bedlow." Andy aimed his six-shooter at Trent's head.

Slowly Trent loosened his grip. Jane climbed down, tugging her skirts over the wheels.

Trent shook his head and sneered at Andy. "So you're the traitor. I almost had George pegged. But he proved himself pretty loyal by putting a bullet in Frank's head."

"No sir."

Jane could almost feel Bedlow's shock as Big George rode into the clearing. Her heart swelled as she realized Franklin was slumped behind him. "Franklin!"

Coop raised his gaze to George. "How bad is he?"

"He got beat up pretty good, but nothing a few days in bed won't fix."

"Jane, you've forgotten something. My men went to Frank's place to bring Danny back. And the baby is with Mam."

Coop clicked his tongue against the roof of his mouth a couple of times. "Your men never got close to the house. Danny and Jenny are having an enormous lunch cooked by the famous Shen Cheng as we speak. And as far as the baby—Andy, you want to take this one?"

"Mam and the baby got out right after you left this morning via the bakery wagon."

Coop smiled at Jane. "Everything is fine now."

Trent glared at Big George. "I can't believe you'd be so ungrateful. You would be nothing without me."

George nodded. "Maybe. But I'm goin' home to Texas and bringin' Sienna back to Mistah Frank's place in Nebraska. I'm gonna work for him. And Mam's comin' with to take care of Miz Jane's babies until I get some of my own."

Shock splashed over Trent's face like ice water. "You're taking Mam?" He laughed. "She would never leave me."

"She already did."

Trent's face was ashen as the buggy rolled through the

two lines of horses. He would be alone now. But Jane had no doubt that he would find more people to buy.

Jane moved to get off the horse, but Coop stayed her. "Wait until we get back to his ranch. The sooner we get him in bed, the better."

She nodded.

"I'm Coop, by the way. Your future brother-in-law."

* * * * *

Franklin woke slowly with sunlight streaming across his face. He could barely remember anything that had happened except for Jane. She had come and held his bloody face in her hands.

Almost before he could get his bearing, the door burst open.

"Hey! You're awake." Before Danny could jump on the bed, Jane entered. "Danny, stop!"

The boy skidded to a halt just inches before leaping. "He's awake, Ma."

"I see that." Her beautiful smile lit his heart.

Jenny came in behind Jane. She carried the baby and beamed when she saw him. "I'm glad you're better," she said, ducking her head.

"Thank you, Jenny. I see you're quite the helper."

She nodded.

Jane slipped an arm about her shoulders. "She's more than that. She's Little Frank's big sister."

The impact of the baby's name went straight to his head, and he laughed with delight. "Well, that's convenient. Getting married and having two sons and a daughter all in the same day. And one of them is already my namesake." Danny leaned against the bed, and Frank slid his arm around the lad's body.

"You're gonna be my pa now?"

"Well, I haven't exactly asked your ma yet. But if she agrees, it's what I'd like to do."

"Oh, her. She'll agree. Right, Ma?"

Jane laughed. "Right."

Frank reached out his hand to Jane, and she came to him. A shy smile tipped her lips. She sat in the chair next to his bed and took his proffered hand.

"Tell me everything that happened that day."

She gave him the shortened version of everything that transpired. "The town is gone for the most part, including your mercantile."

He shook his head. "It doesn't matter." He glanced around at the children and Jane, and his heart filled so with love he thought it might burst from his chest. "Everything that matters is right here in this room."

Franklin laced his fingers with Jane's and pulled her close. "I suppose I should ask you officially. Will you marry me, Jane Albright?"

She caught her breath, and tears sprang to her beautiful blue eyes. "I would be honored." She leaned close and pressed a soft kiss to his lips. "I suppose I'll have to waive the rent on the land, though, as a wedding gift."

"I take it that means we are going back to the homestead to live."

She laid her head against his shoulder. "The sooner we start our lives there, the better."

Reaching up, he caressed her hair. "I couldn't agree more."

About the Author

Tracey Cross, also published as Tracey Bateman, is an award-winning author with nearly one million books in print. Since publishing her first novel in 2000, Tracey has written more than thirty books including *Thirsty*, the Westward Hearts series, the Kansas Home series, the Drama Queens series, the Claire Everett series, and the Penbrook Diaries series. Tracey is an active member of the American Fiction Christian Writers and has served as the organization's president. She lives in Missouri with her husband and four children.

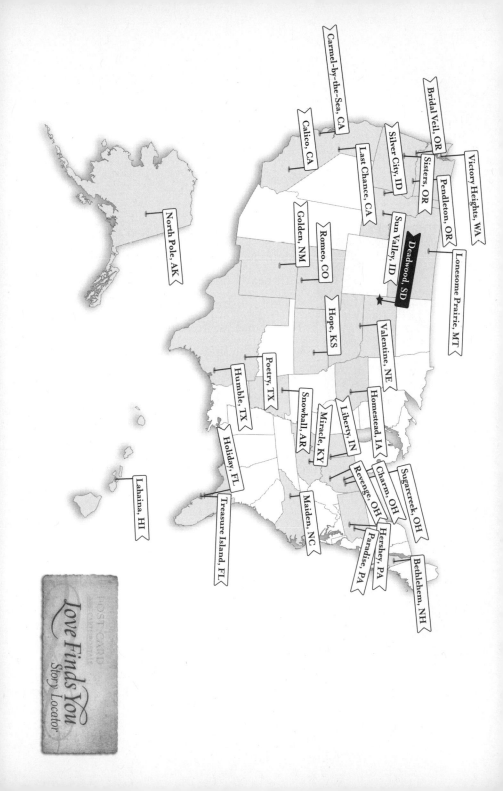